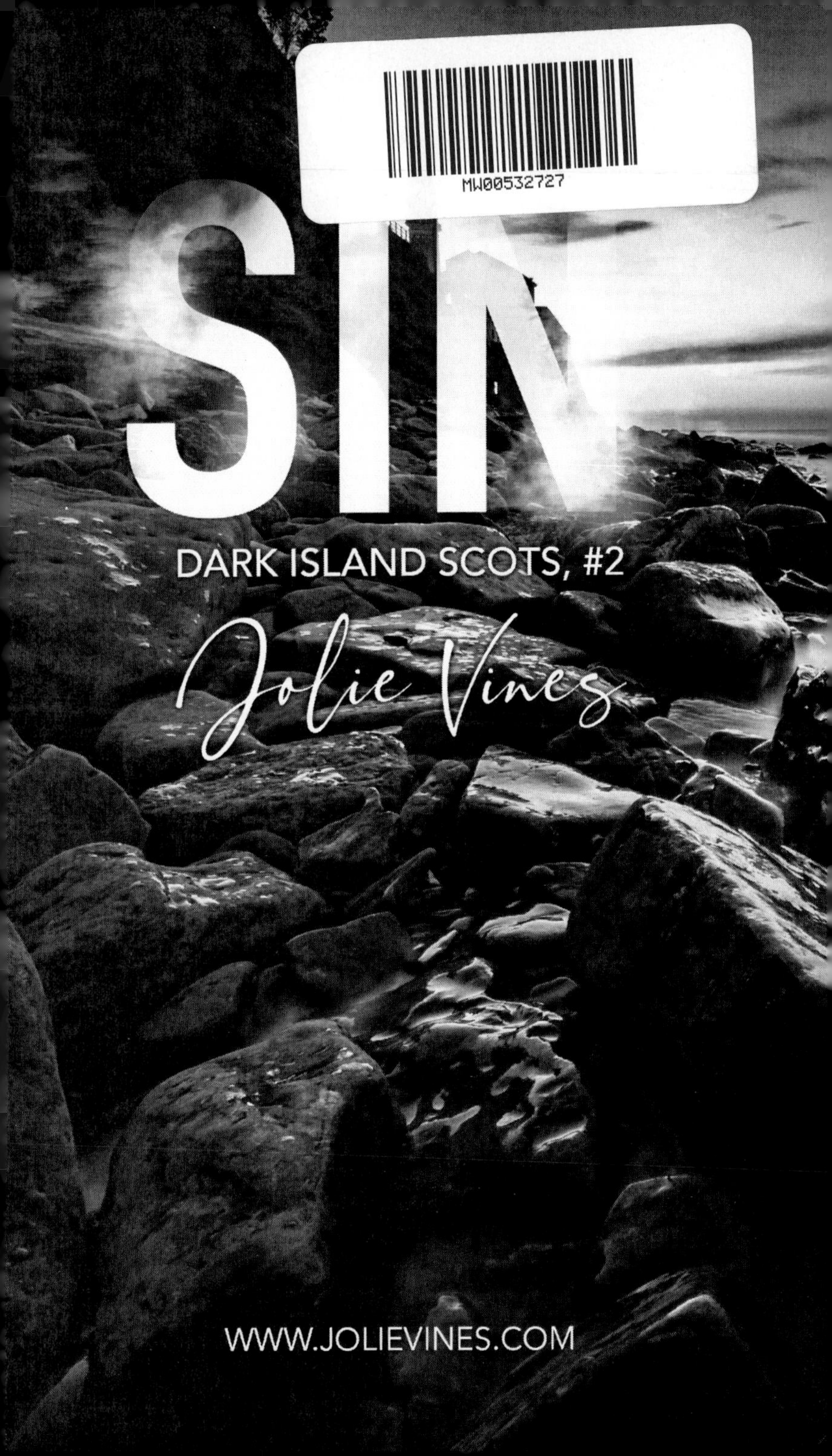
MW00532727
SIN
DARK ISLAND SCOTS, #2
Jolie Vines
WWW.JOLIEVINES.COM

Editing by Emmy Ellis at Studio ENP.

Proofreading by Zoe Ashwood.

Formatting by Cleo Moran / Devoted Pages Designs.

Cover design by Natasha Snow.

Cover model and copyright owner by Andrea Denver.

The bigger they come...

SIN

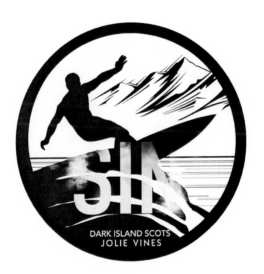

DARK ISLAND SCOTS
JOLIE VINES

BLURB

He was dangerous, but the real sin was mine.

Sinclair was my secret obsession.

The one I dreamed of in a homelife filled with violence and pain.

It was Sin's darkness that saved me, wrapping its way around my heart until it beat only for him.

I helped him escape his island prison.

He asked me to leave with him.

But my mother is pregnant, and I won't let another child be raised in that house of horrors.

The only way to free her is to betray the man I want and the family he's creating.

Love is impossible when my only option is to sin.

--

Sin (Dark Island Scots, #2) continues the story started in Ruin (Dark Island Scots, #1). This is Sinclair and Lottie's romance, so expect exquisite and seductive scenes, a plus-sized heroine and her much bigger hero, and an insidious mystery threatening our tribe of found family.

READER NOTE

Dear reader,

Thank you for picking up Sin. This book is second in the Dark Island Scots series. You should probably read Ruin first to understand what the boys have been through.

Please be aware that this series contains darker storylines, such as domestic violence and threat of sexual assault. An up to date list of trigger warnings can be found on my website jolievines.com

If you like audio, Zachary Webber and Zara Hampton-Brown do an incredible job with this series. I mean, dayum.

Happy reading!

Jolie

1

Sin

Of all the ways I'd plotted escaping my island prison, this scenario had never featured.

High above the black, choppy sea, our rescue helicopter tore up the air.

Every beat of the rotor blades ramped up my alarm.

On the wall seats, Cassie, my six-year-old sister, clung to my brothers while crew members checked us over, and upfront, two pilots held the helicopter steady. Yet we were missing part of our family. With his girlfriend, Struan had made it to a boat, directly below us in the water, but then sent a panicked message. A plea for help.

Someone else was on board with them.

Since then, there had been no reply.

Furious, I glared down the spacious cabin, directing my frustration at the crew. "Try them again. Call their radio. Do something."

"No response to my hail," reported one of the pilots through our headsets.

Max McRae, Struan's friend who'd brought in this

rescue crew, swore and made a gesture to another man. He grimaced, and the two had a kind of staring match.

"Why are ye just standing there?" I demanded. "We're wasting time. Ye heard him. They need to be extracted. Winched off. Whatever the fuck it is ye do."

Max faced me, sparing a glance for my younger siblings. "Cool your temper. We're working out the best approach. The risks—"

"Fuck the risks. Ye came here to save Struan, aye? We aren't leaving without him. If ye aren't prepared to go down there, send me. Hook me up to a cable or I'll do it myself."

"No fucking chance," the guy snapped back, his eyes flashing with frustration. "If ye want to help your brother, let us do the thinking. This is our job."

I knew this. They ran the Scottish mountain rescue service and had flown up here with a helicopter kitted out with equipment. Still, I couldn't just sit back. I leaned in, hot from the need to do something, anything, to end this nightmare.

It was my role, I was the leader, the one who took control. "I can't just wait—"

"Contact," the pilot announced.

Everyone stilled. I clamped my headphones closer.

"Max? Anyone in the helicopter, it's Thea." Static mangled her voice. "Can you hear me? Please help. Struan's hurt."

Hurt. My blood ran cold.

Max held out a hand, attention fixed. "Thea, what happened? Describe Struan's injuries. Who's on there with you?"

No answer came.

"Thea, come in," he tried again.

A long moment of dead air passed. At last, Max sprang into action. Helped by a second crew member, he clipped into a harness.

"Sin," the other crew member said to me. Gordain, Max's uncle. "Arse in the seat and don't move. If Max has to fish ye out of the sea, too, we'll consider leaving ye there."

"I can help," I tried.

"If we need it, we'll ask for it."

My muscles screamed for action, but I relented, throwing myself down next to Burn.

The heli doors slid open, and cold air rushed in. Max got into position at the edge, backed out, then descended into the night.

I counted heartbeats. The in and out of my breath. The thuds of the blades.

We'd fought so hard for freedom, I wouldn't leave without Struan.

Already, I'd had to walk away from another person.

Violet. Or *Lottie,* as everyone else called her. Her father was deep in the conspiracy that had imprisoned us on the remote Scottish island. I'd asked her to come with us, she'd refused. Despite there being no reason to remain. Despite Thea being her closest friend.

Despite the kiss I'd landed on her.

It had been an error in judgement. The more I thought about the lass, the more I knew she'd been playing me.

Her staying behind showed exactly where her loyalties lay.

At the gaping doorway, Gordain crouched, operating the winch. The two pilots kept us steady. I could do nothing but wait.

"Landed, over," Max's voice finally came.

In our position directly over the boat, little was visible from the windows. Only darkness and the edges of our spotlight. Churning water and deadly depths.

Time crawled by.

Max could have found anything. I examined the memory of Thea's voice. She'd sounded strained, but it had been hard to hear.

"Ready for incoming," Gordain announced, flipping something on the winch.

The pilot acknowledged his report.

"Who?" I demanded.

"Max is sending Thea up. Struan will come after. Crouch behind me in case I need a second pair of hands. Don't approach the door."

Nothing had come over the radio, so Gordain must have seen Max on the boat below. I shifted from my seat and got ready, watching the entranceway and the winch cable.

It began winding in.

The helicopter stayed steady, but the wind buffeted us.

In a slow reveal, Thea appeared.

I skimmed a look over her pale face and distraught features, her soaking clothes from her swim in the sea before she and Struan reached the boat. Gordain guided her over the lip without need of help from me, unclipped her, then sent the harness back down.

On her hands and knees, Thea scuttled deeper into the cabin. She mouthed something to me, but the wall of noise drowned her out.

"Headphones and a space blanket," Gordain barked to me.

I snatched up the items and draped the foil blanket over her Thea's shoulders. She pulled on the headset.

Her fingers were red with blood.

"Whose?" I demanded.

This time, she heard, and her reply came over the comms system. "Struan's. Esme stabbed him. He says it's a flesh wound, but I'm not so sure." Her gaze stuck to the open door. "He made me come up first, and Max stayed with him."

"Esme?"

"Charterman's daughter. My old friend. She said all these terrible things about Struan, then she pulled out a knife." The lass shuddered in shock.

Charterman had been our jailor. The main man behind it all. And now nicely dead, thanks to Struan.

I should've comforted her, but the winch motor was moving once more.

All of us seemed to hold our breaths.

Finally, Struan appeared in the doorway, Max with him. The rescuer exchanged a look with Gordain at the winch controls, and between them, they manoeuvred my brother inside the heli.

Conscious, but very pissed off. Thank fuck.

Under the stark light, all I saw was red. Blood streaked his arm, staining clothes already dark from the seawater. He glowered as we hauled him in, relaxing only when he saw Thea.

Struan pulled on headphones, and his words came through clearer. "Get this off me. We need to go."

"Aye, lad. We will." Gordain removed the harness, taking care over Struan's injured arm.

He gestured to Max who closed the door, cutting off the swirling air and black night.

"Tell me where you're injured," Gordain said. He snapped on a pair of surgical gloves from a medical kit.

"My arm, that's all." Struan struggled to sit up. "I used it to block her knife."

The older man examined the deep slice. "The cut needs cleaning. I'll treat it now, and we'll get ye to a hospital for stitches."

Struan's wild eyes focused on mine. We couldn't go to a hospital. They'd ask questions, and we had no idea what kind of lies had been told about us. What the authorities knew.

The truths were bad enough.

We'd left behind one huge fucking mess. A dead prison keeper, buried in the yard, the incinerated house of a perverted islander, maybe with him inside. Burn, the youngest of us, already had an arrest warrant out in his name. He'd just turned eighteen. If caught, he'd go to prison. Maybe we all would. All this aside from the drowned man.

"No hospital," I bit out.

Gordain looked to me. "If his arm becomes infected, it'll get ten times worse."

He was right, but he didn't know the stakes. All we could lose.

"No hospital," I repeated, earning a nod from Struan.

He closed his eyes and sagged against the helicopter's wall. "I'm glad for the help, but we cannae go near a hospital or the police. Max knows this."

Gordain muttered to himself and searched in his kit. "I'll stitch it, but I can't numb the area. I only have over-the-counter meds."

"I don't need the pills. Just to get away from this fucked-up nightmare."

Thea huddled next to Struan, and Gordain knelt beside them.

"What happened to the woman who stabbed your boy?" he asked her.

"She jumped into the sea and swam away, right before Max landed on the deck," Thea replied.

The older man switched his focus to Max, who raised a shoulder.

"I didn't see her. No one else on the boat. Couldn't see a body in the water."

Gordain swore. "We can't leave her in the sea."

Anger rose in me in a hot wave. "Aye, we fucking can. The woman stabbed my brother. Her father imprisoned us. We've barely started to understand why, and there's no way we're waiting around to pull her from the situation she helped cause."

I stared down each of the men in turn.

No matter how Struan knew Max, our rescuers weren't our friends. In their mountain rescue jumpsuits, they looked like officials. Experienced rule followers. People who would hand my group of delinquents over to the cops because it was the right thing to do.

This was one huge mistake.

But it was Thea's quiet, shocked inhale that stole my attention.

She peeled back Struan's shirt. A red stab wound pierced his side, darker blood oozing out. A second injury.

And far, far worse.

My brother slumped, and his eyes rolled.

My dread flared bright. I spun to Gordain. "Is that a good enough reason to go?"

"Aye, to a hospital."

The moment stretched out between us.

He was right. Despite the risks, Struan needed care

we couldn't provide. I gave a sharp nod, Gordain issued orders to the pilot, and at long last, the helicopter tilted then peeled away.

My family had escaped the island. Fled our prison.

All but one. The brown-eyed woman I didn't know how to leave behind.

2

Lottie

The shattering of glass echoed through the house, shocking and loud, even in my bedroom.

"Look at me when I'm talking to ye. Ignorant bitch," Da screamed from the kitchen.

I hunkered down on my bed, out of the firing line but sensing every mental blow. My father had been ranting for hours. He'd arrived home in a fury, his rage giving me hope that Thea and the prisoners had escaped.

My heart needed to know they were far away from here. That Sin was free.

Dawn's light peeked through my open curtains.

By rights, they should be safe by now.

I'd helped them as much as I could, but last night, the situation had grown deadly. My father and his mob of islanders had held the men here, illegally, I suspected. Probably for money. They didn't want them to escape.

Down the hall, Da yelled again, something else smash-

My mother replied in calmer, soothing tones, and a tremble started deep inside me.

He didn't like it when she answered back. I'd learned on my mother's instruction to accept his rage until it passed. Take the hits, hide the bruises.

When he'd got home, I'd stepped between him and my mother. Wanting to protect her and the baby she was expecting.

The pregnancy I was certain she hid from Da.

I'd taken a punch to the stomach for it and had been thrown into my room, phone still confiscated, door locked. I didn't care. It was better for him to use his fists on me.

"Hush, Ma," I whispered, urging her though she couldn't hear.

The voices quietened, either as he calmed or with some new degree of rage. I couldn't be sure.

I'd never known him this bad, and he had a temper that could last for days.

I banded my arms around my knees and tucked my head down, bracing myself for worse.

As often happened, my mind took me to another place. Since I'd been a little girl, I'd dissociated with ease. Drifted away from my horrible home life to someplace better. Recently, it had all centred on the same scene.

A beach. A group of men surfing the cold waves.

My first meeting of Sin.

I'd heard rumours of the prisoners over a year ago. Da had suddenly come into money, and a relative on our tiny island explained that a youth offending scheme would be operating here. That boys with criminal records would be brought to the island to be rehabilitated, away from their former lives.

Da's money had been a bribe.

The reason for the boys' incarceration had been far from true. I hadn't known it back then.

Regardless of the warning given, I'd wandered the beach, dying for a glimpse. I had a romantic soul. A soft heart. I felt bad for anyone taken from their family, though it was all I ever dreamed about for myself.

For many months, nothing, then they were there in the water. Three figures, each carrying a tiny neon light, marking them out in the surf. I knew everyone on the island. We never had tourists here. It could only be *them*. The bad boys.

One in particular caught my eye. He was huge, which wasn't difficult against my 5'2" self, but this man was in a league of his own. At least six and a half feet of muscle. Black hair cropped close to his skull.

Brutal-looking. Easy to imagine as a criminal.

From a distance, I soaked in the sight of him.

It quickly became an addiction. I returned again to seek him out. Then one evening, the tables flipped. By moonlight, he surfed in and ordered the two younger men off the beach, handing over his surfboard to go with them.

I scanned the ground, wondering what had interrupted their late-night surf.

Then he strode right up to my hiding place behind a fall of rocks. The neon green of the surf beacon at his wrist cast menacing shadows over his savage features.

"Why are ye spying on us?" he snarled, his voice deep and deliciously gruff. "Last week. Yesterday. Tonight."

"I… I didn't mean any harm. I saw ye out there and was curious."

"About what?"

"Who ye are. Why you're here."

His lip curled. “Why, what were ye told?”

I barely knew any men. Not like him. I’d gone to school in the village with a handful of other children from the island. Then, because of how remote we were, my studies had switched to online, with only the occasional trip to the high school on the mainland for exams.

I didn’t know how to talk to someone like him. Should’ve had the sense to fear him. Yet my lips moved anyway. “I was told to stay away from the criminals.”

The mild interest in his gaze blinked out. The huge stranger bit out a curse word, turned, and stalked away across the sands.

I should have left him alone. Maybe my father had knocked any sense out of my head. Because a few days later, I found myself back there again.

The moment Da fell asleep, which was often early if he’d had whisky after dinner, I stole out of the house, hopped on my pushbike, and pedalled across the island.

This time, I needed more.

A greater kick of the excitement my spying gave.

The same thing happened. The big man spotted me, dismissed the others, and marched over.

“My name’s Lottie,” I spluttered at his approach. “What’s yours?”

“None of your business. Ye should listen to your da and keep away from us.”

“If I listened to my father, I’d be dead, drowned in that sea.” I meant it as a joke, though it wasn’t.

He looked me over. His scrutiny touched on my braided fair hair. My face. The gap in my jacket where my boobs distorted my clothes.

I’d never been skinny. I loved food, and cooking was

the only thing I did that ever earned praise from my parents. My father used my weight as an insult, but I didn't hate my body. That was a role reserved for others. So I knew what the stranger saw first—the plus size, not the woman.

Yet the expected disgust didn't register. Instead, his gaze lingered before he tore it away to stare at the waves.

Shock danced through my veins. Swift attraction followed, clinging to me in the world's fastest crush.

"Is there anything ye need?" I asked rapidly, wanting to keep him with me. "I'm leaving the island tomorrow with my mother for a shopping trip. I can bring back a few things, if ye like?"

"Are ye serious?"

"I am."

"You'd risk your neck to help us? Why?"

Good question. Because he was viciously handsome. Because the distraction of watching him burned away the murky unhappiness of my existence.

I gave a shrug. "You're not able to leave here, and life is hard enough without snacks."

He smiled at me. A fleeting curl of his lips that was gone as fast as it arrived.

God, I could live for that smile.

The rest had been history. He gave me his name—Sin. I made a couple of trips to buy items for the men. They needed all the basics. Razors. Soap. When a fourth man turned up, my friend, Thea, met him on the ferry, and the two of us even hung out with the criminals by their beach fire. Struan, the newcomer, had kissed Thea, and envy had claimed my heart. Not for him. But because I so badly wanted Sin to do the same to me.

When a little lass arrived to join their numbers, I gave

up any belief that the men were here in any legitimate way. No one could imprison a six-year-old. The sweet black-haired girl had stolen my heart almost as much as her big brother.

Her arrival also brought an end to their stay.

Last night, they fled the hostel where they'd been kept, their keeper dead, and their escape mandatory.

Sin asked me to go with them. I refused. He'd boosted me up to the kitchen counter and sank that hot mouth onto mine. Finally, I got the connection I so desperately wanted, but it was bittersweet.

I couldn't walk away from my mother. Not with her expecting a bairn. And she'd refused to even discuss leaving Da.

Another crash brought me out of my daydream and back to the present.

"Don't try to mollify me," Da blared. "Who do ye think ye are? After all I've lost. All the problems I have. Ye have no idea what those boys have done. And ye have the nerve to tell me to calm down?"

A thud resounded, a soft cry following.

My blood froze.

He'd hit her. I knew the sound of a fist smacking into flesh all too well.

I leapt from my bed and hammered on my door. "Da! Unlock the door."

Another grunt came from outside, and I slammed on the wood harder.

"Da, I need to talk to ye. Please. It's about the men."

Silence followed, then stomping in the hall.

I backed away from the door right as the lock clicked and it flew open. My red-eyed father glared at me.

"What did ye say?"

I had nothing to tell him, I wouldn't give up any secrets. I just couldn't let him hit my mother. "What happened to them?"

Da's eyes narrowed. "Why are ye interested?"

"I only asked."

"Ye little slut. Just like your mother. I knew ye were sneaking off."

Anger built with desperation inside me.

"Which of them did ye open your whore legs for?"

"I never—"

He backhanded me, the hit so fast I didn't have time to avoid it.

Blood pooled at a cut where my teeth pierced the inside of my mouth, but I kept on my feet. Experience had taught me that cringing away only enraged him more. Standing meekly before him and taking the hits got the beating over with faster.

"Don't know why I expected different. Like mother like daughter," he continued. "Dirty. I should have known. Which of them was it?"

I kept silent.

"Answer me!"

"None, Da."

He grabbed my collar to bring my face to his.

I anticipated another punch. More vile words. Instead, calculation registered in his watery eyes. "Ye can find them."

"What?"

He dropped his hold on me then paced away, his gaze distancing. He muttered to himself. "It isn't all lost. Charterman's dead, but there has to be a reason behind it all. Someone still has that money."

He checked his watch then spun back to me. "The ferry's leaving in twenty minutes. You'll be on it."

My chill deepened. I couldn't leave my mother. Not when he was like this. "No."

He turned purple, the broken red veins on his cheeks disappearing under the unhealthy hue. "After all I've done for ye, raised ye, fed ye, put a roof over your head, and you'd still defy me. It's time ye earned your keep. Find those men. Beg, borrow, steal, lie to them, I don't give a damn. Your prissy friend was with them. She'll take ye in. I want to know who they are. Where they are. Why they're important. You've already disgraced yourself with them. This time, make it useful."

He snatched my phone from his pocket and tossed it at me. It hit my head, and I moaned and clutched my hands around the ache.

He wanted me to find and betray my only friends. I could've left with them, been with them now, but nothing had changed. My mother was at risk from Da. If I was here, I could be a buffer. Protect her from the worst of his rages.

I had no idea what he'd do if he found out she was pregnant. Even thinking about it terrified me.

Ma had always wanted another baby, and considering her age, this could be her last shot. I knew she'd lost pregnancies before, and though she'd never admitted it, I suspected Da's violence had been the reason they'd ended. Maybe keeping the baby would give her reason to leave him.

At my hesitation, my father smiled.

"You'll be on that boat. You'll find the men and bring back that information. Don't let me down. If ye fail, you'll never meet that bastard bairn in your ma's belly. And don't ever expect to come back."

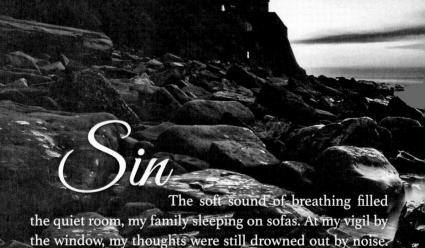

3

Sin

The soft sound of breathing filled the quiet room, my family sleeping on sofas. At my vigil by the window, my thoughts were still drowned out by noise. Shouts. Chopping helicopter blades. The rush of my blood.

I couldn't get my panic to stop. Not while we still didn't know anything about Struan.

He could be dead on an operating table.

A casualty of the war none of us signed up for.

After our escape from the island, the mountain rescue team flew us to a hospital. Struan had been carted away on a stretcher from the landing pad, Thea rushing along at his side.

The rest of us had kept to our seats. Without question, Gordain had ordered the helicopter to take off once more, then he'd brought us here. To a house on his land, apparently used as a ski lodge or cabin but vacant in the summer months.

He'd pointed out the stairs to the bedrooms, a bathroom, a wee kitchen with a box of food magically waiting, then he left us, calling back that he would return the following afternoon.

I didn't know what to do with that. Couldn't be sure if it was kindness or something else.

My brothers and sister slept on, all still wearing their shoes, none of us willing to take one of the no doubt comfortable beds upstairs.

Ready to run again if we needed to.

I twisted my phone in my hands.

Thea had sent a text saying that Struan was going into emergency surgery, but I'd heard nothing since. I thumbed out of the message then brought up a map, checking our position. Gordain had brought us deep into the heart of the Cairngorms National Park in the Highlands of Scotland. The cabin perched on the side of a mountain, near to a snowboarding centre, and beyond, there was a castle and a village, plus other houses dotted here and there in the landscape.

Still remote but far away from Torlum.

The castle was Gordain's home. He'd mentioned that last night.

I zoomed out farther on the map, checking the lie of the land. Yesterday, which felt like a lifetime ago, Thea had given us the news that the man we believed was our father, some wealthy old bastard called McInver, lived in a mansion in the Cairngorms.

Undoubtably, he was the reason we'd been imprisoned.

In a minute, I found his home on the map. McInver's estate was a thirty-minute drive away. I wanted nothing from the old pervert. Except answers.

Specifically, what happened to my mother.

Questions over the identity of my father brought me right back to memories of her. And her death.

Rustling had me raising my head.

Scar righted himself from his sprawl on the couch, pushing back a blanket. "Any news about Struan?"

"No."

"What time is it?"

"Eight."

My brother yawned and stretched his arms. "He has to be out of surgery by now."

I grunted acknowledgement, and Scar climbed from the sofa and took the opposite side of my window seat. Outside, the morning sun lit a tree-lined slope, a hill falling away beyond.

Sunrays pierced our hideaway, illuminating my brother, and highlighting the ridge of a scar that cut down the left side of his face. I didn't know the story of how he'd got the injury, but I wouldn't ask either.

He peered at me. "Jeez, Sin. Have ye even slept?"

"Don't need it."

He gazed at me then permitted a slow nod. "You've been watching over us. I've got this now. Go close your eyes. Sleep before ye pass out. We're safe enough, and we can't make any plans until everyone's here."

Exactly my thinking, and he'd understood instinctively. Together, we'd survived the island. What happened next was a decision for all of us.

Homeless, penniless, but not directionless. I'd keep us together, no matter what it took. I didn't doubt it would be a challenge, particularly with six-year-old Cassie. That changed nothing.

I couldn't shut off the thudding in my ears. The sense

that I should've done things differently. Got us away without help.

Hauled Thea's damn friend over my shoulder and taken her with us.

I stood from the window seat, my blood still rushing. "Ye say we're safe enough, but that's only until our so-called rescuer returns. I can't sit around and wait. I'm going to him. Keep the door locked, and I'll be back when I know his game."

I left the cabin, pausing to hear Scar engage the catch behind me. Then I set off down the hill for the road I knew from the map took me to the castle.

It was so fucking bright out here. I jogged to the cover of trees, following the road through a forest.

The castle was easy to find, the name of it, Braithar, etched in stone beside the huge arched entranceway. I strode up to hammer on the door, but it flew open before I could knock.

A woman appeared in the frame, not much older than me but using a stick to walk with. "Oh! Ye made me jump. Who are ye here for?"

"Gordain McRae."

She gave a warmer smile. "My father. Hang on." The lass leaned back into the castle. "Da? Visitor," she called.

She edged outside and pointed over her shoulder. "Go ahead and wait in the hall. He'll be right down."

The lass crutched over to a car, hopped in, and sped away. I stared in amazement. I could be anyone. Yet she'd just given me permission to walk straight into her home.

Despite the open front door and the wide hall beyond, I didn't move from the spot. Not until Gordain appeared, a toddler on his heavily tattooed arm.

He set his gaze on me, and his eyebrows furrowed. "Did something happen?"

I didn't like any of this. Not their lack of security. Not the implied, probably fake concern for me and mine. "No. Why did your daughter just leave this door wide open? What's up with that? I could rob ye blind and be out of here before ye knew it."

The older man set down who I guessed was his grandchild, holding the little lad's hand. "Aye, ye could. Coming in?"

He led me inside, through the airy hall to an office. He gestured for me to take a seat, then disappeared with the boy, returning alone.

"I left Finn with my wife. Ye have ten minutes until she starts work and I need to take him back, so talk to me."

What the fuck did I have to say? My head swam with exhaustion.

Gordain sighed, sitting back in his leather desk chair. "There's a reason I said I'd come over in the afternoon. After everything you've all been through, I assumed you'd need rest. I know your boy is okay. He won't need picking up today, though."

"You've heard from Struan?"

Gordain shook his head. "Max rang the hospital an hour ago. Struan had surgery, and he's in recovery now."

Everything felt false. Dangerous. Even my flood of relief. "Good to know."

"The police are asking questions. We told them we picked up Thea and Struan on a routine training exercise and knew nothing about them other than the lad was injured and they asked for our help. I don't suppose Struan will tell them the truth?"

I wasn't giving him anything. "What happened is our business."

A rough laugh was my answer. "Thought you'd say something like that. Then tell me what I can do to help."

"Why?"

"Why what, help ye? I trust my nephew. He has good instincts. He believed Struan to be in trouble, and the drama last night proved that out. Ye were imprisoned on that island, aye? Now you're free, and if ye want to stay that way, ye can't go it alone."

In that, he was wrong. For a long time, I'd had no one I could trust. My mother was dead, my life out of control. One by one, my brothers and sister had been delivered to me on the island. Our shared experience, our kinship, enabled me to get over the barrier of trust. But to this man, I owed nothing.

Even if he was genuine, which I doubted, hanging around here would be a mistake.

"All I need to know," I said, "is when to expect a visit from the police. We can be gone, and you'll have done your job."

"No one else knows you're here, aside from my family. We didnae tell the police there was anyone else involved. That doesn't mean trouble won't find us. It's possible that those islanders could make a report. If they looked closely at us or the helicopter, they might have identified our branding."

He pointed at a radio on his desk, a circular mountain rescue logo on the back. It had been on the helicopter and on their jumpsuits, too.

I gazed at it, not buying any of this. "Do ye seriously expect me to believe ye haven't called this in?"

Gordain's concern dropped, and he pinned me with his hard focus. "I'm a family man and laird of the land here. Sometimes it's necessary to involve the police when the law needs to play out in your favour. Other times, it isn't. I don't know what happened to ye, or why believing the word of an honest man is such a problem, but that's your shout. Use the cabin as long as ye need it. If ye want advice and guidance, I'm here for that, too. The only thing I ask is the guaranteed safety of my family and to know you're not at risk, especially the wee girl with ye."

"You're in no danger from us, and our sister has four brothers who'd die to protect her. All we want is to be left alone." I jumped up, weaving on my feet where tiredness threatened my strength.

Gordain stood with me, a hand out in case I needed it.

I couldn't accept it. I had no choice in using his hospitality, but it wouldn't last. The moment we had Struan back, we'd be gone.

At the cabin, Burn and Cassie were awake, and the smell of bacon filled the fancy space.

Scar emerged from the kitchen with a plate for me and a mug of something steaming. I grunted thanks and devoured the sandwich in seconds flat. Had I made a mistake this morning in trusting Gordain? I wasn't sure. Tiredness had become my enemy.

The three of them watched me, our little sister keeping close. It wasn't normal. There was a TV for her to watch. Space for her to play. My resolve doubled down.

"When you're done with that, you're sleeping," Scar decided. "It's either that or you're going to fall over."

"As soon as we've heard more about Struan." Despite Gordain's words, I couldn't rest.

On the table next to me, the phone blared, Thea's name onscreen.

I snapped to answer it and set it to loudspeaker. "Thea?"

"He's okay."

Her words spilled into the room, loud and with instant impact. All of us slumped, relief filling the space between us.

"He came out of surgery, but they wouldn't let me see him while he was in recovery. Nor would the doctor talk to me because I'm not next of kin. But a nurse let me know when he was brought down to the ward. Apparently he was yelling for me anyway, so I was there when the doctor came by."

"Yelling," Scar said. "That's a good sign."

"Isn't it? He said Struan was lucky. The second stab wound missed anything major, but it was deep and needed repairing all the same." Her voice dropped. "The police are here. Struan refused to give his name, and I wasn't about to either. They asked me all kinds of details about how he was hurt and even threatened to arrest me unless I gave them answers."

"What the fuck?" I burst out. "They can't arrest ye. You've done nothing wrong."

"I know! They tried to intimidate me about withholding information on a crime, but I called them on that. Struan was stabbed, but unless he wants to press charges against someone, or they have a suspect, there's been no actual crime reported. He kept passing out, but the minute he was awake, he told them where to go. The doctors don't know what to do with him. They've treated him under a John Doe name. I'm pretty sure as soon as he can walk, he's going to be out of here. For now, they have him sedated so he can't cause himself a new injury."

I palmed my forehead. "Thank fuck he's okay."

A fresh wave of exhaustion passed over me.

"There's more," Thea half whispered. "I heard the police talking in the corridor. They had a picture on one of their phones and they were discussing if that was him. Jamieson, they said. That's Burn, isn't it?"

I shot my gaze to my youngest brother. On the sofa, he heaved a sigh and gave a sarcastic thumbs-up.

"Careful you're not overheard," I said to Thea.

"Don't worry. I've left the hospital. I want Struan to have my phone, which means I need to pick myself up a cheap one. But also, Struan had car keys on him, and I remembered that he'd left your keeper's car in Inverness when he came to find me. I'm trying to track it down. If it'll run, we have a working vehicle."

Until this point, I hadn't been sure Thea would stick with us.

After all, her friend had so easily walked away.

I tapped the screen to drop her a pin. "I'm sending our location now. Drive here. Ye can rest up, and we'll return for Struan later. One way or another, we'll get him out."

"Okay," she agreed. "Got it. You're not that far away."

A pause came, then Thea took a rush of breath. "I just had another text. From Lottie. Holy heck."

Despite myself, my pulse thundered. "What happened to her?"

"I'll tell you when I see you. Got to go."

Infuriatingly, Thea hung up, and I glowered at the phone.

Happier emotion held in the room, and my brothers and sister talked about how Struan was alive. How he was going to hate being laid up.

I should be celebrating along with them, but a warning was building inside me. Violet, *Lottie,* had refused to leave the island yet was now chasing after Thea.

On top of the police, the islanders were our biggest threat.

And Violet was on their side.

4

Lottie

Thea's strained voice sounded on the other end of the line. "I'm at the coach station now. Can you see the old grey car? Find me."

I weaved through the throng of people coming and going from buses and hitched my bag over my shoulder. Thea had pulled up by the side of the road, parking badly and blocking a corner.

I jogged over, and she flung open her door. To the tune of some arsehole laying on their horn, we fell into a hug.

"I'm so glad you got away," my best friend uttered. "I've been so worried. I hated leaving you behind."

The beep sounded again, one long, irritable sound. I stuck my middle finger up to the driver then rounded the car to climb in the passenger side. Thea got us on the road, her hand briefly leaving the gear stick to grip my fingers.

Blood stained her sleeve.

Earlier, when I'd texted her on my long coach trip from Skye to Inverness, she'd called me straight back and told me about Struan getting stabbed and his emergency surgery at the hospital.

"Is there any news?" I asked.

"No. He's still unconscious. We're going to find the others now, which poses a small problem." She shot me an apologetic look. "Sin doesn't want you to know their location."

I shrank in on myself. "*Why?*"

"I think he's worried your dad will somehow find out. I told him that he's wrong and we can trust you."

Briefly, I closed my eyes. The whole way here, I'd wrestled with myself over my father's demands. The threats he'd made.

The only thing I was sure about was that I couldn't navigate it alone.

"Ye can't," I admitted.

"What?"

"Trust me."

Thea's eyes widened, and she took a corner, getting us onto the main road that led out of the city.

"The only reason Da let me go is so I can report back to him about the men," I confessed. "He was so angry that they'd escaped. I'm supposed to find them for him. Betray my friends."

Panic returned to me in a rush, and I swallowed, trying to stop the tremble that started deep inside.

For a long moment, I was lost in my head, going over the violence, the fear. I didn't realise Thea had pulled over until she took both my hands in hers. Her concerned gaze travelled over my brow.

"God, Lottie. He hit you?"

"Do I have a bruise? Nothing new there. That was probably my phone connecting with my head. At least I got it back."

I flipped down the sun visor and slid aside the cover to the mirror. A dark-red welt blended with my hairline, my blonde locks back in a braid which did nothing to obscure the edges. All day, I'd been travelling with that on display. Not that I had any makeup to conceal it, but even so. Embarrassment had me cringing in on myself.

Thea's gaze turned steely. "The bastard. You're safe now. We can make up something to tell him. You won't have to contact him or even go back again."

I squeezed her fingers. "Except I will. He said he'd hurt Ma. She's pregnant, and he threatened the baby, too."

"He'd put his own unborn child in danger? Why am I surprised, he uses his fists on you."

"It doesn't matter about me. Do ye see what's happening here? Sin's instincts were right on the money. I'm a snake in the grass, and you're taking me right to them."

My friend held my gaze, shock morphing to calculation. "Do you trust me?"

I gave an unhappy laugh. "Of course I do. You're one of the few people I care about."

"You care about Struan's brothers and sister. Sinclair most of all. I know that's true because you wouldn't have told me this otherwise. You could've just let me drive straight up to the door, texted your father, and had a welcome party of islanders arrive by nightfall."

I couldn't let that happen. I also couldn't let my mother get hurt. There was no good way out of this. "Da wants to know why they're important, presumably so he can blackmail them, but I wouldn't put kidnapping past him either. After all, he was happy to let them be imprisoned on the island for over a year. He's angry about the money he thinks he's owed for it. But ye have to believe me that I don't want this."

"I know." My friend drummed her fingers on the steering wheel. "Okay. Here's what we're going to do. First, we'll buy you some time. Text him and say you're in Inverness and waiting to meet me tonight. Once Struan's out of hospital, tell your dad that you and I are waiting at his bedside. That gives us time to leave and to think about how to help your mum. We'll talk to Sin—"

"No. He can't know. At least not yet. He'll chuck me out faster than I can blink. I need to work out a way to fix this myself, but I swear I won't throw them under a bus."

Thea stared at me but slowly nodded. "We'll find a way together. I'm going to guess you've had about as much sleep as I have. Neither of us can make a good decision right now. Send that text, switch your phone off, and grab something to use as a blindfold. We'll get to the safe house then talk more after food and rest, and after we've got my boyfriend back."

I was so selfish. Whatever my problems, at least I didn't have the man I loved in a hospital bed. I gave Thea a swift hug, then she got us back on our way.

Less than an hour later, the car shuddered around us, and Thea brought us to a stop.

"We're here. Keep the blindfold on for a moment. Let Sin see."

"He's not going to be happy."

She giggled, the sound anxious. "When is he ever? I don't think I've even seen him smile."

I had. My recurring daydream played it over and over. I'd also felt the edge of a smile on his lips when he'd kissed me. I hadn't told a soul about that. Had it only been yesterday? It felt like a lifetime ago. Everything had changed.

She exited the car, and voices reached me.

Then my door flew open, air rushing in.

"Christ, Thea," Sin snapped. "What the fuck were ye thinking?"

Slowly, I peeled off the blindfold made of one of the long-sleeved tops I'd hastily thrown into my bag before Da kicked me out.

We were parked beside a two-storey log cabin. Thick fir trees surrounded us on a hilly slope, no other houses in sight. Nowhere I recognised.

But all of this paled to the man looming over my door.

Sin glared down at me. My pulse raced, but I forced myself to stand on shaky legs. When he kissed me, he'd asked me to go with them. I'd said no. Whatever excuse I gave now wouldn't hold up.

"What are ye doing here, Violet?" he said, low and dangerous.

I hated lying to him, so I stuck to a partial truth. "I had to leave."

He narrowed his eyes. "Just like that. A day after we escaped. What changed?"

"Everything."

The moment played out between us. He was going to force me back into the car. Probably drive me away himself and leave me by the side of the road somewhere. I had no chance against him. He was so much bigger than me. Well over a foot taller, with a muscular frame I'd long drooled over. Against him, I was utterly powerless.

Then something registered in his expression, and his attention locked on to the mark on my forehead.

A wildness came over his gaze.

"Lottie!" a voice rang out.

A small black-haired girl pushed between me and Sin and threw her arms around my waist. "Oh my God, ye came. I wished for ye, and now you're here."

I sank to my knees and hugged Cassie in return. The six-year-old's warm welcome was the polar opposite to her icy big brother's, and for some reason, tears lodged in my throat.

She took a little shocked inhale, her fingertips drifting over my forehead. "Did ye fall and hurt yourself?"

"Something like that. I'm fine. I can barely feel it," I insisted.

At the door to the cabin, Sin's brothers appeared, both peering at me with a mixture of caution and happier emotions in their expressions. I rose again, and Thea took my hand in hers.

"Lottie's one of us," she announced, drawing me around the car door to slam it closed. "She escaped Torlum just like the rest of you, and now, she's staying with us. Anyone got a problem with that?"

I goggled at her. Thea had hardened up in the past year, but it suited her.

"No problem," Scar mumbled.

"Good to have ye here," Burn added.

Thea squeezed my fingers then marched into the cabin, the others going with her. Apart from Sin. He and I stayed locked in our respective positions.

Like it always did, his gaze travelled my body, briefly centring on my chest. Sin was a boob man, I'd guessed. Something I had in abundance, my only real charm. Maybe if I was lucky, I could seduce him like Da had suggested. It might buy me more time to try to work out what the hell to do.

"I don't know what's going on, but I'll find out. If ye want to stay here, you'll hand over your phone," he finally spoke.

I snorted a surprised laugh, slapping my hand to my mouth to stifle it. "I'm used to that. My da was always confiscating it, too. It's switched off, so ye know."

I took the device from my bag, holding it out. Sin shoved it in his back pocket before moving closer, intimidating me with his size. The top of my head barely came up to his shoulder, so I had to crane my neck to link my gaze to his.

We were so close. Enough to feel his warmth. Enough to see the flecks of steel grey in those dark-blue eyes.

Every hair on my body stood on end. Every inch of skin came alive, burning for his touch. I should feel threatened by him, but impossibly, he only stirred me up.

Sin's chest rose and fell.

"The safety of my family is all that's important now. I will end anyone who threatens that." He dropped each word like a bomb.

Abruptly, he turned and marched away.

Tiredness hit me, and I swayed on my feet. I'd done it, found them, and I had exactly no idea of what to do next. One thing was clear: No matter what Thea had said about me being one of them, that could never be the case.

I was the outsider.

Everything I wanted came at the cost of ruining their hard-fought freedom. And threw me in the path of Sin's wrath.

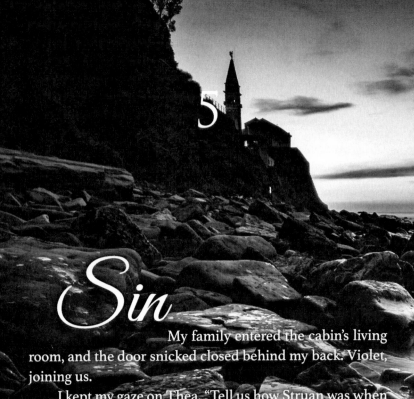

5

Sin

My family entered the cabin's living room, and the door snicked closed behind my back. Violet, joining us.

I kept my gaze on Thea. "Tell us how Struan was when ye last saw him."

Thea perched on the edge of the sofa, her shoulders slumped. "Still unconscious. I snuck the phone in to him and made sure the nice nurse knew it was there. He was hooked up to a drip and monitors. I didn't want to leave him, but they wouldn't let me stay."

Violet took the middle sofa seat and held Thea's hand. Cassie scooted over and huddled in next to her, the three lasses in a line.

Scar jerked his chin at Thea. "So the surgery went well. Did the nurse say how long it would take him to recover?"

She curled in on herself more. "The doctor said he'd need to be under observation for several days, which is when he freaked out and they sedated him. It was awful. I didn't think anything could beat the horrors of the past day, but that took top place."

"And the cops?" Burn asked.

"Still there. I saw them as I was leaving."

"Is Struan going to be arrested?" Cassie piped up.

Thea turned her tired gaze on the wee girl. "I don't think they can. Not unless they make up a reason, and why would they do that?"

"Because Struan looks like a poster boy for delinquency," Burn said on a hard laugh. "All of us do. There's any number of reasons why they could decide to take him down to the station for a friendly chat. Pin shite on him. Let alone if the islanders reported us for crimes they've invented. We cannae let that happen."

"Or crimes we actually committed. Charterman is dead. We ransacked the hostel. Burned down a house." I flicked a gaze at Burn, our pet arsonist, then swept my gaze around the room to include everyone in my thinking. "All of that could be blamed on him. The fact he isn't handcuffed to his bed tells me those reports haven't come their way yet. The minute he's out of life-threatening danger, we need to free him."

Thea nodded. "Agreed. It's all he'll want." She broke out in a large yawn.

It was catching. None of us had slept well, if at all. Scar, Burn, and Cassie had only grabbed a few hours earlier today. Whatever Violet had been through left dark rings around her eyes, as well as the bruise that was slowly driving me mad.

"Here's what's going to happen," I said. "Unless there's a reason to leave, we'll stay in this cabin until we're all back together again. Only then will we make decisions about what the hell to do with ourselves. If Struan is likely to be unconscious until evening, we're all going to rest up until then. One person needs to be on guard at all times, and everyone needs to sleep, eat, and be ready for tonight."

Violet raised her hand. "I can cook."

I gave a single shake of my head, a swift conclusion forming in my mind. "Not now. You're sleeping with me."

Her eyes widened, and pink flooded her cheeks. "I'm what?"

"I don't trust ye, but I need rest. If ye want to stay here, it'll be under my watch. Which means on the opposite side of any bed I'm in."

"Sin!" Thea objected.

But Violet lifted her chin. "No. It's okay. I can handle that if he can."

She stood then made for the stairs. I followed, my heart thumping too fast, but I wasn't going to back down.

Murmurs chased us, but I ignored them all to pursue Violet.

In the hall upstairs, she passed open bedroom doors, peeking into each one. "Which is yours? I can't see your things."

I'd only been upstairs to scout the place. "I don't have any things. Pick the biggest bed. I need the space."

She arched an eyebrow and entered the room at the end, a wide master bedroom with a huge bed. "If it's space you're after, why insist on me staying with ye?"

"Until I can trust ye, you'll stay where I can see ye."

Across the room, I snapped down a blackout blind to cover the window with its panoramic view of the wooded valley, then drew the curtains, plunging us into darkness. Only the open en suite door gave us light to see by.

Violet set down her bag on a chair and eyed the bed.

Tiredness gnawed at my senses. I needed to pass out and sleep hard.

Next to Violet.

My error slammed into me. I hadn't fucked anyone in a long time. While I'd been on the island, the lass now closed in here with me had been front and centre of my fantasies. Every time I jerked off in the shower, it had been with her in mind.

Her pretty face, curvy arse, and tight cunt. Her tits. Christ. They alone had become a not-so-minor obsession of mine.

She chewed her lip and gestured at the bed. "Do ye have a side?"

Aye. Inside her.

I gave a shrug, and Violet bent to remove her shoes. Providing me a view right down the valley of her chest. Instantly, I was rock-hard, my desire for sleep replaced by utter need for her.

On her knees. Or all fours.

Under me and crying out.

Those tits of hers in my hand, mouth, mine to play with.

Without a word, I stormed into the bathroom and closed the door, thumping the switch for the shower to spring to life. Then I stripped, stepped under the hot water, and took my dick in hand.

I gripped myself in the way I imagined how tight she'd be.

Relief came as I fucked my fist. With my eyes closing of their own accord, I let the hot water sluice over me. Back at the hostel, I'd done this too many times to count. Feet apart, one hand braced to the cool tile wall, my mind on the lass across the island while I jerked myself into a fever.

Except now, she was only the other side of the wall.

A smirk spread over my lips. Whatever her reason for coming here, it wasn't good. I couldn't touch her. No matter how badly I wanted to. But that didn't mean I couldn't still use my thoughts of her.

Images I'd created over long months flashed back into my mind. Naked, she'd be a fucking goddess. Curves in all the right places. Taking me in deep when I worshipped her body. Those incredible tits.

It was the curve from the top of them towards the centre that did me in. A guide for me to follow. I'd mentally traced that with my tongue more times than I could count. Following the path down.

In my grip, my dick hardened so much I was gasping for breath, my impending orgasm tightening my balls. The end images of my fantasy were always the same. Her nipple in my mouth. My cum spilling into her cunt. Her crying out, coming with me.

That last glimpse always pushed me over the edge.

Groaning her name, I came into the hot stream of water. Each pulse savage and...fucking wasted. The shower washed away my sin as I jerked my last.

The door clicked, and I raised my gaze to find her in the frame, staring right at me with shock in her eyes. I hadn't tried to hide the sounds I was making. She'd come here for a purpose, and if I couldn't fuck her, I was going fuck with her until I found out.

Violet held my stare then slowly let her gaze slip down my body. I was still hard, and I didn't conceal myself. She didn't look away, soaking in the sight of what she'd done to me.

Her lips parted, and her tongue darted out to lick them. Then she turned and fled.

All the lust I'd burned up flooded right back into my mind.

There was only one way it would ever ease. With her under me. Which meant I was in for a world of pain.

I took time over washing myself and drying off, giving the woman a chance to get to sleep. Then, naked, I entered the bedroom and climbed into the big bed.

There was two feet of space between me Violet, and she slept on her side, facing away from me. I stuck my hands behind my head and forced my eyes to close. With everything that had gone on, the utter mindfuck of the past year and the culmination of it in one twenty-four-hour period, I wasn't sure I'd ever rest peacefully again. People had died. Every one of my family had been in danger in one way or another. Still were.

Yet somehow, lulled by Violet's regular breaths, I passed out into thankful, oblivious sleep.

6

Lottie

Sex fascinated me. Despite having zero experience with another person, beyond the single knee-weakening kiss with Sin, I'd explored my own body. Chased the good feelings it gave me. I'd never felt ashamed, though I had complete terror about ever doing the same with a guy.

Waking in the dark room with my fingers slipping under the line of my underwear wasn't new.

Doing so with a huge man in the bed next to me was anything but.

Sin made a low grumbling sound in his slumber.

I paused my sleep-induced wandering and held my breath. In the shower, he'd said my name. Done so while jacking himself off. I'd stared at his huge dick then scuttled back to bed, hopelessly turned on, but with one fact clear in my head.

I couldn't do anything about it.

Not with him. Not when I might have to betray him.

But what I'd seen... No wonder I'd woken up like this.

I wriggled on the sheets, my fingertips so close to where I needed them. The towering need inside me steadily built. Probably a result of the stress I'd been through. My body needed that natural release. He'd done it—

Sin rolled over in the bed, just enough light in the room for me to see his eyes were still closed. He reached out blindly, and his hand landed on my shoulder.

I froze.

My skin lit up with a lick of electricity.

That hand drifted lower then settled, loosely cupping my breast. I clamped my lips over a gasp. My heart thumped so hard he had to feel it in his sleep.

He was *touching me.* Only the thin layer of my t-shirt divided us.

My nipple hardened, poking into his palm, and a burst of lust shot through me. The tiniest degree of friction from his move generated blooms of warmth, radiating from my nipple to each pleasure point.

Too much and nowhere near enough.

I restarted my breathing, lips apart, then eased my fingers deeper into my underwear. Autopilot drove me to seek my damp centre. I dipped my fingers into my wetness, hitching a breath at how good it felt. Then I drew back to drive a light circle over my clit.

I did it again, resisting the urge to hiss at my surge of heat.

Was this wrong? He'd got himself off using me as his aid. He was touching me now, but... Not consciously. If he was awake, he probably wouldn't get this close to me with a barge pole.

I swallowed, not liking the way my thoughts were leading.

I should stop. Take myself into the bathroom to finish alone.

The hand at my breast tensed. Sin's breathing changed, and he stiffened beside me.

God, he was waking up.

I held perfectly still, waiting for him to snap his hand away. To leap up and shout at me. Instead, he took a short inhale as if shocked by what he was doing. Then his fingertips dug into my soft flesh.

I arched into his grip, a tiny push of my shoulders into the mattress.

In all the things I'd done to myself, working out that my breasts were highly sensitive had only provided frustration. I couldn't play with both my nipples and touch my clit at the same time. Or slide my fingers in and out of myself, seeking an orgasm. I needed another person for that.

For the first time, I had one.

A soft whimper left my lips. I moved my fingers again over my clit. I couldn't help it.

In a rush, Sin lurched up, the blankets falling off us. His hand whipped to find mine skating over my core, and he gave up a growl of need.

For a heart-stopping moment, he curved his massive, naked frame over me and set his forehead on mine. I had no idea what he was going to do or say. Only that I needed this moment more than I'd ever wanted anything. In the dark room, the air charged, some kind of explosion imminent.

He pressed harder, my boob still in his grip, his mouth millimetres from mine.

But then pain burst across my forehead. He was pushing directly on the bruise Da had given me.

"Ow," I whispered.

He recoiled.

At the same second, footsteps drummed along the hall. Someone hammered at the door.

"Sin, Lottie, wake up. Struan's on the phone," Burn called.

We broke apart instantly, and I leapt from the bed, dragging on my jeans before Sin could turn on the light and see my bare thighs.

He was half dressed and out the door when I turned, but I caught a fleeting glimpse of his bare, muscular back as it disappeared under his t-shirt. I chased him down the stairs to find Thea and the others crowded around her phone.

"...no fucking way they can keep me here," Struan's angry voice sounded. "I can walk around fine, but they won't let me get dressed. The doc threatened me with another dose of whatever knocked me out if I didn't calm down. Consider this me fucking calm. Get me out of here."

Sin grabbed the phone. "It's me. Drop your voice and listen up. Play along with whatever they ask. If you're good to walk, you're good to leave, aye? But it won't happen if they're watching ye constantly as a flight risk. Now, repeat this out loud."

Rustling came from Struan's end of the line, like he was sitting taller in the hospital bed. "Good to hear your fucking voice. Go for it."

"Say this: 'Okay, Ma, I'm not going to do anything daft. I'm just frustrated, but I'm not about to bust my stitches. Can ye bring me in some clothes in the morning?'"

Grouchily, and a little louder, Struan repeated the words.

I crossed to stand with Thea, giving her my support. Her boyfriend was a hothead, but he listened to Sin. If we were going to get him out unscathed, we all needed Sin's plan.

The big man dipped his head. "Good, in a minute, call out a couple of things for your fake ma to bring in. That way they're expecting ye to still be there in the morning." He glanced over at a clock on the wall. "It's nine PM now. I don't know what time hospital shifts start and stop—"

I raised a hand. "It's seven till seven for the nurses. They work twelve-hour shifts then have thirty minutes' handover."

A relative of mine, Annis, had been a nurse for years, but recently retired back to Torlum. Her workload had always been punishing, though she'd loved it. For a while, I'd wanted to be a nurse, too, and I'd peppered Annis with questions. I'd even done a work placement at a community hospital for a few weeks when deciding on college courses.

Sin's gaze held mine for a beat. "Which means the new shift has already started, and all those people will be bright-eyed and alert. I'm guessing they won't all take lunch at the same time and leave an empty ward for us?"

I shook my head. "Unlikely. Struan, what kind of ward are ye on? Is it a private suite or an open room with lots of beds?"

"The first option. Bring my charger, too, Ma," he answered, following the game.

It made sense that they'd put Struan into a private room if the police were going to want access to him. It also made things easier for us. I ran over what I knew about hospitals.

Sin kept his focus on me, giving me the floor. A shiver

ran through me at the opportunity to prove I wasn't just a threat.

"Nurses work on systems of checks and observations. They'll have set times to come in and do those, plus to administer any medicines the doctors have prescribed. Adult wards have people coming and going all the time during visiting hours, but relatives can have reasons to hang around after, for example if someone is dying. They don't kick ye out. Our best bet is to sneak in, get to your room between checks, unhook ye from the machines, and walk straight out. They can object, but they can't stop ye from leaving."

"But the police can," Sin interjected.

I had no idea what the police would do, but it felt right to avoid them. "I think the police sometimes have officers permanently posted at city hospitals. If you see them, they'd have no reason to stop you or ask questions, not until you have Struan and are walking out with him. That bit, you'll need to do fast."

A swift nod from Sin gave me a fresh burst of confidence.

"Here's what we're going to do," he decided. "Struan, grab your chart and tell us the time of the last checks. We'll do what Violet suggests and walk in like we own the place, one person in the car outside in case we need a fast getaway."

Scar stood taller. "Who's going? It can't be everyone."

Sin gave a single shake of his head. "Just two or three of us. We'll need the space in the car to bring Struan back."

Thea's lip trembled. "I'm going. Don't you dare say otherwise."

He awarded her a brief nod, then his gaze drifted over the rest of us, finally settling on me. "Thea, Violet, and I will go. Scar, Burn, and Cassie, you'll stay here. Don't answer the door. Don't go out."

An excited thrill danced down my spine. I'd expected him to order me to stay. Lock me up. But no, he wanted me with him. I could be even more useful this way.

Objections sounded loud, Scar most of all, but Sin silenced them with a glare.

"This is going to work, and it'll be by ye all listening to me. Burn can't go out in public anyway, and Violet and I can pass for a couple while Thea plays getaway driver. Struan, we're coming for ye. Be ready."

That applied to all of us.

In the dead of night, Thea drove up to Raigmore Hospital, passing the brightly lit Accident and Emergency department with its line of ambulances outside. On the journey from the Cairngorms, we'd hatched a plan, and my knees jiggled with the need to get it underway. I liked action. I liked being helpful. I especially wanted to reunite my friend and her boyfriend. And to have the hope of one of Sin's smiles bestowed on me.

He and I were playing a *couple.* My fantasy come true.

Thea pulled over and peeked at Sin in the passenger seat, then to me in the seat behind. "I'll be here and waiting. Please be gentle with him. Keep him safe."

"We'll get our boy," Sin assured her.

He and I climbed out into the cool night air.

From downloading the hospital's floor plans, and from

Struan's information, we knew exactly where his ward and room was. The first hurdle was to get past security and into the main hospital building.

Faking confidence, I paced purposefully to the main entrance. The doors opened automatically, but a uniformed guard waited on the other side. She smiled politely, and I swiped a shaky finger under my eyes and reached back to take Sin's hand in mine.

My heart pounded, all my nerves on edge.

"Which way to the cardiac suite, please?" I asked with a shudder in my voice. "My da was in for emergency heart surgery, but they rang to tell me I had to come down right away. I'm his next of kin. There were complications. It was so unexpected. He was doing so well."

The guard's expression crinkled in sympathy. "I'm so sorry, sweetheart. Zone five. Follow the blue markers to the ward. Someone will take ye to him."

I dipped my head in thanks and marched on, towing Sin with me.

The moment we were around the corner, he dropped my hand as if my touch burned.

I peeked up at him. "That was easy."

His so-serious gaze held on me. "Good acting skills."

My answering laugh came out nervous, and I fast-walked down the empty corridor. "Or maybe I spent a lot of time as a child hoping my da would have a heart attack and practiced pretending like I gave a damn."

The corridor opened out into a crossroads with lifts to other floors. We ignored the blue markers to follow the orange zone seven ones, Struan's ward.

Ahead, the lift whooshed down.

A second ahead of it opening, and leaving us in the

path of potentially nosey hospital staff, Sin hauled open the door to the stairwell and manhandled me inside.

Without hesitation, he jogged up two flights. I plodded after him, scowling and half out of breath by the time I reached him.

"Wait for me. I don't have mile-long legs like ye."

He leaned on the stair rail, and his gaze sank down my body. "No, ye don't."

From any other man, I probably would've heard that as an insult. But not from him. Instead, my body warmed yet again. There had been a moment between us in bed earlier. A second of balancing of whether we were going to follow the direction our bodies were leading, or stop.

It was better that we'd been interrupted. He'd hate me less that way. Someone needed to get that memo to my lady parts.

Sin peered out of the door. We were on the right floor now, Struan's ward at the end of the corridor. Together, we slipped out and approached with caution, our target visible through windows in the heavy double doors.

The next bit was going to be more complicated. We had to enter the ward, avoid any nurses or medics, and get to his room undetected. Which meant spotting a gap. But right now, we were out in the open.

The ward's doors swung open, and a man bustled our way, pushing an empty wheelchair. In hospital uniform, he was either an orderly or a porter.

Oh shite. The worst person to encounter.

His gaze locked on us, and I anticipated the question to come, so spun around to face Sin.

"Hug me."

He furrowed his brow. "I don't like touch."

That was news. He'd definitely liked touching my boobs. I moved in closer, determined. "Fake it. Hug me like I'm distraught and need comforting."

"Weep, then," he retorted, but his rigid arms came around me all the same.

Suddenly, I was pressed to his hard chest, right in the place I'd always wanted to be. It didn't matter that it wasn't real, not to my mind and body. The deep scent of him filled my lungs, and I closed my eyes and snuggled in, only remembering to shake with tears a second before the man's voice interrupted us.

"Excuse me. Visiting hours were over a long time ago. Ye can't be here."

Sin loosely patted my back. "We were called in with bad news," he intoned, his voice flat.

God, his acting skills sucked.

I choked on my pretend crying, though my eyes had actually filled with water, and turned to face the man. "I'm in shock. How could this happen? Everything was okay, and now he's... He's..."

I burst into a fresh flood of tears and hugged Sin. I wouldn't get to do this again. Might as well enjoy it while I had permission.

A pause came, then the orderly's voice returned. "I understand. Still, ye can't wait in this corridor. I'll take ye to the bereavement room where ye can have privacy. Or I can call a taxi from the foyer."

Damn it. "No." I shook my head. "We have to stay here to meet the doctor. They need to write something then call in the coroner. What was it called again, baby?"

I peered up at Sin who stared back, baffled.

The orderly stroked his chin, his suspicion mellowing.

"Ye mean the declaration of death. Only a doctor can decide someone is deceased."

I gave a relieved smile. "That's it. Thank ye. I'm sure he won't be long. Though the nurse said it was very busy tonight so we might have a wait."

He sucked his teeth. "You're not wrong. Rushed off my feet."

I made a little 'O' with my mouth. "Yet ye found the time to stop to talk to us. You're so kind."

The suspicion dissolved from his expression, and the man graced us with a smile, resting a hand on the wheelchair. "It's my job to make sure this hospital runs smoothly."

I nodded with enthusiasm. "I'm sure they couldn't cope without ye. Thanks so much for your help. We won't keep ye any longer."

The orderly bobbed his head sagely.

But he didn't leave.

"Lost my own ma at this very hospital. Several years ago now, but the memories never leave."

"Sorry—"

"'Course, she was eighty, so it wasnae a surprise. The list of ailments she had took longer to read out than her eulogy."

I reluctantly released Sin, conscious over him not wanting me touching him and needing to focus on how we were going to get away. We couldn't wait around, not without risking other staff joining us. Struan was in one of the rooms beyond, and all we had to do was get to him.

But just as the orderly started on a list of the treatment his poor mother had received, a siren blared.

In a heartbeat, people were everywhere.

7

Struan – *thirty seconds earlier*

"Motherfucking fuck." The wee plastic tube piercing my arm stung as I yanked it out, liquid dripping. Already, I'd half dressed myself under the sheets. My jeans and boxers were still damp from last night's dip in the sea and bloodied from my stab wounds.

Not much I could do about that.

Swinging my legs from the bed, I shrugged off the hospital gown and pulled on my t-shirt. A hole pierced it.

For fuck's sake.

I stooped to snag my boots from the bedside locker, closing my eyes against the rush of blood to my head. Being upright was messing with me, but I wasn't about to sit on my arse any longer. A text message from Theadora had clued me in to the plan.

Sin and Lottie were about to spring me.

They were going to fail.

Neither would be able to see what I saw. The cop arguing with another patient in the room opposite. Some old geezer who'd been kicking off with the staff.

Through the glass panel in my door, I could see the uniformed officer across the corridor. He wasn't here for me, not this guy, but I'd bet any money one call and my own personal interrogators would be back.

I sucked in a breath and pushed off the bed, straightening to test my balance. I tilted right and scowled, correcting myself. The pain meds were messing with my head, but all I needed to do was get out of my room, off the ward, and downstairs. If I was outside, my friends could find me. I'd even let Sin fucking carry me if it meant getting out of this place.

Which meant causing a distraction.

By the door, a wee red box was my target. With two knuckles, I smashed the glass.

The fire alarm instantly screamed its warning.

The cop backed out of the opposite room, hesitated, then strode left towards the nurses' station. Showtime. I swung open my door, and without pause, went right instead.

Jesus. Walking was a trip. Pain lanced through the fog of medicine, slowing me down. I clutched my hand to my side, blinking to find a nurse exiting a room on the same side as mine.

"Please return to your bed," she said but hustled in the same direction as the cop.

I passed the open door, taking a glance inside. On the raised bed, a man watched TV, ignoring the siren and with his leg in a plaster cast.

A white bag of meds perched on the table next to him.

What were the odds he'd been prescribed antibiotics? I needed those fuckers, the doctor had said.

Making a decision, I pushed into his room, snatched the bag, and backed out.

"Oi!" the guy yelled, but the alarm drowned him out.

I didn't stop.

Had to run.

Tucking the bag under my shirt, I paced on. The entrance to the ward was maybe fifteen metres away. No distance at all. Somehow, every step I took seemed to make it farther. The siren wailed too loud, my breathing came too short, and the edges of my vision blackened.

Oh fuck. I was going to pass out.

A yelp of frustration came from me, and I slumped against the wall.

Slid down it.

I'd got this far, but it was over.

Then hands took me. Lifted me. I couldn't see now, but I picked up the shocked gasp of a woman then a man's grumbled response.

Lottie and Sin. They'd found me. Right at the second I needed them.

"Meds," I muttered, flopping a hand to indicate what I'd dropped.

"Got 'em," Lottie replied.

Darkness stole my relief and knocked me out.

Next I knew, cold air slapped me and an engine thundered. Thank fuck that wailing siren was out of my ears.

"Oh my God. Is he okay?"

Theadora. My lass.

"He passed out. Quick," Sin ordered. "Get in the back with him."

He jostled me, then my head was in Theadora's lap and I was stretched out on the back seat of a car.

"I'll drive," my brother demanded.

"No argument from me," Lottie replied. "I've never even sat behind the wheel of a car."

I missed his reply, but whatever he said pissed her off.

"How? I lived on an island with no cars. What was I supposed to do?"

"How old are ye?"

"Twenty. Now stop baiting me. I need to look at the meds bag. We have bandages. Some painkillers. Oh, antibiotics! Score."

She continued, but my attention drifted. To Thea's warm touch. Her fingertips ghosting over my face and into my hair.

"I was so worried," she whispered. "They wouldn't let me stay with you. Even after you said you wanted me there, they told me I had to go. I thought I'd never see you again."

"The bastards," I said back, hushed. "I'll never leave ye again."

Something splashed on my cheek. Thea brushed her tear away with her thumb, but I caught her hand. Pressed it to my mouth.

"When we can, I'm going to marry ye."

Whatever her response, I lost it to another blood rush then darkness.

No one would keep her from me again.

Not her old friend, Esme, the bitch who stabbed me, not her da, who we all thought was dead before we found out otherwise. Whatever battles we had to come, I meant every word. She was mine. One of my family.

Whatever Thea wanted, I'd give to her. If it took everything I had.

8

Esme

Across the hotel room, the man watched me.

"My dad blew your cover," I snapped at him. "Right before he died, he told Thea you're still alive. Your daughter knows."

His lips twitched, but little emotion showed on his haggard face. "That could pose a problem."

For him. I had nothing now. Dad was dead. He'd always given me direction. A target for my anger. Without that, I was lost.

Augustus Stewart leaned forward, his hands on his knees. He'd aged in the time he'd been in hiding. Dad said he'd been running from debt collectors, which was how he'd entrapped him into the plan in the first place. Augustus needed money. We had been due a windfall, if my father could've manipulated McInver and got him to agree to have my brother as his heir.

All that had been lost.

"Listen, Esme," Augustus said, wrapping his voice around my name.

Despite myself, I inched closer. I'd only made it off that island because he had a boat waiting. Plucked me from the water. He'd saved me.

"Your father was my oldest friend. I cared about him and I care about you and your brother. My daughter...disappointed me. In many ways. You, on the other hand, made your father proud. It is my role now to take up where he left off. You are not alone."

I had my brother and my stepmother. But they were weak.

I'd always needed a firm hand.

A plan. A way to get my due for everything I'd suffered.

"I'm your daddy now," Augustus crooned. "And you are my new daughter."

"Yes," I breathed.

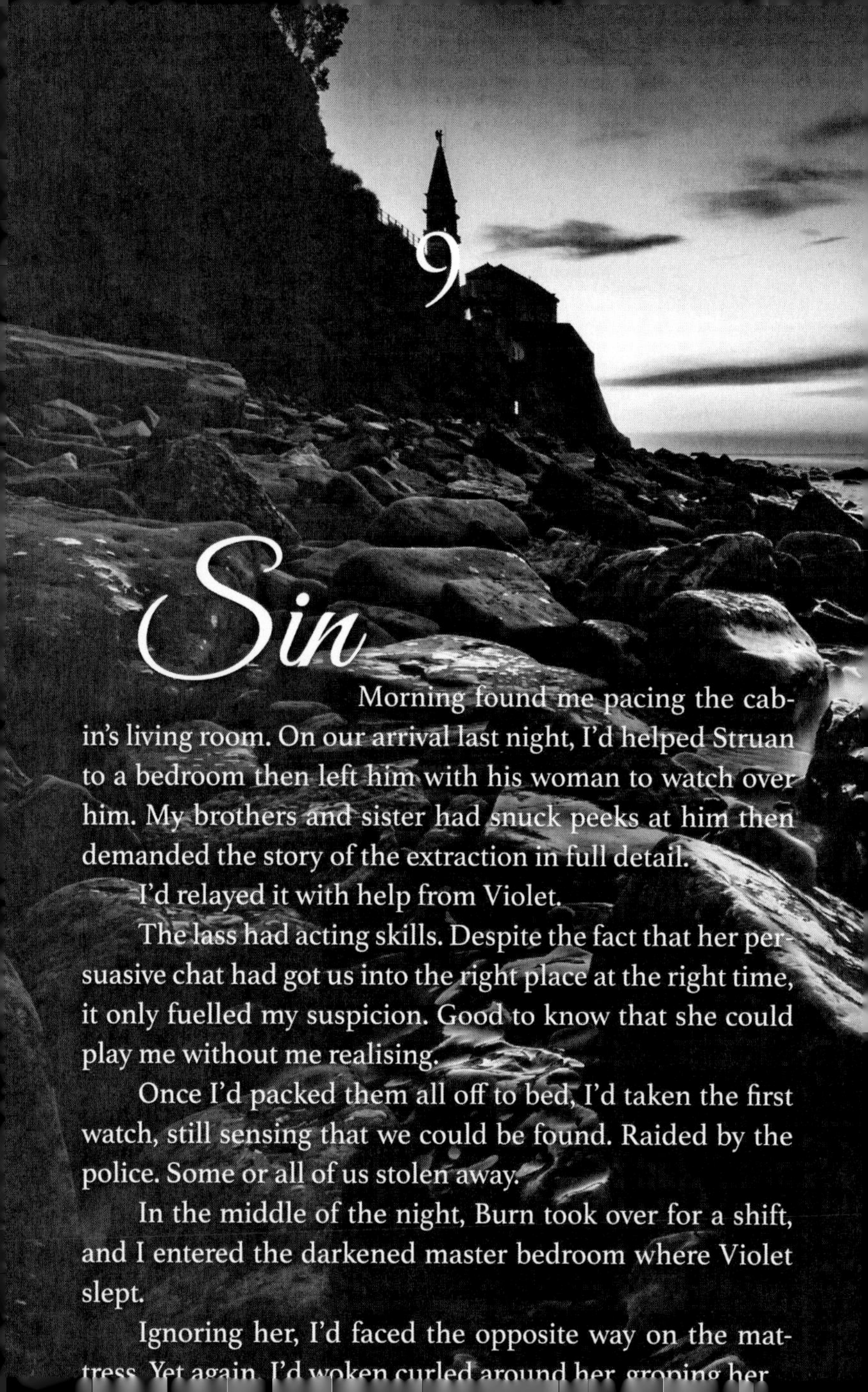

9

Sin

Morning found me pacing the cabin's living room. On our arrival last night, I'd helped Struan to a bedroom then left him with his woman to watch over him. My brothers and sister had snuck peeks at him then demanded the story of the extraction in full detail.

I'd relayed it with help from Violet.

The lass had acting skills. Despite the fact that her persuasive chat had got us into the right place at the right time, it only fuelled my suspicion. Good to know that she could play me without me realising.

Once I'd packed them all off to bed, I'd taken the first watch, still sensing that we could be found. Raided by the police. Some or all of us stolen away.

In the middle of the night, Burn took over for a shift, and I entered the darkened master bedroom where Violet slept.

Ignoring her, I'd faced the opposite way on the mattress. Yet again, I'd woken curled around her, groping her fucking amazing tits and harder than ever for her.

My plan to keep an eye on her had backfired. It had required every morsel of my self-control to climb out of that bed and take out my lust on my fist in the shower instead.

"Hey, man," Struan said from the top of the stairs.

With care, he eased down the first of the stairs, his hair damp, and a warning in his eyes for me not to help him. I got that. His pride was as overblown as mine.

"Where's Thea?" I asked.

"Drying her hair. Should be down in a minute. What the fuck is up with this place?" He gestured to the plush, striped dressing gown he'd put on over his boxers, the front hanging open and displaying white bandages plastering his side.

"A luxury holiday rental." I curled my lip.

I'd never once been on a holiday, but my mother had taught me the trick of how to find empty holiday homes. More than once, we'd used them when we were between houses.

"You'd know better than me," I added. "We're on your friend's land."

He reached the bottom of the stairs, taking a second to breathe through obvious pain. "That so? I've no fucking clue what planet I'm on, let alone where we are."

Scar emerged from the kitchen, carrying a fistful of mugs. "Does it matter where we are? We're free."

Free. I couldn't accept the statement.

Struan swore. "Temporarily, maybe. Catch me up. What's happened?"

He lowered himself onto one of the grey sofas, pale, but alive. Not bleeding anymore.

I stared at him for a second to reassure myself of the

fact, then put my hand to my mouth. "Family meeting," I bellowed, summoning the others.

Cassie scampered in from the kitchen with Burn hot on her heels. At the top of the stairs, Thea emerged with Violet, and the two women trotted down.

At the base of the stairs, Violet stood in a patch of late-morning sunlight. She'd taken a shower, and her fair hair was loose, golden in the sun, gleaming as she divided it into strands then started braiding it. I'd never seen her with her hair down. She always wore it twisted in neat plaits around her head.

For some reason, I couldn't stop staring.

"Earth to Sin," one of my brothers said with a laugh.

I snapped out of it and picked up one of the coffees Scar had brought in, taking a deep sip. Then I addressed the room. "Now we have Struan back with us, we can finally have this conversation."

My pulse picked up, the next part of what I had to say not about to be comfortable.

"First of all, before we talk about what we're expecting to go down, I don't want to make plans on anyone's behalf. I've kept us together, and that's what I want. My family with me. But if anyone else has somewhere to go, or people to be with, I'll help ye get to them."

Silence met my words.

My intention was to give them the option to leave, even though it was the opposite of my instincts. I hadn't had a family in a long time, and I wanted to pull them closer. We'd made it off the island. They had a choice.

I needed to know everyone was all in.

"I was in foster care when I was kidnapped and taken to the hostel," Burn said slowly. "There's people I want to see again but naw for good reasons. Unless ye kick me out, you're all my family now."

"Same," Scar said. "Even if I had somewhere else to go, I wouldn't."

Cassie gazed at me with rounded eyes. "I don't want to leave."

Burn set an arm around her and gave her a squeeze. "No one's going to make ye. You're our sister. Ye belong with us."

Struan glared at me. "Is this a serious question? After everything we've been through together, you'd consider walking away?"

I rolled a heavy look at him. "Did ye listen to what I said? I want us to stay together. I'm giving ye the option not to, if that's what you'd prefer."

"Fuck that." He reached for Thea and eased her down on the sofa next to him.

She curled her legs underneath her. "What he said. I'm just as mixed up in this as anyone else. My father caused many of the problems we're facing. I vote that this is us. A family."

At the edge of my vision, Violet shifted on her feet. I'd deliberately included her in this debate. Wanting to see her squirm.

"I'm not one of your kin," she said slowly. "I know that. And I've got my own objective in leaving Torlum."

There it was. The reason for her being here was nothing to do with escaping her da or following her friends.

I lifted my chin. "And I don't imagine you're about to share that secret?"

Thea's eyebrows dove together. "Don't talk to her like that. She's already explained everything to me."

"I'd rather hear it from her."

I stared Violet down. She didn't drop my gaze, some inner turmoil in her eyes. I didn't like it. Hated not knowing her mind. Hated even more that my need for her was only growing.

"I'll tell ye, if ye insist. But I'd rather not. At least not yet. Give me some grace to handle it. I promise that standing here today, I'm no threat."

What the fuck kind of answer was that?

But everyone was staring at me as if I was the bad guy.

The moment played out, then I breathed out through my nose. "Whatever."

The lass gave a small, apologetic smile, then dropped her gaze. "I'm going to make lunch while ye talk. I noticed someone brought supplies. Cassie, if the conversation gets too boring, come and join me. I could use a hand."

Violet shot me another look, and I pulled my head out of my arse for a second to see what she did—a discussion about violence and threat probably wasn't best for Cassie.

"I'll come now! But can ye do my hair first? I want it just like yours." Cassie beamed and danced away to the kitchen.

I watched them leave, then turned my attention to Thea. "If she's a risk to my family, I need to know."

"Watch your tone," Struan snapped.

Thea jutted out her chin. "Lottie isn't a danger to us. God knows we have enemies on all sides. She isn't one of them."

"I'll be the judge of that."

The lass cut me a hard stare. "You know it's true, or you wouldn't have ordered her into your bed."

I shrugged, happy to be the arsehole in this. "Didn't hear her objecting."

"Would ye quit arguing?" Scar snapped. "I don't know about the rest of ye, but I'm on day two of apparently being free, and I feel anything but that. We're off the island, but where does that leave us? Are we on the run?"

He was right. We needed to get down to business.

I drew a heavy breath and sat in an armchair, regarding the others. "I don't know, but a priority has to be finding that out. What do we know for certain?"

Struan adjusted his position on the sofa, drawing the dressing gown closer around him. "We know why we were kidnapped. At least we have a theory. Rich and decrepit McInver is our father, and either he or someone else with him wants to stop us claiming an inheritance when the old goat kicks it."

Thea nodded agreement. "We know more than that. When I was in the sea fighting off Charterman, he was screaming things at me. Like the fact he married a relative of McInver's just so he'd have a son who could be in line for that money. He and Esme were working to put Henry in that spot."

Her boyfriend gave a dark laugh. "Look how well that turned out for him."

Struan had drowned the man. I'd watched them tussle in the water then Charterman's body get carried in by the islanders. My brother was a murderer. Good for him.

He turned to Thea. "Is that the reason Esme stabbed me? She said I was in the way."

Thea paled. "She's twisted up. Her dad made her that way. I don't know what was going on in her mind, and I don't really care. But somehow, I'll get revenge for her hurting you."

His gaze softened, like her getting vicious on his behalf

turned him on. "It's only a scratch. I'll live." Then he rested his forehead on hers and palmed her cheek, saying something too low for me to hear.

It was uncomfortably like the pose I'd found myself in with Violet before the hospital rescue. When I'd hurt her by pressing on the bruise her father left.

I cleared my throat, breaking the moment. "As I see it, we have a number of questions that need answering for us to have any kind of life. First is what kind of heat is on us. Was Charterman's murder reported? Also our keeper is buried on the island. Her death could be blamed on us."

"We didn't kill her. The daft cow electrocuted herself," Struan said with a laugh.

Scar and I swapped a look. No one but us knew exactly what happened, and it was up to Scar to tell his story when he was ready.

I continued. "Then there was the fire set at Jenkins' house."

Burn, my youngest brother, grunted from his sprawl on the second couch. "We know the police are after me, even before I did that. Thea heard them say so at the hospital. If it comes to it, I'll take the rap for everything, not just the fire at that pervert's house. At some point, I'm going down anyway. Might as well pile the rest on top so ye can all breathe easier."

All of us protested.

Thea shook her head. "No one is taking the fall for anything. We're still speculating. We need facts. I can call Charterman's office. The island is mine now, and they were dealing with the paperwork. I have a legitimate reason to ask after him and find out what they know. Next, we have Lottie. She knows everyone on the island and she can ask questions on our behalf."

"No way," I refused.

"What about Daddy dearest?" Scar asked before another argument could start. "Is anyone here interested in his money? Considering how much effort went into keeping us from it, others will be expecting us to go after him."

We looked between us, no one leaping to make a claim.

"I never had money," I admitted. "I'll make a wild guess and say that none of us did."

"Cassie will need it," Burn added slowly. "We're all adults and should be able to find off-the-books work in some way or another. But how do we keep a six-year-old? Someone will have to act as her parent if she's going to go to school, and that means having a house. An income. Without something formal in place, the authorities will find out. She'll be taken from us."

We all went quiet for a moment and let that fact sink in. Over my dead body.

"I'll go to visit Struan's mother in prison," Thea said quietly. "She might be able to tell us something about McInver. I'm not saying you should be thinking about his money, but it could be useful. Particularly if one of you intends to become Cassie's legal guardian. But from my perspective? You're owed it. That old bastard is a serial abuser of women, and he's responsible for all of you being alive. Therefore, if he's at death's door and there's an inheritance due, it needs to go to you. Not someone else. It would be unfair for Charterman's son to claim that huge house and all the money. Particularly after the way his family and mine went about securing it. They don't deserve it. You do. Cassie does."

Begrudgingly, I nodded.

"I'll go see McInver," I replied slowly. "Struan, it can

wait until you're better. You're the oldest by two weeks."

He sneered. "I've got exactly zero interest in going anywhere near that man. I'm happy to go along with the plan, whatever it is we agree on, but count me out of meeting him."

As he moved, the sleeve of his dressing gown slid up, revealing his tattooed arm. Struan furrowed his brow and gestured at Scar. "My ink needs redoing."

In the hostel, Scar had designed a tattoo—a line drawing of a surfer in front of an island, with a circle around it. All of us four men had it in plain ink on our arms. Mine was a faint sketch now. Struan's had been wiped away entirely, probably by someone at the hospital.

Scar found a black pen on a desk then crouched next to Struan, refreshing the design in easy strokes.

As he worked, he peered at me. "I'll go with ye to meet McInver. I'm interested in a morbid kind of way."

I dipped my head in agreement then spared a glance for Burn. When we'd first met, after he'd been delivered to the island, I'd recognised him. He was the little boy my mother scowled at whenever we saw him out with his ma. Except he was eighteen now, and I knew for a fact the police weren't chasing him for no reason.

I had so many to protect. I needed to do right by all of them.

When Scar was done with Struan, he moved on to Burn, redrawing the same design.

Struan rotated his arm, admiring the work nestled in among his multitude of other tattoos. "Once I'm able to walk more than ten feet without wanting to kill someone, I'm going to get this done permanently."

Scar's cheeks turned pink. "For real?"

"All of us will," I said.

He hid a smile, then scooted over to do mine.

"Last point," I continued. "Who are our enemies now? The two people who tormented us for the past year are both dead—our keeper, and our jailor, who we now know was Charterman."

"My dad is still alive," Thea said quietly. "For months, I thought he was dead. If Charterman is to be believed, my father was as much a part of it as he was. Presumably chasing the money, too. Which means he'll still be trying to get it, and trying to stop us."

"The islanders. They're chasing a payout," Burn added. "That's what the head guy said when they surrounded the house—they just want what they're owed, I guess for enabling our prison. And then Jenkins might come for me for my little act of arson. If he's still alive."

The islanders. My gaze jumped to the kitchen door. From inside, music played, the occasional sound of Violet's kind, encouraging voice and Cassie's higher one filtering back.

One islander in particular had led up the pack. Forbes Hunter. The head guy, as Burn named him.

Violet's father.

And in a rush, I formed my suspicion of exactly why the lass was here.

10

Lottie

It was strange the way memory worked. How it constructed patterns behind the scenes.

The whole time the family had their meeting, and Cassie and I had been examining the remainders of the box of food, and drumming up lunch, my brain kept drifting back to a different place.

When Sin kissed me in the kitchen at Thea's grandmother's house on the island, he'd demanded first that I put my hands behind my back.

What came next, the warmth of his lips on mine, the taste of him, had all obliterated that small part.

He didn't like touch. He'd said so at the hospital. He'd liked me enough to want to kiss me, but not to have my fingers caressing him or running over his buzz cut short hair.

How could anyone not like that? Not crave someone else's hands on their body? It was all I'd thought about with him for a long time. Not just for sex but needing that connection. Feeling up his thick biceps. Enjoying the safety of is arms.

Touch was huge for me but a problem for him.

In many ways, it was the least of our difficulties, but I couldn't stop running over it again and again.

The kitchen door opened, and two hungry boys burst in.

"God, the smell has been driving me wild." Scar homed in on a large platter of cheese-and-tomato toasties, picking it up with one hand while simultaneously grabbing a tray of sausage and bacon sandwiches in the other.

There hadn't been much to work with, no healthy vegetables in sight, but it was enough to feed everybody. I'd had Cassie grating cheese while I grilled meat and buttered bread.

"Take it to the table," I commanded.

"Yes, my lady," Scar quipped back with a smile.

Burn snuck up to me and gave me a light and entirely unexpected hug. "Thank ye." He pressed a smacking kiss to my hair then took the tray of drinks I'd made and followed his brother.

I stared after him, a little dazed from the affection, then felt the weight of someone watching me. Sin leaned against the wall outside the kitchen, his arms folded.

I flicked my fingers for him to shoo. "Go eat or it'll all vanish, and we don't have anything else."

He glowered for a moment longer then disappeared. I took a couple of minutes to clear up the tiny kitchen, loading the dirty utensils into the first dishwasher I'd ever used, then joined the others.

The downstairs of the cabin was all open plan, aside from the kitchen. Seated around the wide dining table, the family devoured the food. All aside from Struan, who, on the sofa, had closed his eyes and appeared to be sleeping again.

I liked watching people eat a meal I'd prepared. It gave me a warm feeling inside. Even Sin seemed to be enjoying my basic offering.

"There are some practical matters we need to discuss," I said, drawing attention my way. "We're out of food now, so someone needs to do a supermarket run. I'd like to go." I waited for Sin to raise his head and refuse, but he merely glanced at me. "Tell me your favourite foods and I'll cook whatever ye like."

Scar pointed with the edge of his sandwich. "You're golden."

Burn's lips curved into a grin. "All those months deprived of choice, and she just casually says something like that. Marry me, Lottie."

I giggled, swapping an amused glance with Thea.

"We also need to change the sleeping arrangements," I continued.

At the end of the table, Sin stiffened.

I hid my smile. "Cassie, Burn, and Scar, there's two more bedrooms upstairs. Cassie should have one, the boys in the other."

Cassie knelt on her chair, her eyes wide. "I get my own room?" Her shoulders shrank. "What if there's a storm in the night and I get scared?"

I crossed to stand behind her seat and smoothed a few strands of hair back from her face. In the kitchen, before we'd made the food, I'd twisted a French braid into her black hair, the same style as mine.

"I'm scared of storms, too." I smiled down at her pretty, heart-shaped face. "We can huddle under a blanket together if it happens."

Burn reached out and shook her arm lightly. "Or I can sleep on your floor. No reason to be afraid."

The youngest of the brothers was a mixture of sweet, cocky prankster, who obviously adored his family and would do anything for them, and dangerous arsonist. Even now, his Zippo lighter sat on the table next to him. Every now and again, he'd flick the wheel, generating sparks. His angelic face hid a dark side.

Next to him, Scar was the opposite. He wore a deep gouge down his cheek like a battle injury, marking him out as dangerous. On the inside, though, I knew him to be smart and kind. The two older brothers were similar in projecting attitude that told you to steer clear. I knew Struan loved Thea, so he had it in him, but Sin seemed to have two ways of seeing people: those he trusted, and were therefore under his protection, and those he didn't, which bundled me in with every stranger on the street.

Scar finished his last bite of food and took up a pen from beside his plate. "I'll do it now," he said to Cassie.

I'd missed that part of the conversation but quickly got clued in when she shot off her chair, went to him, and stuck her arm under his face. Scar sketched a circle on her forearm, then drew a little surfer on it with craggy landscape behind.

They all had them. Scar's on his left forearm, Burn's on his right, and Sin had his tucked on the underside of his upper arm, just visible beneath his t-shirt sleeve.

A branding. Another way of them reinforcing how they were a family.

If Thea had one, I couldn't tell. A long-sleeved shirt covered her arms, and I wasn't about to ask.

"Can I have Skittles from the shops?" Cassie asked me.

"Small problem with that plan," Sin grouched. "We need money. I'll try to find work, but it could take a while to get cash in hand."

Thea pushed away her plate. "I have some. My grandmother hid bundles of notes in her house. I used half of it to pay for my last term at uni, but the rest is in my bag that you took onto the helicopter and brought here for me. It's sitting upstairs in our bedroom." She held up a finger to pause any protest. "Don't refuse it. My father helped imprison you all on the promise of a payout. It's only right to spend his mother's money on you in turn. Everyone needs clothes. A phone each to keep in contact. Food and basic goods. I was lying awake last night thinking about how little you all had at the hostel. Lottie's right. Now is the time to eat the favourite foods you've been missing. Indulge in small luxuries."

An unsaid implication rang out. *Before you lose the chance.* No one was safe, still.

"I'll make a list." I crossed the room to collect a pen and pad of paper. Two covered plates sat on the sideboard. "What are these?"

Thea angled her head. "I set aside a plate for Struan when he wakes up. Sin did the same for you. I've got a couple of phone calls to make, so eat up or someone will nab them."

I was too busy staring at my plate to reply. Unless my father demanded I sat down with them, I avoided eating at the table with my parents. Da wouldn't fail to comment on my portion size and whether he should buy smaller dinner plates. How I'd never lost the chubby cheeks I'd had as a bairn, and how no man wanted a fat girlfriend. My mother would try to take the sting out of his words by chattering about the science behind a calorie-deficit diet. Her way of offering support I'd never asked for.

I usually ate in the kitchen by myself. Away from prying eyes. Was this a kindness or a test?

When I glanced over at Sin, he was half standing, his attention down the room.

"Fuck off," Struan said, awake now. "I don't need help. But thanks."

He made his way to the table and dropped into a chair, wincing.

"Quit swearing in front of Cassie," Burn griped.

Struan's dark eyebrows beetled. "You're seriously asking that of a man with a stab wound to his gut?"

Cassie sniffed, examining the line art on her arm. "I know all the bad words, but I don't say them."

Struan snorted. "No one would blame ye if ye did."

"Aye, she hears them enough," Burn snapped back, his lighter wheel scratching.

A shadow fell over me. Sin collected the two plates and gestured with a jerk of his head to the spare seat at the table.

I crept to it and sat. Like a waiter, Sin served us our lunch, taking away the plates balanced on top to protect the food.

He'd saved me one of each type of sandwich I'd made. They were still warm.

My *thank you* got stuck in my throat, so I gave a tiny nod instead, forcing back the feeling that I was about to be judged for eating.

Struan picked up a sandwich and bit into it. "God. Meat."

I took a daintier bite and assessed him, then scribbled on my pad. "Green vegetables. Red meat. More painkillers."

Struan squinted at me. "What?"

"You're healing," I added. "Which requires good quality protein and fresh vegetables for vitamins and minerals."

"Roast chicken," Scar suddenly blurted from my other side. "Can we have that one day? With roast potatoes, stuffing, and gravy."

"Ready for mine?" Burn stood and braced himself, both hands on the table. "Every time we had food discussions in the hostel, I made a mental note of what we craved. I've been preparing for this moment for a long time."

I grinned. "And now ye have a personal chef on site who loves to cook. Bring it."

Rapid-fire, he launched into his list. When I'd been sneaking them goodies on the island, I thought I'd had an insight into their lives. This was giving me so much more. They all craved hearty meals. Real food. Lots of meat. My mind ticked over with ideas. The sheer amount I'd have to cook was beyond anything I'd done before, but I relished it.

"And beer," Burn finished. "I'm finally legally old enough to drink. Fuck, I want a party night of getting drunk to celebrate all the birthdays we missed in the hostel. Then I want to go surfing with a full belly and enough alcohol in my system so I drown as a happy man."

"Drown?" Scar asked. "Let's try to stay alive for at least a few weeks so we can enjoy freedom for a change."

But Burn's happiness had shrunk back to some other less pleasant realisation, judging by his expression. "You're free, with any luck. I'm not. If Lottie's going to go shopping, I'd bet any money Sin won't let her go alone. Which means another road trip I can't go on." He swore and pushed away from the table. "Ignore me. I have no idea where my head is at, but it isn't good. Don't mean to bring everyone down with me."

He strode away and climbed the stairs.

I watched him go, my heart hurting. They'd all suffered so much, and there was no point pretending that the situation now was safe and secure. It wasn't.

And a big part of that threat was me.

"Struan," Sin said, drawing everyone's attention back. "There's something I need ye to do. Your friend, Max McRae. Call him up and sound him out. I want to know how the land lies with them. I went to see his uncle, and he said he'd leave us alone, but I can't trust him."

Struan chewed his food and took a swallow of drink. "Will do. He texted us earlier about Thea's car, which is in their garage. I don't know him well enough to trust him either, but he and his family proved themselves good so far." He gestured around. "We're in their house. No cops have swung by. What's worrying ye?"

Sin drifted his focus to me and held me captive. "What's worrying me is the pretence of being allies when they're just waiting for their moment."

Struan grumbled a reply, but I didn't hear it. Inside, I ached. I was supposed to be reporting back to Da. Yesterday's message before Sin confiscated my phone only gave me so much time.

No amount of preparing delicious meals for the nutrition and taste-starved prisoners would quiet the demons haunting me. And I had the idea Sin could see every one of them.

Thea paced by the front door, making her calls. She hung up and rejoined us, taking her seat with her jaw slack in confusion. "Huh. Two things. I called Charterman's office. His associate came on the line and told me there had been a terrible accident. Charterman drowned. This new guy was taking over my case, and he'll call me with any updates on getting my full inheritance sorted out."

"Drowned? As in an accident?" I asked.

Struan went completely still.

"He didn't elaborate, but that's good, right? Drowned isn't killed," she added.

It was...unexpected. Da had been so angry. He could've used the death as a reason to get the police pursuing the men.

Swift realisation followed. "If it hasn't been reported, the islanders don't want the authorities to find ye," I said.

"Aye, so they can do so themselves," Sin cut in.

Thea swapped her gaze between us. "At least for now, that means no one is chasing Struan. Which is a flipping huge relief." She reached and took his hand.

So easily, they touched. He didn't push her away or drop the hold. In fact, his knuckles stood proud, like he was gripping on to her hard.

"The other thing," Thea continued to him, "is the jail your mum is at. It's a low-security unit. She's allowed drop-in visitors. I asked if I could go this afternoon, and they said yes."

A stormy expression formed on Struan's face. "Fuck. She's alive then."

I had no idea why he expected her to be otherwise, and I looked away from the emotion being shared between them.

That was true love. Fire, devotion, and unhidden feelings.

"Lottie?" Her voice took me out of my reverie. "Will you go with me? I'm nervous, and you're better with people than

I am. They said it would be okay for us both, and it would be good to find out as much about McInver as she remembers."

"Of course I will."

Sin would have something to say about that, I was certain, but whatever his opinions, he kept them to himself.

I finished my food, keeping my gaze down. When I went to clear up, Sin took over, ordering me to go wait in the living room. After I'd gone, he asked something of Thea, his features set in their usual glower.

She came and joined me at the window seat.

"He told ye not to let me out of your sight, am I right?" I asked.

"Correct. He's going to go with us to the prison then shopping, and Scar wants to as well."

I sighed and dropped my voice. "He's driving me crazy."

"I assume not in the good way. Are you okay sharing a room with him?"

I peered out of the window to obscure my mouth. "No problem there, aside from utter frustration. Last night, he was in the bathroom, and he said my name, so I opened the door."

Thea took a shocked rush of breath. "What was he doing?"

"What do ye think?" A giggle rose in me, and I pressed my lips together, hiding my expression from the room. "I saw everything. Then ran. I wasn't brave enough to do anything about it."

"But you wanted to?"

Several months ago, I'd told Thea I had a crush on Sin. That's all it was. Scorching new emotion, worse for being unrequited. Except weren't crushes meant to burn out? Mine was only getting stronger.

I groaned and hid my face. "Yes, I wanted to. I know he only said my name last night so I'd walk in and feel uncomfortable. It's his way of messing with my head because he doesn't want me here. He was probably thinking I'd go running back to the island at the sight of his act. Joke's on him that I actually liked it."

"Are you going to do anything about it?"

"Nope. I'll suffer in silence, like always."

Thea's eyebrows rose. "How bad is the suffering, exactly?"

I dropped my voice even lower. "So bad. His body... I can't even explain it but I feel like I might explode every time I look at him. Sleeping beside him is torture. Another night of it, and I'll probably self-destruct in a fireball made of horniness."

"Oh, sweetie, take matters into your own hands."

"I wish I could. He does things to me I can't take care of by myself."

Her expression turned devious. "That gives me an idea. I'm going to buy you something when we're out."

My mind boggled. Across the room, Sin muttered something about being ready to go in thirty minutes, raising his voice so we'd hear.

Him coming with us presented me with a problem.

I leaned in to Thea. "I need to use your phone when we're out."

"I hadn't forgotten. We'll have to make sure Sin doesn't see." Her eyes narrowed. "I heard Struan tell you all about my car. Max is a mechanic in his day job, and he said it's still broken, but they have one I can borrow. It's at the garage now. I can pick it up anytime."

I stared at her. "A second car would be really useful."

"Agreed."

A moment played out where we tested each other's resolve. We were going to sneak off. Sin would no doubt chase us, but it would give time for me to talk to Da away from prying eyes.

"Let's do this thing," I whispered.

Operation Betrayal was a go.

11

Lottie

With Thea behind the wheel of a neat little Kia, we set out for the jail. I put on a blindfold just in case we were caught, but removed it to watch the road behind us, expecting an enraged Sin to zoom up in the rear-view. Yet he didn't appear. Somehow, we'd gotten away with it.

After fifteen minutes, I finally relaxed.

"Here." Thea fished out her phone and handed it over. "Make the call. Get it over and done with."

A chill trickled through my blood as I dialled the number, using the code to conceal who was calling, then waited for the connection.

"Hello?" my mother answered.

My heart gave one big thump. "Ma, are ye okay?"

"Lottie? Of course I am. Why wouldn't I be?"

I sank against the seat and closed my eyes. "Because of how Da was. I thought he'd..."

Ma didn't fill in the blanks. "No need to be dramatic

He was just a little upset."

This was the way it always went. He'd be outrageously out of line. Dangerous. Abusive. The next day, my mother would dismiss or minimise it. I wasn't having it anymore.

"No. He hurt me. I have the bruised forehead and stomach to show for it. He threatened to hurt ye, too."

"In the heat of the moment," Ma continued over me. "He calmed down right after ye walked out."

"Ma! I didn't walk out, he kicked me out. Listen, I want ye to do something for me. Pack a bag and go get on the next ferry. It's the only way I'll know you're safe. I'll meet ye and find somewhere for us to stay."

I sensed Thea focusing on me and opened my eyes to see emotion in hers. I hadn't meant to ask my mother these things. I hadn't expected her to answer the call at all. But the opportunity was there, and I had to take it.

My mother took a shocked inhale and dropped to a whispered hiss. "Why would ye even ask that? What wrong with ye? This is my home."

"It's not okay to live like that. It's definitely not okay to raise another baby like that. We can build a life away from him. A happy one."

Something sounded on the other end of the line, a click, like a door opening, then the thud as it closed.

My mother went quiet, the line muffled as if she'd placed her hand over the receiver. Then she came back. "Your father's home now. Talk to him."

Talking to him was the last thing I wanted, but I'd taken my shot and been knocked back.

"About time." Da came on the line. "I assume there's information for me?"

I pressed my fingertips to my temple, trying to get back

to my script. "I found Thea in the hospital in Inverness. She's with her boyfriend who's badly hurt. They're releasing him tomorrow or the next day, we think."

"Where are the rest of them?"

"I don't know yet. Hopefully I'll find out once he's out."

Da made an off sound. "What's this number you're calling from?"

"A borrowed phone. Mine broke when ye threw it at my head," I snapped, more venom in my tone than I'd planned.

Da laughed. "Always said ye had a thick skull."

God, I hated him. In no way was I like my father. Not in looks, I had my mother's fair hair and shape, nor in personality. We didn't move alike, talk alike, and I was so glad.

"If I find the men," I gritted out, "I want Ma off the island and away from ye the same day."

My father hummed. "Your mother won't leave me."

He wasn't wrong, except, "She will if ye kick her out."

I was taking such a risk. All of this was unrehearsed. I'd never spoken to him like this, knowing it would come back to me in his fists. But finally, I had something to hold over him. Information he wanted.

I still had no intention of giving that information up, but the bargain was out of my mouth anyway.

My father went quiet for a moment, and when he spoke again, his voice was bitter. "Look who's finally grown a spine. Aye, ye can have her. I've put up with her for too long anyway. Two days, Lottie."

"Da," I said, ready to beg him not to hurt her.

But he'd hung up, and I had a new deadline.

Thea kept on driving. "I think I understand now. You asked him to release her—she won't leave on her own?"

"Nope. I've asked so many times before, even found

her a place in a refuge for women facing domestic violence, but she turned me down flat. Now she has a bairn on the way, I hoped it would be different. I can't let that little one be raised like I was. In fear of getting hurt. Of watching Ma cower and him ruin our lives on a daily basis. I get that she's scared of leaving, but isn't her baby worth that? Wasn't I?"

Water filled Thea's eyes, but I couldn't cry. I'd done that far too many times.

I swallowed my regret. "To get her away from him, he has to kick her out. For him to do that, I have to give up Sin and his family. You. All the people I care about. It's impossible."

"We'll find a way," Thea promised.

I could only hope that was true.

An hour later, still with no sign of Sin, but with several attempts at calling Thea's phone, we arrived at the prison. We left the car and entered the building together, approaching the security desk.

Through the first gate, we were given a pat-down search, taken to the reception area, then instructed to sit on fixed plastic chairs to wait.

At the end of the room, a uniformed officer strode in and called our names. I followed her with Thea to meet yet another woman down on her luck.

In a wide room, populated with other families meeting, we took seats at a table. Then a small woman was led in and directed to the seat opposite. She peered between us. She couldn't have been more than forty, and she had the same features as Struan, but a different colouring—light-brown hair to the black he shared with his brothers and sister.

"Which of ye is Theadora?" She examined us in turn.

Thea pressed her fingers to her chest. "That's me. This

is my friend, Lottie."

"I would've said your sister, you're so alike. I'm Davina. How's my boy?"

I gave my own smile then settled back as Thea updated Struan's mother on some of what happened to him. She left out key details, likely on Struan's instruction, and though I listened politely, my mind was elsewhere.

Once, a relative of mine had told me Thea and I looked alike, a fact I'd instantly denied.

Thea had long dark hair and was willowy. Beautiful.

I was fair, short, and much curvier. I'd never taken the time to look past our body shapes to our faces.

Even so, it wasn't true. We both knew exactly who our parents were. Unfortunately, in both cases.

"Davina, there's a specific question we have today," Thea continued as I tuned back in. "I really wanted to meet you, but we also need to know some things about Struan's dad."

Davina recoiled. She darted her gaze between us, her hands clutching together. "Why?"

Thea took a shuddering breath, and under the cover of the table, shot her hand to grab mine.

I took this as my cue. "We believe Struan has been targeted because of who his father is," I said carefully. Calmly. "He's the heir to this old man's wealth. So it would be useful for us to know something about the man before we visit him."

Thea hadn't mentioned anything about Struan's brothers or sister, so I wouldn't either.

The woman cringed. "I don't want him to see him. I never wanted him to know."

I reached and took her hand, too, connecting the three

us. Shitty father figures had hurt us all. "It's okay. Struan is strong. McInver can't hurt him."

At the name, Davina shrank back, withdrawing her hand right as the guard started towards us. The woman gave me a stern glare. *No touching.* Right.

"I haven't heard that name in a long time," Davina uttered. "Don't go to see him. Ye seem like nice girls. Send a brother or your father. Don't go yourselves."

I knew few decent men, Struan and his brothers aside. And they were victims, too.

"Because he's dangerous?" I asked.

"He's twisted. Doesn't even pretend to hide it."

"I've met him," Thea said suddenly. "I'm so sorry you suffered at his hands. We have to see him. There's no choice. Can you tell us what you remember about him?"

Davina gulped, but slowly, she gave over her account of being bought for a few days at a time by McInver. He'd pick her up, sometimes by herself, sometimes with other women, and take them to his house.

They'd be locked in. Imprisoned.

Though she didn't call it assault as he'd paid for her time, there was no confusing the fact.

"He had rules. We weren't allowed to look at him, just be docile and soft, no matter what he did. Unless he specifically told us to fight him. Whichever he picked, he'd have his way then let us go when he was through. I'd earn a tip if I didn't flinch. I won't tell ye sweethearts what he'd do to get a reaction."

And she was the one in jail after that bastard had messed up her life.

"He was often in a frenzy," she went on. "That's the best way to describe it. He'd rant about a woman who'd rejected him. Call us by her name, sometimes. Rhona, she was."

Thea and I swapped an unhappy glance.

It was Thea's grandmother who rejected McInver, first when they were young, then again after her husband died—the start of his rampage, based on when the boys were born. I'd loved Rhona when I'd been a little girl. Though Thea and her da only visited the island a couple of times a year, I'd see Rhona often. She was the grandmother I never had.

"Good for whoever this Rhona was," Struan's ma continued. "She did the right thing in running from him. He was so full of rage, and he'd take that out on me and whoever else was there."

Considering the timings, that had to include Sin's mother. The two men were born a couple of weeks apart.

"Do ye remember the names of any of the other women?" I asked.

She set her head to one side, her shrewd gaze suddenly all Struan. "Maybe. Why do ye want to know?"

"I might know another woman who was involved."

Davina tapped her lip. "We didn't use our real names, so it probably won't help, but there was a tall lass I saw more than once. He liked her. Edie, he called her. It didn't sound like a street name, so it stayed in my mind."

Tall. She had to be Sin's ma.

I knew nothing about her, except the fact she'd died. Surely he'd want any information he could get.

"Do you remember anything else about her?"

"Nothing good." Her gaze set on someone over my shoulder.

I glanced around to see the guard gesture to the clock. Our time was up.

"Tell my boy to leave it alone. If he needs money, he

can steal cars. Anything other than this. Don't go to McInver's house," Davina begged. "He has rooms set up for girls. Locks on the doors. Chains on each post of the beds. It's not worth the risk."

"He has what?" I slapped my hand over my mouth.

"That's not all. He's sly. Not harmless, no matter how he looks. Don't be fooled."

On that ominous note, Struan's poor mother was led back to her cell.

Thea and I returned to the car, quiet and caught up on all we'd heard.

In a space opposite ours, Sin was already waiting.

12

Sin

From the passenger seat, Scar gestured at the prison entrance where two lasses exited the grim building. "Aren't ye worried?"

I grunted instead of answering.

"I mean about Lottie calling her da."

For most of the trip chasing them down here, both of us had brooded in silence. The women had gone rogue, fucking infuriating me, but my hands were tied. The moment I'd realised they'd got a car and run, I'd turned to Struan.

He knew.

They'd had a thirty-minute head start, and the fucker hadn't said a word. Instead, he'd beckoned me closer and told me, in no uncertain terms, to back the fuck off his girlfriend.

If she trusted Violet, that was good enough for him.

Well, it wasn't for me.

At my lack of a reply, Scar twisted in the seat to face me. "You've been on Lottie's case from the moment she showed up. Ye took her phone, told her ye didn't trust her, had her wear a blindfold to come to the cabin. What comes next?"

I huffed a frustrated laugh. "Why, are ye concerned over what I'll do to her?"

"I like her. We all do. I just want to know what ye think."

He wanted my judgement. I stared out the windscreen as Violet and Thea crossed the road and slowly moved closer. "I'm pissed off that they came here alone, and aye, she could've made that call, but I'm also very sure that no matter how close Theadora is to her, Struan's safety comes higher. She won't help her."

He chewed on that. "There's holes in that plan a mile wide."

I sighed and half turned. "Life lesson. If people are going to fuck ye over, there's nothing ye can do to stop it. Sometimes, it's better to let them go ahead and be prepared to handle the consequences."

"Keep your enemies close? Do ye really see her that way?"

Of all my brothers, Scar was most like me, apart from being far kinder than my grumpy arse. He thought things through. Planned ahead and could anticipate trouble. Except he did it to try to keep shite positive, not wanting to let in the darkness that threatened him. I did it because I knew nothing could stay good for long.

The two women reached our row of cars, both with downturned expressions.

Despite every reason why I shouldn't go there, I soaked up the image of Violet with uncontrolled appreciation. The warm afternoon meant she'd left the cabin without a jacket, so I had full sight of the outline of those incredible tits.

I'd had my hands on her. Wanted to do it again.

I didn't want to see her as the enemy either, but that went against all my instincts to keep my family safe.

Before the women reached us, I gave up my thoughts to Scar. "If she's going to call us in to her da, she'll find a way. I can't control that. What I need to know is why. Then I can anticipate what he'll do."

"How will ye find out?"

"One way or another, she'll tell me."

He scowled but hopped out. The lack of surprise on either woman's face told me they'd expected us and already seen the Ford.

Without pause, Violet climbed in next to me, and Scar joined Thea in a blue Kia—the women's escape vehicle.

The lass who raised my blood like no other watched me.

I kept my expression flat, resisting the urge to soften for her. Perhaps Scar had been right. My watch-and-wait approach had risks. Those were mine to take.

I started the engine, following Thea out of the car park. We had the shopping trip next, and as much as I wanted to just drive Violet away to lock her up somewhere, we needed food.

"Why did ye run?"

Violet swallowed but didn't answer. Instead, she changed the subject. "Struan's mother told us a whole lot about McInver. Thea will be telling Scar right now. Want the details?"

I should push her. Demand answers. Get her confession. Yet something more than Struan's warning stopped me. Her softness. Her care. I *liked* her, just like Scar said, and I didn't want to know.

I gave a short nod, and she started on her tale.

A short while later, we arrived at a retail park with a large supermarket. Violet had filled me in on our genetic father's habits, and I'd descended into a dark fog of picturing my mother in his house.

He tied women up. Hurt them.

I couldn't handle that shite.

I parked up and swapped a look with Scar. He obviously didn't like what he'd heard either.

Violet's attention locked on to the supermarket.

"Scar will go with ye," I told her, needing space from her calm, fake friendliness. From my need to throttle her.

"Actually, I need him with me," Thea replied. "I'm going to pick up clothes and phones for everyone. I know Struan's size, and Scar can help with the rest of you."

My brother cast a glance down me. "For yours, I'll just pick the biggest in the range."

I'd always struggled with clothes, so there was nothing new there. "Don't worry about me. Get the rest of ye sorted," I ordered.

Thea slipped over to Violet and whispered something in her ear.

The woman's cheeks pinkened. "Ye can't do that."

Thea arched her eyebrow. "Can and will. It's my gift to help with that little problem you told me about earlier."

"What problem?" I demanded, but neither looked at me.

"Thea," Scar interrupted, his gaze settling on a building across the car park. "If I give up on having a phone, can I ask for something else?"

"Anything. Burn already asked for something specific. I'm serious about us all living like we're free now. We should be celebrating life. Whatever you need, we'll get."

She linked her arm through his, and the two walked away. Leaving me with Violet.

"What did she say to ye?" I asked.

"Nothing. Well, nothing I'm going to repeat to ye. Let's go buy food."

In the bright supermarket, Violet grabbed a trolley and consulted the list she'd written. I took the trolley from her and played security guard as we walked up and down the aisles. Into the basket went all the things my brothers and sister had asked for.

Packs of meat. Vegetables. Junk food. Soap, razors, deodorant.

Violet even picked out a stuffed toy dog for Cassie. She grinned over a Velcro pouch in its belly that opened to reveal three little puppies, commenting on how my sister was going to find it so cute.

I couldn't smile.

I'd seen Thea hand over cash to buy it all, but my head was swimming with the sheer amount of shite available on the shelves. The whole time we'd been on the island, I thought myself immune to the deprivation. I could withstand hardship. I was tough enough to live through cold nights and too-few calories. To shoulder the violence of the place and protect my family.

But now, suddenly, that was all gone, and I was surrounded by plenty. Rows and rows of bright consumerism. Feast after famine.

Sweat broke out on my back, and I fought away the strange and overwhelming feelings.

They kept coming.

All this because I'd been fathered by some rich man. Not only had my mother suffered at his hands—those images were only getting worse—but the hits were still coming. At my brothers and sister, at me. I had to protect us all and I didn't have enough information to do that.

I was out of my depth and drowning, and on the shelves all around me, fucking boxes with smiling people printed on them wanted yet more from me.

Gentle fingers pressed briefly on my arm, and I blinked to find Violet peering up at me. "Sorry. I know ye don't like touch, but ye didn't answer when I said your name. Is something wrong? I mean other than me."

My breathing came too hard. I didn't have an answer.

Her pretty eyes took me in. "I'm finished now. Let's go."

I managed a swift nod, and she directed us to the checkout, packed up and paid, then finally, we were outside again.

I sucked in a breath of early evening air, needing to get out of this place. I'd grown up in a city but now hated being in the middle of civilisation. Hated the people in their cars, carrying on their dull lives.

At the Ford, I manhandled the bags into the boot. Violet gazed in the direction Thea and Scar had gone.

"I don't think they're finished yet. Why don't we take a walk? Just around the perimeter. Beats staying still."

She was doing this for my sake, I knew. We fell into an easy pace, slower than I normally would, but it felt good to move.

"Must be weird being off the island," she said. "It wouldn't be strange if ye were disorientated and finding it hard."

Great. I was easier to read than a book.

"If ye want to talk about it, I'll listen."

"No."

Violet cast another look at me, her expression more pensive now. “There’s something I wanted to talk to ye about. I asked Struan’s mother about other women she might have seen at McInver’s house.”

I stopped dead on the path. “She met Ma?”

“I figured with the two of ye being so close in age, they were probably there at the same time. She confirmed it. At least I think so. She met a woman there named Edie. She remembered her being tall, so I put two and two together.”

Edie. The name socked me in the gut.

No one had said my mother’s name to me in years. She’d disappeared then turned up dead, and I’d been passed around foster homes until I aged out. I didn’t get to go to a funeral. I didn’t know where she was buried. The only clue I’d had on what happened to her was an overheard conversation between two cops. They’d joked about sex workers and how often they ended up murdered on the job. As a young lad, I hadn’t understood that, but the phrase stayed with me until one day, it registered. It meant she’d been killed by a client.

Violet’s careful attention took me to pieces. “Was that your mother’s name?”

“Yes,” I choked out. “What else did she say?”

“She didn’t really want to talk about her, but she remembered Edie was his favourite. I thought you’d want to know. It wasn’t all bad.”

“Not all bad?” I scored my scalp with my fingernails. “Ma was murdered. Maybe by him.”

Then I shut my damn mouth, because I’d already told her more than I’d ever told anybody else.

Instantly, tears sprang up in her eyes. “Oh my God, Sin. By McInver?”

My whole hidden agenda had been blown. All because I got freaked out in a supermarket. Anger rose in a hot wave, at myself but about to be directed elsewhere.

I crowded Violet, moving in on her until her back hit the wall of yet another fucking shop. "That is none of your business. Stop talking. Keep out of it."

She kept her gaze directly on mine, and her hand came up to hold the back of the one I'd unknowingly gripped around her throat. Her touch...

I didn't hate it.

Her fingers slid over my knuckles, and my breathing only came harder. There was nothing in my head apart from holding on to her. Pinning her down. Keeping her from running from me again. All my blood had rushed south. Every piece of me was magnetically drawn to the infuriating, interfering lass in my hold.

I leaned in.

Violet pushed up on to her tiptoes and closed the distance, then pressed her lips to mine.

Instant relief channelled my aggression, my confusion. I needed somewhere for all this energy to go. To turn this chaste peck into more.

Her soft body was the perfect target.

But as quickly as she'd landed her mouth on mine, Violet broke the kiss.

"No," I gritted out, only seeing her.

Her mouth curved in a smile. "Scar is calling us. I think they're done."

With staggering effort, I straightened and released her. Thea and Scar waited by the cars, staring at us with unhidden amusement.

Instant regret rushed over my error.

What the hell had I done?

Messed with the enemy. I'd lost my head and couldn't do it again. No matter her sweetness, care, and all the other fronts she'd put on to draw me in.

Yet all the secrets swarming around us whispered that I was going to lose this battle.

13

Lottie

We arrived back at the cabin under cover of darkness. I slipped off the blindfold Sin insisted I wore on the silent drive back, and climbed out, rushing to carry the bags inside. For tonight, Burn's party evening, I wasn't making anything fancy. Beer, burgers, and music were on the cards.

We were met at the door by a very excited Cassie. I held out the bag of Skittles and the toy dog, but she threw her arms around me, mumbling through tears about how she'd missed me, and how she'd worried I wasn't coming back. I hugged her hard and showed her the plushie again, finally getting a smile. Struan sat up from the sofa, an arm ready for Thea. She danced past me and dropped carefully into his embrace.

Burn was nowhere in sight.

In the kitchen, I unpacked the shopping, Sin a quiet shadow at my back. He carried the heavier bags and crates of beer but neither spoke to me nor made eye contact.

I didn't care that I'd overstepped and kissed him. In that moment, he'd looked so lost, I couldn't help myself.

Besides, the gift Thea had threatened to buy me had been on my mind.

A vibrator.

I'd complained about getting worked up over Sin, and she'd given me a solution. Part of her living-free plan for us all. She was also buying one for herself, citing how Struan was going to kill himself by overexertion if she didn't.

It had given me the image of using my gift with Sin in our room. Teasing him like he had me with his shower show. Not that I had the nerve.

God, I needed to hide it before he saw it.

Something clicked in the living room, then a vibrating sound filled the air.

A laugh followed, and I clapped my hands to my mouth and darted out, horrified.

On the floor next to the sofa, Scar crouched, showing something to Struan. In his hands was a device attached to a cable. I squinted at it, slowly recognising...a tattoo gun?

Christ on a cracker. My heart pounded.

"I got it secondhand from a tattoo parlour," Scar was saying. "Just walked in and asked the guy if they had a spare. He started to argue, but Thea flashed the cash, and he was smiling. He said it sometimes starts funny, which is why they don't use it with customers, but otherwise it's good. He even gave me black ink, disinfectant, and plastic wrap."

Struan's eyebrows lifted. "Ever inked anyone?"

Scar shrugged. "For a while, Ma had a boyfriend who did tattoos. I know the basics."

"Ye can finish my sleeve for practice, then brand us all with our surfer logo. Fuck, when my scars are healed, ye can go over those."

Burn appeared on the stairs. He glanced behind me to the giant at my back. Sin brushed by, cans of beer in his hands. He handed them out to everyone except Cassie, starting with Burn, then ending with me.

He lifted his, drawing the attention of everyone assembled. "Happy belated birthday, Jamieson."

Burn smirked then cracked his beer and took a deep drink to the sound of the rest of us repeating Sin's words.

A thump came at the door. We all froze.

Cassie darted to me, hiding under my arm, her puppy abandoned. "Don't let them take me."

I pushed her behind me and looked at Sin. Halfway between us and the door, he was clearly torn over which way to go.

The thump came again, but this time a voice with it. "Hey, joyrider. Are ye alive in there?"

Struan drooped on the sofa. "It's Max. Holy fuck. I called him earlier, but he was working. Someone let him in."

Thea obliged, and the mechanic turned rescuer stepped into our temporary home. I used the opportunity to take my package from Thea and dart upstairs with it, hiding the bag in the little chest of drawers beside my and Sin's bed.

Back downstairs, I set myself up in the kitchen, shooing away any offers of help. I cooked, pictured all the ways in which I wanted Sin, and got overheated from both activities.

An hour on, and I'd fed everyone, including Max who chatted to Struan, then cleared away.

With no further reason to hide, I slipped into the living

room, then did a quick tidy up of the cans that now littered every surface. I passed Sin, and he reached out to grab my wrist, but I evaded him and went to the front door, stepping out to the warm evening air to find the recycling bin.

I'd just disposed of the cans when footsteps crunched on the gravel path. I swung around to find a stranger approaching. A man in his early thirties. Tattoos. An easy swing to his walk.

He raised a hand in greeting. "I'm Smith. Max asked me to come up."

"Hey," I replied. "I didn't know we were expecting anyone."

"A happy surprise for both of us. I didn't know there were lasses here."

Then he did that thing that guys do, a quick blink where his gaze dropped to my chest then back up again. He'd checked me out. Blatantly, too.

"What's your name?"

"Lottie."

"Bonnie name for a beautiful girl."

Amusement curled inside me, but before I said another word, the door flung open and Sin barged out.

The newcomer backed up a step, his flirty smile vanishing as he took in the huge man. "I'm Smith. Max said he had a friend who needed a lesson in using a tattoo gun. That ye?"

"No." Sin turned to me, his expression flat. "Fetch Scar."

I hid my grin and entered the house, leading an excited Scar back outside with me. He jogged over and shook the guy's hand, thanking him for coming up.

A sentinel by the door, Sin glowered on. I guessed he wasn't happy with this arrangement, but for whatever reason had allowed it anyway.

"Smith," I said. "Can I get ye a beer?"

"Thanks, pretty darling."

I went to go back inside, passing Sin in the doorway. This time, when he reached for me, I let him catch me.

He pulled me against him and ducked his head to my ear. "No more fetching and carrying. You're not our servant."

"Didn't ye just send me to get your brother?"

"That's different."

"Because it was ye and not some other guy?"

He breathed through his nose then shot his gaze to where Scar and Smith examined the tattoo gun.

There was no way he could be jealous. Not over me. Not of some complete stranger who'd barely said a word to me.

I was imagining it. He'd be worrying about who this guy was. Make sure he didn't overhear anything or ask questions.

Still, a strange vibe was coming off him.

Taking a step back, I hailed the new guy again. "There might be some food left, too. Want a burger if I can rustle one up?"

Smith's eyes widened. "I'll love ye forever."

To my shock, Sin unleashed an actual growl and towed me into the house. Through the living room, we marched, passing his family, and into the kitchen. There, he slammed the door closed and turned to me.

"What are ye doing?" he demanded.

I cocked my head at him. "In what respect?"

"Ye know what I'm talking about."

"Do I? Explain it to me. Because I was just being polite to a guest. You're the one acting crazy."

"He was eyeing ye up."

"So? What's wrong with that?"

Sin didn't answer, and instead, swore and backed up, watching me like I was dangerous.

Irritation grabbed hold of me, and I stalked towards him. "No, don't stop. Tell me exactly why I can't talk to other men. Thea tells me I'm free and should be acting like it. Ye just want me to leave. My whole life has been one long act of repression, so forgive me if for once, I choose to do whatever the hell I please."

"Which is what? Run away? Flirt with strangers?"

"To be normal! To act like I'm twenty and have experience of life. To know how to kiss without scaring a guy away."

Damn. That last part wasn't supposed to have come out.

Sin's eyes darkened all the more. "There's nothing wrong with the way ye kiss."

"I disagree. From our non-moment earlier, I obviously need the practice. All ye did was glare at me."

I was breathing hard, steamed up from getting angry. I so rarely lost my temper, but he brought it out in me.

That first kiss we'd shared had been in Thea's grandmother's kitchen. I couldn't stop the memories flooding in.

Sin prowled closer, so big against me I had to stretch my neck, sending my senses haywire.

"I glared because I was two seconds away from dragging ye down an alley and forcing ye to your knees for me."

My body flushed hot at his harsh admittance.

I wanted to run my mouth and call him on it. He didn't really want this, I was almost certain.

Except the dark light in his eyes scared me to silence.

Slowly, his hand came up until his fingers curled around the base of my throat. Like earlier, it was a light hold, but possessive and controlling at the same time.

I held perfectly still.

With the stealth of a predator, he lowered his face to my level. My eyes shuttered closed of their own accord, but Sin shook me lightly by the neck.

"Hands to yourself."

Then his mouth took mine.

His lips moved, testing, even careful. To start with.

The fingers gripping me tightened, and he gave up a low, urgent sound that sparked as much pleasure as his touch.

There was something so carnal about him tasting me. Like I was wounded, and he was coming in for the kill.

I followed his lead, tilting my head. Sin groaned but didn't stop. His tongue slid over the seam of my lips, and I opened for him. He invaded my mouth, seducing me and taking ownership. His taste branded itself in my mind.

If I thought the press of his lips against mine decadent and delicious, his tongue entering my body was something else entirely. It delivered me smack bang into the zone of wanting everything at once. His hands in my clothes, feeling up my breasts. His mouth going lower.

Him fucking me.

I whimpered, and he surged, holding me to him to take repeated plunges. Harder kisses.

Needing more, I backed up, taking him with me until my rear hit the kitchen table. I scrambled onto it and spread my knees to bring him into the gap. He didn't want my touch, but I grasped his t-shirt in my fist so I had some grounding. Sin didn't stop me. Between my thighs, he pushed until I dropped back onto an elbow, him leaning over me.

I wrapped my legs around his.

For a second, both of us took a breath, our chests heaving, my heart pounding. We'd gone from nothing to being arranged in a sex position in the space of a few minutes. If this was supposed to be a kissing lesson, it only taught me where he wanted kissing to lead.

He held my throat. I gripped his t-shirt.

"Roll your hips into mine," he ordered.

"W-what?"

"Grind into me."

At my lack of action, Sin surged his hips against mine. "Like that. So ye understand where this will end up if we don't stop."

The door swung open down the kitchen, the sound of music getting louder with it.

Whoever interrupted us laughed, and the door closed again.

Sin stared down at me, then abruptly stood. He swore and scrubbed his hand over his shorn black hair.

With hot cheeks, and even hotter other parts, I scrambled up and avoided his gaze. "Thanks for the lesson. I think I'll go to bed."

"You're forgetting something." He backed up and swung open the fridge, collecting a beer can. Then he handed it to me.

I blinked at it, the metal can icy to my touch. "Um, thanks?"

Sin snorted, then gripped the back of my neck and marched me from the kitchen, through the living room, and out the front door.

He put his lips to my ear. "For your friend, pretty darling."

Then he landed a hard, possessive kiss to my lips in front of Scar and the new guy, released me, glared purposefully at the man, then stalked away from the cabin.

14

Lottie

Scared, excited, and red-hot, I left the party to hide upstairs. If I'd been braver, I would have chased after Sin. Finished what we started against a tree, or down on the forest floor, but I couldn't read him. I didn't know if he liked the kiss or if his reaction was just typically male.

What he'd really meant by that warning.

After a quick check in on Cassie, who was fast asleep in the first bedroom, I entered my room and closed the door.

There was no way I could rest. I was too worked up. Which meant I needed release, and I had my new toy to help me get there.

Silently, which was unnecessary because the thudding music hid most of my sounds, I opened the drawer, then holding my breath, I extracted the box and unpackaged the device inside.

She'd bought me a bold purple vibrator, ridged like a dick, and with multiple speeds. God, it pulsed, too.

Living at home, I wouldn't have dared buy something

like this. But everything was different now. Life wasn't real anymore. I could be the liberated woman who took matters into her own hands.

A quick read of the packaging while I rinsed it over in the bathroom assured me the product was almost silent, but even so, I stripped to my underwear and climbed under the covers to muffle it.

Then I shot up, ran to the door, engaged the lock, and flung myself back in bed.

If Sin had wanted to take things further, he'd be here now, not off on the prowl. If he returned while I was midway through, he'd have to wait.

Wriggling down the bed, I got comfortable. Then I grabbed Sin's pillow, putting it under my hips to cant them higher.

I wanted him here. Doing this with me.

I'd have to cope solo instead.

Closing my eyes, I summoned the image he'd given me last night. Him in the shower stall, hefty dick in hand. A pulse of warmth spread through me, and I hit the on button for the toy, taking it straight to my chest. I pulled up my cami and set the end of the vibrator against my nipple.

Instant pleasure spread, and I sucked in a soft breath, closing my eyes. Drawing it back, I slid it over, pushing harder while squeezing my other nipple between my fingers.

Already, this was so good.

The vibrations added something extra, and I was already so sensitive. Kissing Sin worked for me in ways I'd never anticipated. If I had time, I'd play like this for longer, but the small matter of anxiety over his return set a ticking clock in the back of my mind.

Keeping up the action at my nipple, I grazed my knuckles down my body, over my soft belly.

Without even getting to my centre, I could already feel how wet I was. How wet he'd made me.

It wouldn't take me long to get off. Again, I summoned the image of his dick and wriggled my fingers into my underwear to reach my clit.

The door handle rattled.

I scrabbled to turn off the vibrator.

It rattled again. "Violet. Open the door," Sin snapped.

No! I couldn't take another night of unfinished business. "Leave me alone," I called back, too late realising how strained my voice sounded.

"Open the door now or I'll break it down."

Shite. I squeezed my eyes closed and rolled up from the bed. If I let him yell, he'd wake Cassie. Draw the attention of everyone. I trudged to the door and unlocked it.

Instantly, it swung open, and he was bearing down on me, the door kicked closed behind him.

I expected some new anger, but in a shadowy room, Sin's expression was...concerned.

"You're upset." He peered at me.

"I'm fine." I turned on my heel and marched back to the bed, hating being mostly undressed in front of him. My top half, concealed only by my tight cami, I could handle, but not my thighs.

A peek around showed him standing in the centre of the space, not moving, not yelling but waiting.

"Did something happen?"

I didn't understand this version of him. The one concerned with my emotional state. He didn't trust me. I assumed he couldn't care less about me.

I flung back the covers. "Seriously, leave it."

But his gaze shot to the bed. Too quickly, I realised my mistake. The cushion and the vibrator peeked out from under the blanket, visible even in the low light.

I bristled with embarrassment. "I just..."

"Just what?" He strode two long paces until he was across the bed from me.

I lifted my chin in defiance. "Had to finish what ye started."

Sin smirked, dropped to sit on the sheets, and toed off his boots. I stood there, unsure what to do with myself.

"Lie back down in the same position," he ordered.

"You've pissed me off."

"And you've turned me on. Lie down," he repeated.

I could refuse. Throw the pillow at him to handle my overbrimming frustration. But I didn't. I sat cautiously on the bed. At the action, my boobs bounced inside my skimpy top, and Sin's full attention fixed on my chest.

He licked his lips.

For some reason, after everything else I'd seen and done with him, that did me in. Fresh heat blazed, chasing away my other emotions. Emboldened, I raised my hand to my breasts and cupped myself, sliding my hard nipple between two fingers over the cami.

I'd never been alone with a man apart from him. Never shared my body with anyone else. I only knew what I liked.

And Sin's gaze was glued to where I touched myself.

God, that was a trip. I shaped and moulded myself, loving his rapt focus.

"Strip the top," he ordered, low and dark.

"You're far too dressed for me to do that," I challenged back.

Sin reached back and ridded himself of his shirt in one

easy pull, exposing his solid upper body. He had a V-shaped frame—bulky shoulders and thick upper arms leading down to a narrow waist. Mouthwatering. So much, I had the urge to lean in and sink my teeth into his muscle. Yet, I knew the no-touch rule still held strong. Which meant I could look but nothing more.

And since he'd done what I'd asked...

I tugged one of the cami straps down my arm, then the other, revealing my breasts to his ravenous attention. I left the top to pool around my waist, covering my belly rolls, but it barely claimed any of my thoughts. I was lit up from the way he devoured me with his gaze. How his breathing came harder and the room charged with electricity.

Like before, I cupped my tits for him, pushing them up and together, and creating curves and a deep valley.

"Fuck," he drawled. In a rush, he popped the button of his jeans and tore them down his long legs, taking his underwear with them and freeing his heavy, hard dick.

Holy shite. Up close, it was a monster. Had to be ten inches long, if not bigger, and thick, too.

He laid back on the bed, legs wide, and took himself in hand.

"Does this scare ye?" he asked.

"Yes," I confessed.

But only fitting it inside me. His earlier threat about putting me on my knees for him held less fear. He could do *that* to me right now, and I'd love it.

Instead, he reclined. "Pick up your toy. Make yourself come before I finish."

I hesitated, so new to this I had no idea what I was doing.

Sin stroked himself. "On your back. Now."

I hustled to obey, returning to where I'd been right before his interruption. I wriggled the cushion under my hips again and arranged the top over my belly.

A buzzing sound drew my focus back to Sin. He had my vibrator in his hand.

I let out some kind of whimper then, unthinking, reached out and grabbed his wrist, bringing the vibrator back to my nipple.

He groaned and pushed it into my flesh, leaving me to concentrate on my other breast while my spare hand returned to my underwear. Finally, I had what I wanted. Both nipples attended to while I could play with my clit.

With my gaze firmly on him, I finally got back to where I'd been.

Grazing over my so-sensitive core, I hissed in pleasure. Sin fucked his fist faster. It turned me on even more seeing his reaction to my body. To sharing this with me. Open-mouthed, I sank my fingers into my wet slippery centre, drawing them back to rub circles. Winding myself higher. Writhing in heat.

The whole time, he moved the vibrator in a pattern. Surge and retreat, tease and play.

It was a proxy for him to deliver pleasure while controlling touch.

And I was the lucky recipient.

I alternated sliding my fingers inside myself and teasing my clit. I kept my gaze on Sin's body, on his actions to himself. How he'd do similar by reaching to grab his balls.

"What do ye need?" he bit out. "The vibrator's to fuck yourself with, aye?"

"I don't want ye to stop touching me," I admitted. "I love ye playing with my nipples."

But the thought of using the vibrator lower down was enough to make me crazy, too.

He swore and rolled closer, urgency in his moves.

Ducking to my breast, he took my nipple in his mouth and sucked, groaning with the pleasure of it. I bucked up, arching my back. His hot mouth, the sound he made... I couldn't even imagine.

At the same moment, he drew the vibrator down my body and to my core. Despite it remaining on the outside of my underwear, it sent spiralling delight out in waves. So close. So intense. One glance at his avid expression, and I was done.

My orgasm detonated. Pleasure flared, stealing my awareness of everything but my body and the man next to me. Every cell lit up. The warmth of his mouth at my breast became my whole focus, even when I drifted back and realised he'd tossed the vibrator to the sheets.

Sin lurched over me, still with my nipple in his mouth, jacking his dick harder. With a deep groan, he came, spilling over my belly and thighs, soaking my cami. He notched his forehead to my shoulder before sinking back to tongue my nipple in lazy swoops.

I came down to earth, dazzled, startled, and a lot relieved.

I expected him to climb off me, to stop touching me, but instead, Sin nudged my boob then sucked hard on the skin underneath. He kept going, grazing me with the edge of his teeth, until I realised what he was doing.

Leaving a mark.

Finally, he drew back, gazing down at what he'd done in the faint light. Then he dropped onto his side of the bed and closed his eyes.

I sought the vibrator and pressed it off.

He'd left me sticky, so I crept to the bathroom. In the brighter light, I examined myself in the mirror. My first time with a man, though not all the way, and I figured I'd somehow look different. I had the dark-red mark on my boob as evidence enough.

This bruise, I was proud of.

Taking my time, I showered, rinsing off my ruined underwear and giving him a chance to go to sleep. When I returned to bed, I snuggled down under the blanket, blissfully tired.

He rolled over, reaching for me. His regular breathing told me he slept, but yet again, his hand snaked out to curve around me.

And I drifted off to sleep with Sin holding on.

15

Sin

Thump. Thump. Thump.

Violet's heart kept up its beat under my hot palm, the backdrop to my terror. Again, I'd taken possessive hold of her while unconscious, my hand splayed across her chest, my body curved in her direction.

Her soft breathing was as regular as that thudding pulse.

All while I heaved in air, panicked, my nightmare still owning me. It lurked at the forefront of my mind, constricting my muscles.

A dark and twisted memory buried in the back of my mind had unlocked.

Days ago, I'd realised I had a chance to find out what happened to my mother. Knowing who my da was gave me a route into the mystery.

But with it apparently came a fuckton of childhood trauma.

Shite I hadn't thought about in years. In waking hours,

I didn't waste time on the past. Between me and my brothers, we'd been forged in the worst experiences. If any of them wanted to talk it out, great, I was there for them, but that didn't work for me.

I wanted it all buried.

A fresh wave of imagery threatened me, and I clamped my jaw.

My mother, returning, drunk or high after a night of work under some guy. She usually woke me so I'd know she was home, but this time, she was bitter at the world. Ma had a resentful temper. I'd always known my father was someone wealthy, because she'd seen Burn's mother in the street and told me that bitch had stolen her man. It was the first time I'd suspected I had a brother because of the little lad at the other woman's side.

On this night, Ma crawled into my bed. Made sure I was awake. Ran her arms around my small frame and crushed me to her as she spoke.

Deep in her anger, she ranted about some old boyfriend.

It had to be McInver. He was the only one she'd ever mentioned on repeat, though without a name. He made her aggressive.

Or it was the drugs she took. She didn't realise she was hurting me. I didn't tell her either. Not at the start and not when her outburst built in power.

She muttered about people fucking her over. Disrespecting her. Taking what was hers—a reference to the other woman stealing McInver's attention, I guessed.

Sometimes, she'd shake me. Tell me it was my fault, too. That pregnancy had lost her money. Ruined her perfect body.

The more she got into it, the harder she squeezed, her long nails cutting into my skin, and her perfume poisoning my air. I closed my eyes and tried not to move. But it hurt. Constricted my limbs until pins and needles started. Still, I didn't interrupt. Eventually, she ran out of steam and dropped me, rolling away in sleep.

It was cruel of her. I knew that now.

But I still craved that touch. She never hugged me other than on these dark occasions. The gentler start and end to her assaults were where I felt loved.

I didn't know any different until she'd died and I was in a foster care home. The staff there were firm, kind, and rarely physical. Different people would come and go, but none of them ever did that same grab-and-hold action. I even watched some of the younger children who couldn't get placed with families receive hugs and comfort when they needed it.

As a consequence of my mother's actions, I hated people touching me.

I kept my hair buzzed short because I could do that myself and didn't need a barber. At fourteen, I'd been taken to the doctor's office for my booster vaccines, and I'd waited until the nurse approached me with the syringe, then snatched it and injected myself. It earned me a telling off, but I'd kept myself safe both in body and mind.

Lasses posed no problem either. Sex was always on my terms. I'd never had a girlfriend, but with my size and attitude, it was no challenge to pick up someone if I needed release. Condoms kept me from real touch.

Violet gave a gentle sigh and rolled my way. She huddled in, fitting neatly against my body and dislodging my hold on her.

Her arm slipped around me.

My pulse jackhammered. My mind fled the remnants of my nightmare and gave me back control.

Anger woke in sharp stabs.

I jerked away and stood from the bed. Silently, I dressed, grabbed Violet's phone from where I'd stashed it behind the dresser, and left the room, jogging downstairs.

I expected everyone else to be sleeping, but Scar raised his gaze from the window seat. Thank fuck someone had the sense to take watch. Signs of the party were still apparent in the room. Clusters of beer cans. Plates and food packets on the table.

What the fuck had I allowed?

In the car yesterday, Scar had pointed out that Violet could betray us if she wanted. After, I'd allowed everyone to get drunk. Strangers to come here.

I'd been sleeping on the job.

I needed to go on the offensive, in all areas. In resolving the mystery of my mother's death but also with my family and Violet.

I'd been exhausted and now I had my strength back.

"What's wrong?" my brother asked.

"McInver is a threat, and I'm just sitting here while he lives thirty minutes away. I'm going to check out his house." Anything to stop standing still.

Scar leapt up. "I'm coming."

We woke Burn to take the watch then drove out into the dark. My sense of purpose swept away all the emotion that had arisen from my night terror.

My phone's map directed us through the mountains and out to McInver's place. When we were near, I pulled off the highway and trundled the car down a lane, headlights off. Moonlight filtered through the trees. My eyes adjusted to the pitch-black.

The entrance to McInver's was a mile down the track, but a low wall marked the edge of his territory.

I'd read online that he owned a large area of land in the Cairngorms. His home, the Great House, had been standing for centuries, and McInver allowed hunting, grouse shooting, and salmon fishing on his land, presumably for a tidy profit.

The subtext to that was the old coot probably had a gun licence, and there could be firearms in his house.

We climbed from the car, shutting the doors silently, then crept down the lane until we reached an opening in the wall. Old estates usually had public rights of way through them, and this was a well-used track.

Scar and I followed it, emerging through trees into open parkland.

Down the slope, a massive house dominated the land. The half-moon gave us enough light to pick out its features. Three storeys, pillars outside the front, formal gardens to one side. A couple of cars on a wide gravel car park.

We sprinted to a stand of trees then on to another, circling the house. When we were closer, I gestured with my chin.

"Tell me what ye see."

Scar paused for a moment. "The cars suggest McInver isn't there alone, which makes sense because that place is huge. He'd need help managing it. But there's no lights on either, suggesting everyone's asleep and not expected to be wandering."

He was right, not even a glimmer of a hallway night-light made it through the black windows.

My brother continued. "We know he's in his eighties, so I'm going to assume that whoever's there with him is paid staff, not family."

"Give me your reasoning."

"The cars outside are cheap and functional, not fancy, as ye might expect from a relative of a very wealthy man. They could use that separate outbuilding, which I assume is a garage, but it's a warm night with no rain, so why go to the effort? My bet is the old man is a penny pincher and the first runaround is his. The second is for a nurse or some kind of assistant. Also, there's no signs of life, at all. A family living there would have an impact. We're getting into summer, but there's no toys or bikes outside. No boat on that wee lake. The gardens are untidy, and the grass isn't mowed. My grandparents used to love their garden. When they got sick, they stopped maintaining it. This feels like that. There's no young blood around."

I'd reached similar conclusions.

Scar kicked a foot against a tree, leaning back. "So what now? Want to go in and say hi?"

I considered it. "No. This was about information gathering to form a plan of attack. We're not stealing from him. When I meet the old bastard, it will be face to face. I willnae hide myself."

He jabbed his fingers into his hair and swore. "You're seriously going to just walk?"

"Aye. The timing is wrong."

"He's an abusive fuck! The timing is never wrong. We should end him like we did…"

He spun away. In the rigid set of his shoulders, I picked up on something new. Stress I'd suspected him of carrying after what happened with our keeper.

"If ye want to talk about Keep—"

"Ye mean the day I became a murderer? No, I really don't."

"Camden." I used his real name.

He wheeled around. "The fuck? I haven't been him in a long time. Camden died on the island. There's a whole reason for that, and we're standing on the land of the man who started it. That's where our focus needs to be, not on the fucking island prison which we're never going back to again. This arsehole here hurt our mothers. Ye heard what Thea and Violet told us. It's been playing on my mind all night, the things he did."

Hence why he couldn't sleep.

My brother moved in on me. "If Burn was here, he'd pick a wing and start a fire. Burning the place to the ground might even improve his miserable mood. But we can do better than that." From out of his pocket, he slid a shiny object.

A hunter's knife.

Our dearly departed keeper at the hostel had given my brother his nickname in reference to the deep gouge down the side of his face. Scar had told me it was the result of accidental knife crime.

Judging by the weapon he'd somehow taken ownership of, I wasn't so sure.

It was damn clear he needed to use up some of his angst. Besides, it would do McInver good to be afraid. To know someone was coming for him.

"How about we leave a warning?" I allowed.

I turned, ready to go inflict some damage, but Scar grabbed my arm and stopped me with a hiss. He dragged me down to the grass.

"Car."

I snapped my attention to the driveway, where headlights snaked around a curve from the trees, the sound of the engine following. Two cars. Big off-roaders.

Hidden in the dark, we watched as the drivers approached the house.

From the vehicles, men emerged. The front door of the house opened, a hunched figure in the frame.

"It's him," Scar whispered.

It had to be. The shrunken man with a cane was McInver. He exchanged a few words with the men, then one returned to the first car. From the boot, he lifted something heavy-looking, threw it over his shoulder, then jogged into the house.

"What the fuck was that?" Scar asked.

I had no good answer. A roll of something, like a rug? A small body?

A second man opened the back door of his car. Three dogs leapt out, circling him. One barked, and Scar sucked in a breath.

"If they go on patrol," he said, "those dogs will find us in a minute."

"Time to get the fuck out of here."

Up the hill we jogged, keeping low and not stopping until we reached the tree line that led to the lane and the car we'd hidden well away from the main entrance road. No shout followed us, or rabid barking, and I paused to stare back at the house.

We'd come with the purpose of fact-finding but left with only more questions.

Our next visit would be better informed. He wasn't as defenceless as we'd thought.

Dawn brought a pink sky as we parked up the car outside the cabin, back on the McRae estate.

Scar went in while I planted myself on the bench outside in the cool air. At long last, I'd woken up. Days, we'd had, and I'd let too much slide.

From my pocket, I took Violet's phone.

The device powered up, and messages appeared on the screen.

The soft, sweet, sexy-as-fuck lass had no password protection. And soon, no protection at all. Not from me.

Da: I need that location as soon as you get it. Don't let me down.

Ma: If you can, stay away for a while. Your father is still a little unsettled x.

My gut roiled, but I stared at the first message until it burned into my mind. It had been sent last night, which meant Violet had done exactly what I'd suspected. Been ready to betray us to the islanders. But I'd left it. Ignored it on Struan's request and on my worst judgement.

I was a fucking idiot.

I deserved every bit of the pain clamping me now.

In the house, Struan limped from the kitchen, a mug in his hand. He saw me and stood taller. "Couldn't sleep?"

At my lack of a reply, he furrowed his brow. "I was going to waffle some boring shite about how I've had too much rest, but what the fuck? Has something happened?"

I glared at him. "Pack up. Get everyone else to as well. We're leaving in an hour."

If she'd called her father this morning from Thea's phone, they'd be on their way.

My brother stared for a beat but nodded and climbed the stairs for his and Thea's room. The trust in that simple act could've floored me. He didn't question my decision or demand an explanation. But I couldn't feel his loyalty. He'd given the same to Violet because of Theadora, and he'd been wrong.

Outside the cabin, I returned to the bench then I took up my phone and repeated the lesson my mother had taught me years before.

In half an hour, I'd located a target.

My family congregated in the lounge. Among them, Violet gazed on with the same wonder in everyone else's expressions. Bags surrounded them, all the things we'd bought packed up. A bin liner of rubbish by the door and cash on the table for a cleaner.

We were ready to leave, and I was the only one who knew why.

Except for Violet.

I stared at her, disgusted with myself.

I knew Violet was here for her own agenda.

I also knew that to some respect, she cared about us. Her friend, and my little sister, definitely.

I'd never asked her the direct question of why. Instead, I'd trusted Thea's explanation and carried on blindly waiting for the betrayal. Why bother, when all I had to do was ask? Violet wouldn't deny me the truth. She'd said so herself, but it had been buried by other needs. Last night had seen those removed.

"Where are we going?" Thea asked.

I kept my focus on her friend. "I have a question."

Violet swallowed, standing. "Ask it."

My damn heart pounded, desperate for this not to be true. "Did ye call your da yesterday?"

Silence filled the room.

Violet pressed her fingers to her lips, and pain filled

her expression. "Yes."

Everyone focused on her, shock clear.

I held my ground though my muscles shook. "To report on us?"

Tears filled her eyes. "Yes."

I knew it, but too much of me was caught up in attraction to her. I'd let it happen, and I hadn't asked her a thing.

"Why would ye do that?" Burn asked her. "Do ye want him to find us?"

"No! I'm sorry," she whispered. "I had to make the call but I told him nothing. I'm so sorry."

"She didn't," Thea confirmed.

I shrugged, ice-cold for Violet now. "Everyone grab a bag. Get in the cars. Thea, you'll drive and follow me."

If she thought to challenge me, the woman decided against it.

With whispers and exchanged expressions of shock, everyone complied, all except Violet.

I stood in front of her, arms folded. "Problem?"

Those big eyes had no effect on me now.

"I'm just waiting for ye to go, then I'll leave separately."

I gave a hard laugh, though this was anything but funny. "Do ye seriously think you're walking away from this? No, my little traitor. You're mine now. Ye cut me, now you're going to watch me bleed. Get in the damn car."

We were going, but she was going with us. I'd woken up and taken control. Violet Hunter belonged to me.

16

Lottie

We left the cabin behind us. Thea drove Struan, Burn, and Cassie. Sin put me in the back of the Ford behind him and Scar, like a prisoner.

Maybe I was.

Perhaps the gentle giant I'd seen under his skin didn't exist. Or maybe he just didn't exist for me anymore.

At the main road, Sin put his foot down and muttered something to his brother.

Scar reached into a bag by his feet and handed me a shirt. "Blindfold yourself."

He didn't smile. There was no emotion in his words.

I hadn't looked at anyone other than Sinclair when he'd revealed my shame, but of course, the rest of the family felt it, too.

Darkness descended over me.

We drove for a while, no conversation in the car, and I kept my thoughts to myself. Instead, I focused on the things I knew as fact. My mother was at risk. Da had hurt her in the past and would do so again. I had to get her away.

Without a location from me, he could get angry.

Yet in the past couple of days, I hadn't come up with a solution. I couldn't give him what he wanted without hurting people I cared for. It was stalemate.

The sound of the engine changed, then we stopped.

"Out," Sin snapped.

I didn't have to ask to know he meant me.

I plucked the blindfold off, blinking in the bright daylight, then climbed from the car to join him. We were in a lay-by, under trees. Hills obscured my view. No street signs clued me in to where we were. Just another green, nameless mountain road.

Thea's car pulled up behind, but Sin raised a hand to indicate them to stay inside. Then he grasped my shoulder with one large hand and marched me into the trees.

If this was a movie, I'd be walking to my execution.

We kept going until we were out of sight of the others and at the edge of a steep drop. Sin stopped and released me, then pulled something from his pocket. My phone.

He powered it up and held up the screen. "Read the last message."

I scanned the text from my father, demanding the location of the brothers.

Right. That's how Sin knew for sure. Heat rushed in me, a product of embarrassment, fear, and utter conflict. Sin's gaze burned into my skin.

"I called because I had to, but I didn't tell him anything he could use," I repeated my truths.

"I don't believe a word ye say."

"I'm not a liar. It was for my mother—"

"I don't fucking care. Your mother doesnae deserve your care. She let your da beat ye for years, so don't give me that shite. The people who matter are back there in the cars. If your da tracks that phone and the islanders find us, my brothers could be hurt. Jailed. We could lose Cassie. Do ye understand?"

I stifled a sob with my hand over my mouth but nodded swiftly to show him yes, I knew exactly what it meant. "He wouldn't have the first clue how to track a phone. He can't find us."

Purposefully, and letting me see, he attached a picture to the text then sent it as a reply to Da. It was an aerial view of the cabin we'd just left. No message. Probably enough in the image to hunt it down.

Then he moved in close, his thick fingers sliding into my braided hair to grip the back of my head. He held me still in front of him.

"If he wants us, he's going to have to chase us down. I am more than happy to lead that dance. I will do anything to protect my family. Fight anyone. Hurt anyone. But let me make one thing clear, Violet Hunter. I control it. Not ye."

I winced, his threat stinging.

Sin didn't let me move away. "I made a mistake with ye, but it willnae happen again." Then he placed the phone in my grip and backed off. "Throw it."

"What?"

"Ye heard. Hard as ye can."

I didn't care about my phone. I hadn't missed checking it. But I'd earned the money myself to buy the thing. Whenever I could get part-time work, I'd done so. Last summer, every week, I'd cared for the two young grandchildren of an island resident, taking them out so she could rest. She'd paid a pittance, but it added up until I had enough for the device I'd wanted. But there was no point explaining that.

I pressed my trembling lips together, pulled back my arm, and hurled my phone down the slope, losing sight of it in the dense trees.

Sin watched it go then strode off in the direction of

the cars.

For a foolish moment, I considered running. But even if I found my phone, and it was usable, I had no money. I'd have to call my father to pick me up, and that was out of the question.

Even if I had another option, I wouldn't take it.

Slowly, I trudged after him. Very clearly, Sin had placed me outside of his family group while forcing me to stay with them.

And the most pathetic part of it? I was unbearably grateful for the fact.

Another hour on, and a new sound met my ears. Like a good little prisoner, I'd kept my blindfold complete, but there was no mistaking the sound of the sea.

We were at the coast. Burn would be happy if we were staying round here somewhere. Last night, he'd talked about surfing with such rapture, the misery he carried temporarily shifting.

The car stopped, and my door opened. I climbed out, blindfold off, and smiled thanks at Scar who held my door. Then I took in the pretty scene.

Ahead, a horseshoe bay curved into a narrow stretch of coastline, rugged cliffs behind. Seaweed-strewn rocks met a tiny pebble beach where an old concrete dock stretched out to deeper water. Light rain fell, though the sun still shone. It sparkled on the calm sea.

The deep scent of brine washed over me.

Sin had chosen somewhere perfectly isolated. Instantly calming. *Breathtaking.*

I peered at the single-lane, rutted track that had brought us down here, then behind to the house at our backs. It was another holiday home by the looks of it. Set alone in this beautiful place, and a little run-down with peeling paint on an outbuilding and salt built up on the glassed-in porch.

Thea's car bumped down the road, and before she'd even fully stopped, Burn half fell out of the rear passenger seat.

He stared at the water, then his gaze snapped to Sin. "Are ye fucking joking?"

The big man stood at the front of the car, a distance away from me. The ghost of a smile curved his lips. "We'll be here for a night or two."

Burn yelped then took off across the beach to the water's edge. He ran in, fully clothed, and sank to his knees in the shallows. I pressed my hand to my heart, the expression of utter relief on his face somehow painful enough for me to feel.

Cassie giggled and ran after him.

"Shoes off," I called on instinct.

It was one thing Burn putting up with wet boots, but another thing if she got sore feet. Dutifully, the little girl kicked off her trainers and jumped into a wave, squealing with delight that matched her brother's.

Thea and Struan left their car, and my friend joined me. I gave a little headshake to say *not now,* and she directed an annoyed glance at Sin instead.

Struan lifted his chin at the big man. "What is this place?"

"Does it matter? It's empty tonight, and we needed somewhere to go. It's big enough for all of us, and nobody knows we're here. For now anyway." Sin sliced a look my way, then continued, raising his voice. "Take your things inside. Claim your space. Leave the biggest room for me."

I didn't miss the fact that this time, he hadn't included me in his sleeping arrangements.

At the front door of the holiday home, it took thirty seconds of Sin and Scar working a key safe screwed to the wall for them to extract a set of silver keys and let us inside.

Through the deep tiled porch, warmed by the sun

and containing wicker furniture on which to sit and watch the ocean, another door led us into a main living space. It was a typical seaside home, with a 'gone to the beach' sign hanging on the door, blue-and-white pottery, and seascape paintings here and there. Comfortable and homely. Whoever owned the place kept it well-maintained. I had no idea how Sin found it or how he knew it would be empty, but I wasn't about to ask.

Blue-painted stairs led up to the bedrooms, but a peek down the hall showed me a wide kitchen taking up the whole back of the house, with tall seats set around an island, and a dining table to the side. A big American-style fridge buzzed, and I widened my eyes. The cabin we'd just left had been lovely, but the kitchen had been tiny in comparison. Not designed for preparing large meals. Here, I'd be in my element. I could cook with people sitting at the island, chatting. We could eat dinners around the big table.

"Holy shite." Struan's voice drew me back. "A surfboard."

Sin rumbled a low reply from right behind me.

I spun around to find his gaze on me, then he turned to his brother who was still in the porch.

"It said on the listing that this place was equipped for surfing. Have Burn check out the outbuilding. I'm pretty certain he'll find boards and wetsuits."

Scar took off at a scramble down the track to the beach, hollering his brother's name.

Struan passed me and leaned heavily on the banister, easing himself upstairs. Thea joined him, and they disappeared into one of the bedrooms. Exhaustion hung over both of them.

It was just Sin and me left now.

I didn't make eye contact. "I'm going to get the food into the fridge so it doesn't spoil. Then I'll make lunch."

"Take your stuff upstairs first."

"It's fine. I'll sleep on the sofa. I don't need to claim a bedroom."

A mistake.

He rounded on me and crowded me against the wall, dislodging a small painting that fell to the floor with a clatter. He lowered his face to mine, one hand splayed next to my head, the other coming up to grip my chin, forcing me to look at him.

"Why do ye think you're here? As our personal chef? Our maid? You're in my bed. Understand? Every fucking night. No creeping around. And if I think Thea or anyone else is going to hand ye a phone or leave theirs unguarded, I'll take the lot and throw them in the sea. If ye thought I was controlling of ye already, I'm going to be a fucking monster now."

I closed my eyes against the onslaught of too much feeling. It should be fear chilling me, but instead, stupid girl that I was, I only felt the shock of lust at how close we were.

Sin gave an irritated growl and shook me. "Answer."

"Was there a question?" I sassed back.

"Open your eyes." He set his forehead on mine, right onto the bruise he'd accidentally hurt.

Too easily, he could injure me. The slight buzz of pain from his pressure now was nothing to what those huge hands and bulging muscles could inflict. Yet when I peeked at him, reeling in the sight of his dark regard, the scent of him deep in my lungs, I couldn't name the emotion pouring off him. It wasn't pure anger, or hatred, but something else. A combination I didn't understand.

My breathing turned heavy, my chest rising and falling with each pant.

"I'm not sleeping next to ye," I said on a breath, solely to get his reaction.

"Aye, ye are."

"What, you're going to make me?"

"Now she understands."

"Fine, then don't expect me to lie there frustrated. If you're not going to touch me, I can take care of myself."

Sin inched back and switched his gaze from my eyes, down to my breasts. Wetness pooled at the juncture of my legs. Warmth radiated through me.

He breathed just as hard as I did. "Who said I couldnae change my mind about touching ye?"

A gasp left my parted lips.

Happy shouts came from outside. "Sin! Come and see. Ye were right. Fuck!"

With a cruel smirk, Sin pushed off the wall and walked away. He didn't look back, and I took a second to put myself back together.

In the space of everything being wrong, that moment of push and pull had felt only too right.

17

Sin

Out of breath, I strained, stretching for my goal. My muscles shook with the effort. Sweat poured off me.

One more push and I'd be there.

Clenching my jaw, I reached and finally grasped the handhold in the rock face. Relief nearly floored me, but I hauled myself up onto the top of the cliff behind our house.

Sprawled on the rocky ledge, I panted in the sea air.

Above the level of the roof, I had a view to the bright water, my brothers two dots in the waves.

While they'd spent the afternoon surfing, only breaking to eat the lunch Violet prepared, I'd been on a recce. I'd scouted the coast for a mile in each direction, noting every distant fisherman's cottage and smuggler's nook. Footpaths. The stretch of road.

Farther south from us was Catterline Bay, which I only knew because Ma had a print of a painting some artist had done of the place. She didn't have a romantic bone in her body but said the picture had made her feel some thing. North was Stonehaven then Aberdeen, where Burn and I had grown up.

Maybe that was why I'd started and ended my search here. It felt like coming home.

Aside from that, there was safety in the location.

The position of our surf house was at a gap in the coastal path, so passersby would be few. Even so, I'd scaled this cliff, which loomed metres from the back of the house, just to check if anyone could break in while we slept. It had been a challenge for me, even at my height, so my concerns had reduced. With no footpath down it, only a determined fucker would manage it.

Voices drifted from an open window at the back of the house.

"Do ye still love me?" Struan asked.

"Yes!" Thea's shocked voice replied. "Why do you think I wouldn't?"

Shite. I didn't need to hear this. Easing up, I twisted around, searching for a way through the dense shrubs at the cliff's edge. I'd planned to walk back along the road, but now had to scramble away in a hurry. And quietly.

"I got hurt. I couldn't protect ye," Struan explained.

"I would've taken that knife for you."

"Don't fucking say that."

"Why not? I would've let her stab me to keep you safe. Love doesn't go away just like that. You're mine for good."

"Clothes off. Now. Tell me all that love shite while ye ride me."

For fuck's sake.

Giving up on stealth, I crashed through the bushes, putting distance between myself and whatever they were getting up to in their bedroom.

I half fell through a dead tree, branches cracking under my weight.

"Who's there?" Struan's shout followed.

Ah Christ. "It's Sin," I called back. "Just patrolling. Go back to...what ye were doing."

Whatever he replied, I missed, but I caught Thea's giggle.

Out of earshot, I took my time exploring the ridge then descended again to the bay. In my mind, I played over the fact that Violet had been so ready to betray us. In the same circumstances as my brother and his girlfriend had been on that boat, Violet would never have taken a knife for me.

When I'd finally made it back to the house, I hesitated. I needed a shower and to change my clothes. I had new ones thanks to the shopping trip—joggers, long-leg jeans, boxers, and even a couple of shirts—but hadn't yet tried anything.

The clothes I'd worn at the hostel—a threadbare black t-shirt and frayed jeans—had been the ones I'd been captured in. It felt like a lifetime ago.

But before I went inside, my attention was diverted by a small shape clinging to the end of the sea wall.

"Cassie?" I said.

My little sister peeked up. She'd been staring at our brothers in the surf, her eyes rounded.

I tilted my head. "Want to go out on the water?"

She shrank back. "I can't swim. They've gone out too deep."

"Come on. I'll take ye for a lesson." She could perch on my board like a car ornament.

"For real? Thank ye!"

"Cassie? Oh, there ye are." Violet stepped out of the house, a goddamned apron tied around her.

Instant heat rose in me.

How the fuck was an apron a turn-on? I had no idea, but it cinched around her waist and curved over her tits.

I wanted her in nothing but that. So I could peel it off

her.

I dragged my gaze off her and back to my sister. "Go to the shed. We'll hunt down a wetsuit in your size."

"Lottie, will ye come with us? Sin's going to teach me to swim," Cassie said.

Violet recoiled. "Um, no. I've got things to do."

She was playing maid again. I pointed at the outbuilding. "Naw, ye don't. Both of ye, get changed. I'll grab a board and meet ye out there."

"Don't ye want a wetsuit, too?" Cassie asked.

I needed to cool off. A dip in the sea in my underwear would help. I shook my head, found myself a board, and headed down to the water.

A few minutes on, Cassie joined me where I waited in the shallows, waves lapping my ankles.

She was alone.

I gazed past her to the outhouse. "Good to see there was a suit to fit."

She gave a bashful little grin, turning on a toe. Violet had even strapped a float around her and found sea shoes so the pebbles wouldn't hurt her feet.

"Lottie isn't coming. She said nobody would want to see her in a wetsuit so she's going to make a start on dinner." Cassie hitched a breath and jumped a wave.

On autopilot, I grabbed her hand and towed her deeper. The only way to enjoy the cold Scottish sea was to get right in and adjust to the temperature drop. Except I was hung up over my sister's last statement. Never in my wildest imagination had I considered that Violet would be body conscious. Her body was fucking insane. Curvy and gorgeous. Every man's dream.

Then again, I'd shared a bed with her and never seen her completely naked, despite all we'd done.

How could she make that statement? Had it been throwaway, or was there a reason behind it?

It pissed me off that I cared.

Ridding myself of the emotion, I put my mind to the swimming lesson I had to give.

Over the next hour, Cassie practiced treading water and floating on her back in the calmer spot behind the old dock. Then I sat her on my surfboard and paddled out deeper.

The minute they spotted us, Scar and Burn moved closer, no doubt keeping an eye on my teaching efforts. Like I'd let our sister out of my sight for even a second. They joined us in the approach to the beach, just riding waves into the shore. Cassie squealed with excitement, rising on her knees then toppling into the seaweed-heavy break. Scar scooped her up and set her on his board, jettisoning her away and swimming after in pursuit.

The afternoon sun warmed us.

The rain had gone now, summer in play.

Burn's expression was entirely blissed out. Droplets of seawater slid down his overlong hair, and his cheeks were red from a combination of salt and the sun.

I caught his attention. "Happier now?"

"Aye. I needed this."

I knew it. He had two things he loved, surfing and setting fire to shite. Those opposing elements reflected the fun and twisted sides to his personality.

Something in his expression changed, and his gaze fixed on the house. Violet stood at the front door, dusting off her hands.

She untied her apron then fastened it again, cinching the strings around her waist. Her tits vanished under the cloth then suddenly strained it once more, swelling over the top and around the sides in one of the hottest, unintentional moves I'd ever seen.

Goddamn it.

"Ho-ly shite," Burn muttered.

He watched her, and his stare intensified.

I swept water at him. "What the fuck?"

He blinked. "I wasn't... Okay, I was."

Instant possessiveness had me sitting taller on my board. "After everything she's done, ye need to keep your eyes off her."

My youngest brother choked on a laugh. "Yeah, because that's the reason."

"She isnae one of us," I warned.

He regarded me for a second, then spread out on his surfboard. "I'm staring at her because she's got fucking amazing tits and I'm a horny arsehole. But—"

I snatched hold of the front of his board and flipped it, sinking the wee fucker into the ocean.

He surfaced, spluttering with laughter, and flicked back his sodden hair. "There was a 'but' to that sentence."

I growled, and he laughed more.

"*But* she's also kind to me, and I'm a little bit in love with that. Tell me to think of her like I do Thea and I'll shut it down."

I gritted my jaw.

She wasn't like Thea, who'd gone all in with us. Given over her inheritance to support us. Violet didn't have that unswaying loyalty, either given or received. Or she shouldn't do.

Except I was the only one who seemed to think so.

Burn's mouth fell open in delight. He eased back onto his board and started paddling. "Grand. Exactly as I thought. See ye back at the ranch, bro."

I let him go.

He was wrong, but I didn't have the words to correct him.

At the house, Violet had gone inside, but another figure emerged. Struan. He strode to the wall and leaned on it, watching us.

I checked that Cassie was good to hang out with Scar and paddled in.

My brother tracked me as I stowed my surfboard then stood next to him.

"Wanted to join ye out there," he said.

"Sucks that ye can't."

"Aye. Lottie said it was a bad idea for a day or two. Thea agreed."

I joined him on his lean on the wall. Someone had left a stack of towels, and I wrapped one around my waist, using a second to scrub the seawater from my arms and chest. "You're whipped."

"Fuck off," he said, but it was without real venom. "I own her. She owns me. Call it whatever ye like, but she's mine. That means something."

Neither of us spoke for a minute. I tried to blank out what I'd overheard, but I couldn't deny a kind of envy over what he'd found.

Following that train of thought prompted my next question. "Did Thea know what Lottie was going to do yesterday?"

I could have questioned the lass, but my brother would've brained me.

He stared at the horizon where the sun dipped low. "What if she did?"

I blew out an exasperated breath. "It wasn't for naught that I had everyone pledge to let me lead this. To keep us all safe. And to do that, I need to know everything."

"I can guarantee Theadora wouldn't threaten that. Have ye asked her? Lottie, I mean. Got the feeling she won't refuse ye anything."

"No," I confessed.

"Are ye going to?" At my lack of an answer, he changed tack. "Why's she still here?"

I could've given him one of many bullshit reasons, but

it came back to that point that dogged me. The thing he had that I didn't.

"I can't let her go," I admitted.

He scrutinised me and ticked off on his fingers. "Can't let her go, won't trust her, been in love with her for a year. Yeah, sorry it isn't working out."

"I'm not in fucking love with her."

The fucktard smirked at me. "Yet she's yours."

Mine. Because I wanted to use her. Or maybe I wanted her to use me.

"For now," I muttered.

He clapped me on the shoulder then turned for the house. "Or maybe forever. In ten years, we could be standing like this while our wives and bairns play on the beach."

I curled my lip and gave him a look to show exactly what I thought of that idea. "Babies? What the fuck is wrong with ye?"

Struan's smug expression grew. "Try the thought out for a second. The lass of your dreams getting pregnant by ye. Her belly rounded. A family the two of ye make together and keep safe and happy."

"Sounds like a trap."

"Bullshit. It's addictive."

Footsteps sounded on the path behind us. Violet and Thea approached.

"Dinner's ready," Violet informed us.

Struan pulled Thea into his body and landed a kiss on her. "We'll call in the others."

They ambled down the beach, leaving me alone with Violet.

My head was in a weird place. I had the competing mix of what she'd said about her body to Cassie, Burn's overeager attention, and Struan's fucking pregnancy comment.

I faced her and allowed myself to indulge in that last

point, testing his insistence. Addictive, he'd called it.

I soaked in the sight of Violet's curves, picturing them all the more full from pregnancy. Her tits would be even bigger.

My dick throbbed, and my balls tightened.

Jesus fucking Christ.

"Why are ye staring at me like that?" she asked.

Yeah, no way was I answering.

Violet's cheeks reddened, and she propped her bag on the wall and rifled through it, as if to give her something to do other than face off with me.

A round, silver packet dropped to the concrete path. She yelped and snatched it up, but not before I saw what it was.

A pill packet. Contraceptives.

I took it from her in a quick swipe. "What's this?"

Her blush deepened, and she tried to grab it back. "None of your business."

After the thoughts I'd been having, and her betrayal, it felt very much my business. I held the packet out of her reach. "Thought ye were a virgin. Did your da send ye to seduce me as well?"

I was being an arsehole, but Violet stalled, her eyes wide.

No way.

I was right?

No refusal came. The lass's lips were firmly closed. Pressed together.

Rapid-fire, I joined the dots.

Her father wanted our location, but that wasn't all. I closed in on her, unease spreading. "I'm right, aren't I? How was that supposed to work? He ordered ye to sleep with me and gain my trust? Just me, or would any of us do?"

I swung out a hand to indicate my brothers, approaching from the beach.

Violet's jaw dropped. "No!"

I stalked down the path, away from our audience. Beyond the house, the track ended at a rock fall below the cliffs, the sea closer here.

Violet followed. She said something, but I missed it over the roaring of blood in my ears.

Burn had called her kind, but it was all a front, designed to lure me in. Sixty seconds ago, I'd been picturing her pregnant with my bairn. Her trap was working, and I couldn't allow it.

"How far are ye prepared to go, Violet?" I snarled.

"Please stop."

"Fuck me. Fuck me over. All the same to ye."

Her rounded, teary eyes did nothing for me.

"Why don't we test it?"

Trapping her gaze with mine, I waggled her pack of contraceptives. Then I pulled back my arm and hurled it as far as I could into the sea.

The silver packet disappeared beneath the waves.

Violet stared after it. Shock decorated her features.

Good.

I'd upped the stakes. Now I'd have fun seeing her response.

"What, did I help or hinder your little plot?" I snapped.

"You're a jerk."

"Run your mouth again and I'll pick ye up and throw ye in after it."

Her outraged expression changed to a glower, she turned and stalked back into the house.

I stayed outside, welcoming in the cool evening. I was still too hot. Too bothered.

I couldn't play happy families and sit around the dinner table, eating the meal she'd lovingly made.

It would only taste like ash and deceit.

18

Sin

Darkness had fallen by the time I joined my family. They sprawled on sofas and chairs in the lounge, beer cans open, and a film on no one was watching.

Violet was missing, along with our sister.

“What’s your take on McInver?” Struan asked me.

Scar gestured with his beer. “I was telling everyone about our trip last night.”

I dropped into a seat. “Small. Shrunken. Sinister.”

“Pretty much my words,” Scar added.

“Not unprotected, from the sound of the men who went in.” Struan adjusted his position, Thea tucked in against him. He seemed paler this evening, probably doing too much today in our relocation here.

“What was in the roll?” Burn asked in a spooky voice.

“The what?” I asked.

Scar snorted. “He means what the guy carried from the car. I have this weird feeling it was a body.”

I shook my head. “Too small, unless he’s in the habit

He didn't appear convinced. "Wouldn't put anything past him. Next time we go back, I'll scout around and try to find it."

Burn looked between us. "When will that be?"

I shrugged, urgency to act still in me. "Soon. Tomorrow, perhaps."

Struan grumbled. "I don't know why you're bothering. We don't need him or his money. I still vote we leave it alone, particularly now we know he has men there."

If it hadn't been for the mystery over my mother's death, I might have agreed. But I couldn't ignore the chance of getting answers.

Thea cut in. "No way. If you don't inherit, Charterman's son will. It isn't fair after all you suffered at that man's hands. I can picture Henry now, mobilising to charm McInver. If his sister gets to him, he'll be easily persuaded."

Struan pushed her hair aside to kiss her cheek, muttering something soft.

Then his gaze returned to me. "On the subject of coming and going, I've got a message ready to send to Max, telling him we've left."

He'd waited on my approval. After our words earlier, it gave me a fresh sense of leadership.

"Send it. Before we left this morning, I texted his uncle the same. I want to know the minute the islanders turn up."

I'd also promised the man no risks to his family, which meant no surprises either.

"Why are we expecting them to show up there?" Struan asked, a flick of his thumb sending his message.

"I used Violet's phone to tell them where we were."

My brother choked out a laugh. "Love it. Did Gordain reply? Will we find out?"

"Aye. He offered his support, again, and I told him we'd be lying low for a few days."

Scar gestured to the house. "Got to know, how the hell did ye swing this place? And how long do we have it for?"

"I'd tell ye but I'd have to kill ye."

Violet entered the room, something in her hands. She ignored me entirely and stopped in front of Struan. "Cassie's asleep. Next on my list is ye, big fella."

Struan arched an eyebrow at her, then took the item and held it up to the light. A thermometer. "Really?"

"Really. In your ear until it beeps. Have ye been taking the antibiotics?"

Thea nodded for him. "Not the painkillers, though. He thinks that if he can't feel the pain, he'll make the injury worse. Or that it's somehow unmanly."

Violet planted her hands on her hips. "That's ridiculous. The whole point of the painkillers are so that you're comfortable. But I'm not about to argue with ye. There's enough testosterone in this house to sink a ship."

The thermometer beeped, and she took it and peered at the wee screen.

I didn't like her playing nursemaid to him. Unwanted feelings rose that were dangerously like jealousy. Beyond the possessiveness that saw me dump Burn in the sea earlier just for looking at her.

"No fever. Can I see the operation site?" she asked.

I swore under my breath and switched my gaze to the window so I didn't have to see her raise his shirt and peel back the bandage.

Black night obscured my view of the sea, and the window only reflected the room. In the glass, Violet had her fingertips on my brother's fucking stomach.

Touching his damn skin.

Too much. I leapt to my feet and strode away, finding myself in the kitchen. In the fridge, a bowl covered with a saucepan lid waited among the packets of vegetables and healthy shite. I snatched it out, finding a large portion of chicken seasoned with something spicy on a bed of fried vegetables and rice. Along the side of the bowl, Violet had layered sliced avocado with something sprinkled on top. I searched the drawers for a fork then dug in, standing over the sink, not bothering to heat the dinner.

It was fuel. I didn't intend to enjoy it.

Couldn't help the fact it was delicious, every bite.

Someone entered the kitchen behind me.

Thea opened the fridge and took out a beer bottle, removing the lid to take a swallow. She eyed me. "Enjoying your dinner?"

I shrugged, ate the last bite, then opened doors until I found the hidden dishwasher.

"Tell Lottie. She likes to know."

"For all I know, she could've poisoned me."

I felt rather than saw Thea's outrage. "How can you say that? She spent hours today cleaning this place, making up the rooms, and then cooking. Then she cleaned it all up, put Cassie in the shower, and took her to bed."

I set my expression to neutral. "Guilty conscience will do that for ye."

The lass glowered at me. I had no idea if Violet had told her what I'd done outside with tossing her contraceptives, but either way, I wasn't about to take a scolding.

"She isn't our maid, and she needs help as much as the rest of us do."

I'd said the same, but now, only shrugged. "You've left her in the lounge, up close and personal with your boyfriend. What gives?"

"What gives is I trust her, with Struan or any of you. Because she's trustworthy. One of the best people I know. Do me a favour and ask her about her reasons. I know she'll tell you."

"She already did. It was for her mother. Doesn't make any difference." I only knew what she'd blurted out to me this morning, and I hadn't asked for more.

If I didn't have the details of her domestic disaster, it couldn't pollute my goal of keeping my family safe. And my secondary one about interrogating McInver.

Thea cursed me. "And you're still blaming her? What the hell is wrong with you?"

She stormed away.

I helped myself to a beer and took a minute before I followed.

In the living room, all the lasses were now absent, and Struan had moved to sit at the table by the window. Scar settled next to him, a pen in his hand and his tattoo gun on the table.

"Start by extending some of this." Struan traced over his tattoo sleeve, unfinished at his forearm. "If ye fuck it up, it's not so noticeable. Then when you're practised, all of us can get our brand."

Scar dipped his head, concentrating on the job. I took my seat again, adjacent to the couch where Burn laid out, watching TV.

I wanted to go find Violet. Instead, I kept my arse to the seat and brooded. To the buzz of the tattoo gun and the low conversation between my brothers, I sat in my darkened corner.

Soft footsteps brought me back into the room. Violet, returning. At the edge of the couch, she hesitated, casting her gaze over the four of us. Burn smiled and patted the sofa cushion next to him.

I leaned up and caught her wrist.

She tugged to get free, so I pulled harder, landing us both on my chair, her on my lap. Then I set a possessive arm around her middle, the other hand on her thigh, pinning her to me so she couldn't escape.

Fuck, those curves of hers...

"What are ye doing?" she whispered.

Driving myself slowly insane with the feel of her body.

With my lips against her hair, I let her in on a secret. "My brother has a crush on ye."

Across the room, Burn groaned. "Fuck off, Sin."

Scar gave a laugh, not looking up from his work.

I ran my hand under her tits, brushing the plump swell with my knuckles. "He likes these."

Burn twisted to face away from us and turned the TV up.

I kept my hands on Violet, lowering my voice. "Cassie told me what ye said about the wetsuit. I'd say ye have an audience ready to admire ye in skin-tight clothes."

"Let me go," she demanded.

I held her closer, enjoying her plump arse against me.

Maybe too much. Under her, my dick hardened.

Hidden by the sounds of the movie's car chase playing out, Violet's breath hitched.

She gave up the battle of getting away and reclined onto me. Her fair hair brushed my cheek. Then purposefully, she wriggled, getting comfortable.

Fuck.

Stifling my surge of lust, I tried to retain control. I squeezed her thigh over her cut-off leggings, then slid my hand higher under the hem of her long shirt.

"Tomorrow is going to be different." I drew circles on her inner thigh, nudging her leg to give me room.

She inched her knees wider, her breathing faster now. Then as if to hide what I was doing, she lifted her feet to fold her legs across my lap.

Giving me full access to the apex of her thighs.

An open invitation that went straight to my balls.

Slightly, she tilted her head to mine. "Different how?"

Another soft circle took me another inch to where I wanted to go.

"No more cooking and cleaning for us. These arseholes can make their own food."

Keeping his gaze fixed on the screen, Burn shook his head, his expression panicked. "Speak for yourself. I'm begging ye not to cut off our supply of excellent meals."

"I like cooking," Violet replied, a little strained. "And all of your family offered help."

"Which ye didn't take," I guessed.

She pouted, an expression I'd never seen on her before. Deliberately, she braced herself on the sides of the chair and ground into me.

A punishment for my words? I'd take that any day. But I had to answer.

"Want to get up?" I asked.

"What do ye think?"

"That either way, it's tough."

I palmed her directly between the legs, and she sucked in a quiet gasp then swiped to pull the hem of her loose shirt over my hand.

It suited me. One short move, and I slipped my hand into her leggings and behind the elastic of her underwear. My fingertips grazed her clit, and Violet shivered.

Still, she didn't stop me.

I glided them down into her already wet pussy. "Proof," I accused.

Without hesitation, I slid my index finger inside her tight heat. She clenched around me and dropped her head back onto my shoulder, her mouth open and her gaze on mine.

Warmth spread through me.

With calm menace, I added another finger, stretching her.

Her hand landed on my forearm, and she gripped me. A warning? No. She kept up the eye contact, nothing but need in her gaze.

I fucking loved the challenge.

This was hardly discreet, and she wasn't calling me out. The darkness of the room and the arrangement of our bodies only went so far to hiding my actions. I had no doubt my brothers knew exactly what I was doing.

I could finger-fuck her to an orgasm now and I bet she'd allow it.

Violet's chest rose and fell, and I shifted the hand I'd used to pin her so I was openly cupping her tits.

In a heartbeat, what had started as a tease turned to dark need. I had my fingers inside her and my thumb ready to graze her nipple. Those heavy tits of hers were my downfall. There was only one way to go from here, and I didn't need an audience for that.

With difficulty, I eased back.

"Listen up," I snapped to the room. "As of tomorrow, work out a rota for cleaning. If Violet wants to cook, that's her contribution to the household. Don't take advantage."

"Yeah, you're doing that for us," Burn quipped.

Violet came to her senses. She righted her clothes and shot up, then skipped out of sight. Her footsteps ascended the stairs.

More slowly, I followed, hunting her down.

One of my brothers muttered something that made the other two laugh, but I couldn't hear it past the blood rushing in my ears.

And the absolute certainty about what was going to happen next.

19

Lottie

I took to the dark bedroom and yanked open the drawer of the bedside table. Inside, I'd concealed my vibrator under a shirt.

Sin had taunted me almost to the brink with just a few not-so-sly touches. After everything that had happened today, I didn't know what to expect next. For him to follow. Or stay away. Or try to stop me from burning up the need he'd generated.

Well, fuck him. I wasn't going to wait to find out.

The room I'd picked for us was at the front of the house with views over the ocean. I'd left the curtains open, and there was enough moonlight to see by, as well as watch the hushed waves.

In the bay window, I paused.

Back home on Torlum, despite being surrounded by water, our house was inland by a field. The ocean just out of my reach. The view here was stupendous. Not in the way of a mountain range with soaring peaks, but with endless waves, the entirely calming, *safe* feel.

I'd never had that.

Staying put with my view of the sea, I unclipped my bra and slid the straps down under my shirt then tossed the item aside. I pulled down my leggings and knickers and stepped out of those, leaving myself in just my long, loose tunic.

A pulse beat between my legs, an ever-present pressure from being around Sin. From him touching me. His fingers had been inside me, and it had taken everything in me to hold still and not move my hips to chase the incredible feelings.

I thumbed on my vibrator and braced one hand on the little table in front of the window. If anyone passed by in a boat, they might catch sight of me. But chances were minimal I'd be seen.

I lowered the buzzing device between my breasts, shivering at the sensation. But this had to be quick, so I kept going down to skim it over my thigh.

My pussy clenched in anticipation, even though the thought of using it inside myself scared me.

The door flung open behind me and slammed shut.

Sin.

It wasn't in him to sneak around or be quiet. I kept facing the window, the buzzing so telling, yet I wasn't about to stop.

A click told me he'd engaged the lock, then in a few strides, his hulking form pressed against my back.

One hand curled around the base of my throat, and the other travelled down my arm. He swore, and his fingers spread over mine, feeling what I was doing.

Anger stoked my desire.

Already today, he'd forced me to throw my phone away, then tossed my contraceptives to the waves. Everything was a test. Always challenging me.

I didn't blame him, but one point messed with my head.

He'd performed that second act with a purpose. It was designed so he couldn't fuck me.

For some reason, that pissed me off more than anything.

I went to shift the vibrator higher, but his grasp on my hand tightened, holding me still.

I wrenched against it, but he held firm.

Tension built.

"What's your problem?"

He didn't answer, nor did he move.

"Is it because I can't lose my virginity to ye now?" I taunted. It was a guess. He had to be as conflicted as I was.

His reply was a growl, and the fingers around my throat gripped harder. "Fuck ye. Lose it to this lump of plastic, if ye want. But you'll do it naked and sucking my dick."

Lust streaked through me.

Challenge rose in a hot wave. I turned into his body, dislodging his grip, then I sank to my knees in front of him. Still holding the vibrator, and with my knees wide, I unbuttoned his jeans.

A dim voice in the back of my brain reminded me he was touch sensitive, but he'd asked for this. Couldn't give a blow job without contact.

Sin slapped my hands away and freed his thick cock. It bobbed under its own weight, and he gripped himself hard, his knuckles proud.

Faced with it, I had a sudden panic. He was so huge, his dick in proportion to his massive frame. My hand wouldn't fit around him. How would he ever fit inside me?

Good thing he'd decided it wouldn't happen.

"Take off that shirt," he ordered.

"Are ye going to let me touch ye?"

"Not with your hands."

"Then no."

He stared down at me. My top covered me to my thighs and concealed my shape.

Sin caught my chin with his hand. "I want to see ye."

"And I want to have my hands on your body, so choose."

For a moment, he just kept up his intimidating stare, then his fingers squeezed my jaw until I opened my mouth. He ran the head of his dick over my parted lips.

I opened wider and took him inside, flattening my tongue.

He was so hard, and smooth, too. The taste of him musky. Unique. I liked it. I dipped forward, taking him into my mouth and closing my lips around him.

Sin gave up a groan and speared his fingers into my hair, otherwise holding still.

I sucked, at the same moment, bringing the vibrator up to press it to the base of his dick.

Again, he pushed my hands away, this time leaning in to brace himself on the table just behind my head, his other hand taking hold of the back of my neck, forcing me to arch backwards.

Opening my throat.

He jacked his hips, thrusting into my mouth. I grappled his wrist beside my head, and this time, he didn't stop me. On my knees on the hard floorboards, I could only take, my balance supported by his hold.

He didn't stop, fucking my mouth again, cutting off my breathing. Using me.

Fresh heat flashed along my veins. Something about my lips stretched wide around him, or maybe the sheer need in his act, woke my blood.

I needed this. More.

My eyes watered, but I stroked him with my tongue, loving the way he tensed up. The scent and taste of him obliterated everything else.

With my free hand, I returned the vibrator to between my legs, testing it against my skin but still not placing it anywhere vital.

The sense of getting myself off in a hurry had gone. Urgency built in a different way. From breathing while he fucked my mouth. From the pulses of pleasure in me.

I drove the tip of the vibrator up to my bare pussy and whimpered.

Sin withdrew his dick, breathing hard. He released me. "I want to fucking see."

I wiped the saliva from my mouth with the back of my hand. "Not happy just choking me?"

I wasn't stripping for him. It was too much when I was already in virgin territory in every other way. He might be able to treat it as just sex, but under the surface, it was bigger for me. If I thought about it too much, my chest ached. Exposing myself to him completely meant trust, and that was non-existent.

His dark gaze took me in, then he stooped, lifting me with arms under my legs and around my back.

"Stop!" I yelped. "You'll hurt yourself."

"How?"

"I'm too heavy."

"The fuck ye talking about?" He carried me to the wide bed and placed me on the quilt with more care than I thought possible.

I flushed hot and scrambled up among the pillows, tucking my legs up with my shirt over my knees. "Ye know what I mean."

"Am I not strong enough?"

"That isn't... I mean..."

Sin stepped back to collect the vibrator from where I'd dropped it on the floor. He switched it off and set it on the bed next to me, his jaw locked tight.

Then he stripped his jeans and boxers and plucked

his t-shirt over his head.

God above.

I stared, taking in his long, lean form. Strength cried out from every hard muscle. He was more powerful than I could comprehend. My brain screamed predator, and I was the stunned bunny.

He knelt on the bed and straddled me, pulling me down the mattress to arrange me how he wanted. In the face of his utter, unashamed nudity, I turned to putty. Astride me, facing the head of the bed so his dick was in my face again, he took up the vibrator, turned it on, then twisted to set it directly to my wet centre. I yelped, and he swept it over me, nudging it lower.

My shirt had ridden up to my hips, out of the way so he had free access to stare.

I could handle this. It was dark enough to be sure the stretch marks on my thighs were hidden.

I bucked against the intense vibration but kept my hands flat to the bed, mixed up over what I was doing but in no way wanting this to stop.

"Widen your legs so I can slide it inside ye," he demanded.

"No. It's too big."

"I'm bigger. If I fucked ye now, you'd take me."

I already knew the truth of that. "But that isn't going to happen."

Sin took the vibrator, slick with my juices, to his mouth. Deliberately, with his gaze holding mine, he licked it then tossed it to the sheets.

"Whatever. I'm going to fuck your pretty mouth until I come down your throat, so do what ye like to get yourself off."

With that, he rose and angled over me, clamping my jaw in his thick fingers again. He slid into my waiting mouth without pause. In this position, I was better able to receive him. I closed my eyes and sucked him when he was in shallow and stroked my tongue over him when he went deep.

If my unpractised technique was lacking, it didn't signify. He rumbled approval, and his pleasure spiked mine.

I crept my fingers to the vibrator and again brought it to my clit. I rubbed it over myself and through my folds then flicked the switch and jerked with the added vibration.

Sin thickened in my mouth.

He muttered curse words and twisted to watch.

I cruised the tool up and down, teasing myself and pushing more firmly with every pass.

We fell into sync, me matching his moves, echoing what he was taking from me and delivering it back into my sensitive flesh.

Sin picked up the pace, driving into my throat, so deep my eyes watered. Like before, I could only take now. But it was no hardship. I liked surrendering to him. Him calling the shots. It worked for me that he wanted me in this way.

Desire built into unbeatable need, driven on by his rapt attention. The hint of him losing control. Over me.

He worked harder, and I copied him until a tight coil of heat wound deep in me.

I moaned, and Sin gave up a guttural sound. He crowded over my head and drew out one last time. That huge dick of his pulsed.

"Fuck, Violet," Sin gritted out.

He came over my mouth. Shallow, so the essence of him coated my tongue, spilling over my lips and chin.

Dizzy, I revelled in the new taste.

At the last throb, he withdrew and rolled off me. But he wasn't done. His hand landed on mine where I still held the vibrator. I hadn't come yet. I'd gotten lost in his release.

He took control, moving it to my entrance.

I wrestled it away. "I said I didn't want that."

"Why not?" he said, his voice thick with challenge.

"It's too big!"

"Ye are more than wet enough."

I yanked my hand from his grip and brought the vibrator to my mouth. Just like he'd done, I licked it, then coated it in the dribble still on my skin, all the while glaring at him.

I rubbed his cum all over the pulsating toy.

"And if I use ye as lube?" I tested.

Sin's expression darkened impossibly further.

He'd thrown away my pills. Couldn't fuck me. I wasn't at any real risk of pregnancy from him, surely not if I just missed a pill tonight, yet...

That tiny possibility sent a new wave of heat through me unlike anything else.

Slowly, I delivered the vibrator back to between my legs.

This was stupid.

I didn't care.

He had every chance to stop me, but the arsehole only breathed harder, his nostrils flared.

I touched it to my clit and gasped. Drawing it lower, I notched the cum-soaked end to my entrance, all while keeping my gaze on Sin.

His attention fixed to my pussy. Trembling, I pushed past the slight resistance until the vibrator penetrated an inch inside me.

At the same second, Sin leaned in and sucked my clit.

In shock, I dropped the device to the sheets. Sin clamped me still and sucked harder, holding my hips flat. I grasped my neglected breasts through my shirt. Pinched my nipples.

My orgasm hit me like a wrecking ball.

My head swam. My chest rose and fell.

Delicious feelings danced along every vein, and I lost the use of my muscles and drooped.

There was something so decadent and dirty about what we'd done. Sinful but perfect, too. Later, I'd take a minute to work those thoughts through, but right now, all I could manage was to live in it and enjoy the moment.

Sin rested his face on my thigh, his deep pulls of breath cooling my hot skin.

Without warning, he muttered something then jerked up to bury his face in my pussy, spearing his tongue inside me.

I groaned in shock and lust. Whether he was licking me out or pushing his essence further in, I had no clue, but it only added to the sexiest evening of my life.

Then he climbed from the bed, snatched his boxers from the floor, yanked them on, and left the room.

We had our own bathroom attached to the bedroom, but I didn't move. Instead, I stayed on my back and found the vibrator again, this time giving myself another orgasm with the toy on the outside and my fingers thrusting in me.

If Sin missed this one, that was on him.

20

Lottie

I woke early, Sin a dead weight next to me, his heavy arm thrown over my waist and pinning me to the bed. I'd had the idea to wake up and make breakfast for everyone, but Sin's warning yesterday kept me to my place. That, and I really like the fact he was touching me.

I closed my eyes again and held still, just enjoying the hug.

I must've drifted back to sleep, because next time I woke, he'd gone. Last night, Thea told me they'd be going back to McInver's today. I hurried through washing and dressing, wanting to get downstairs before he left.

In the living room, Cassie and Burn watched cartoons from either end of the sofa, a blanket over them and the remnants of their breakfast on the coffee table.

I hustled into the kitchen where Thea and Struan talked at the island over steaming cups of coffee. A glance down the hall showed me an empty porch.

No Scar. No Sin.

My heart sank. They'd already gone.

He could look after himself, I knew that. He was capable of keeping himself, and the rest of us, safe, yet it was dangerous. All kinds of things could happen.

I might never see him again.

My heart raced, and I started when fingers touched my shoulder.

"Here, drink this." Thea passed me a coffee. "Sin called a family meeting in ten, so it'll be good to be caffeinated."

"He's still here?" Relieved, I warmed my hands on the mug then took a gulp.

Struan jerked his chin down the hall. "Outside."

I took a second to take in his colour and the way he was holding himself—all looked good—then retreated to the front door. The glassed-in porch was already warm from the morning sun, but outside, a stiff breeze drove the waves higher than yesterday. Seabirds squawked, flying in and out of the spray.

Sin paced the sea wall, his phone clamped to his ear.

He spotted me and changed direction to come right at me.

"How many were there?" he said to whoever was on the line.

I lifted my mug to take another sip, but Sin reached out and claimed it from me, drinking half down with a big swallow.

"And you're sure the name he gave was Hunter?" he added, his gaze fixed on me.

Hunter. In a heartbeat, I knew exactly who he was talking to. Da had come looking for him from the photo we'd sent yesterday. No messing around. He'd assembled a gang and gone out in pursuit.

I shrank in on myself but didn't budge.

Sin confirmed a few more details, thanked his caller, then hung up.

"They're out there looking for ye," I said, my voice dull.

"So many of ye want a piece of me."

He leaned in, and I held my breath. One big hand slid to the back of my neck, then Sin

manoeuvred me around the porch door and back inside. By the scruff of my neck, he marched me to the lounge.

"Living room, everyone, now," he shouted and guided me to sit on an armchair.

Burn switched off the TV, and Thea and Struan entered from the kitchen.

"What happened to your coffee?" Thea asked me.

I shrugged, and Sin glowered at the mug he'd appropriated as if realising he'd stolen mine. Had he thought I'd brought him one after ordering me to stop fetching and carrying? That was rich.

Scar thundered down the stairs, scrubbing his wet hair with a towel and dressed in only his jeans. On his arm, black inkwork scrawled, the start of a tattoo.

Sin frowned at his brother until he shrugged on a t-shirt. "First, early this morning, the islanders turned up looking for us. Gordain McRae was waiting for them."

Fear chilled me all over again. Cassie squeaked, jumped from the sofa, and ran at me. I received her in a hug, and the little girl huddled into my body.

Sin continued, regarding his family. "Gordain told them he'd offered us a place to stay but we'd done a runner. He didn't know where. Which is all true. He also suspected they'd scouted the place last night but raided at dawn in order to surprise us. The head guy, Forbes Hunter, asked specifically if Violet was part of the group." His gaze fell on me. "He had your picture and implied to Gordain that ye were with us not of your free will."

I widened my eyes. "He said I'd been kidnapped?"

Sin's gaze intensified. "No. He didn't go that far. But if he does—"

My breath left my body, my disappointment gutting. "I'll leave."

Cassie gasped. "No!"

I gave her a squeeze, my mind racing. "I'll have to. If he sparks a missing persons hunt with the police, that means none of us will be able to go out in public without risking everyone being caught. I'm right, aren't I?"

They swapped glances.

I dropped my gaze to the floor, despairing over my father's actions. The warning he knew would no doubt reach me.

"As things stand," Sin said, "only Burn and Struan are of interest to the police, that we know of. If Violet's father ups the ante, we'll handle it. The only thing we need to be aware of now is that they are on the hunt, which we knew anyway."

"Just a couple of hundred miles closer than they were before," Struan muttered. "Are ye still planning to go to McInver's?"

Sin gave a short nod. "I'm not changing my plan because there's a mob somewhere out there."

I goggled at him. "McInver's place is close to the McRae estate. Ye could be driving into a trap."

"And none of this will be resolved without solving the problem of our birth," he retorted. "Thea, I want to borrow your car. They might recognise the Ford."

My friend nodded, her fingers twisted and intertwined.

Sin snapped his gaze to me. "What car does your da drive?"

"A dark-blue Skoda." I ran through the few cars other men from the island could be driving. Not everyone owned one, and not everyone was in on the conspiracy, but it was better to be safe than sorry.

He jerked his head. "Then we know what to look out for."

"Are they going to come here?" Cassie peeped.

I brushed over her dark curls. "No, sweetie. They won't find us. We could be anywhere in the country."

Sin held my gaze for a moment, and I tried to impress on him no, I wouldn't betray them. I'd never intended to.

"Violet's right, they've no way of knowing where we are," he continued. "While we're gone, if anyone comes to this place and tells ye to leave, don't fight to keep it. Unless they're a holidaymaker, in which case they might be persuaded the place was double-booked. But if it's someone official, stay calm, pack up, then wait somewhere until we can reunite and find another place to stay."

"How likely is that to happen?" Burn asked.

"Unknown. This house has an owner, but it's managed by a holiday company that has gone bust, so neither the owner nor the company can use it until the legal situation is resolved. Ye can argue that ye booked it, which is why you're here, and that might buy us some time. But with any luck, the owner is an investor who doesn't give a shite about the place."

We all stared at him.

He gave a shrug. "Ma taught me the trick of finding these kind of places. The longest we ever stayed in one was a year and a half, and the shortest a week. As long as ye cause no damage, the owner won't call the police if you're prepared to leave."

I'd lived in one house my whole life. Not happily, but securely. I couldn't imagine Sin's world of not being sure where he'd be sleeping that night.

He jerked his chin at Scar. "Ready to go?"

Scar clambered up, muttering about finding his shoes, and Thea grabbed her keys.

I gave Cassie another hug then trailed Sin to the porch. He leaned past me to close the front door, shutting us in.

"Going to tell me to be careful?"

I chewed my lip. "I'm trying to work out what my father will do next."

"So ye can warn me, or him?"

"Don't be a jerk. Ye, obviously."

The corner of his mouth tipped up in the tiniest start of a smirk. I stopped moving and stared.

After everything we'd done last night, I had the strangest urge to thank him. Or to at least talk about it.

It battled my still-rising fear that if he left, I might not see him again.

In that moment, I would have given anything to have the ability to throw myself into his arms. To kiss him. To hug him and keep him safe.

But I didn't have the right. He wouldn't want it, so I kept my hugs to myself.

The front door burst open, and Burn appeared. He threw an easy arm around my shoulder, grinning at his brother. "Don't worry, I'll keep the lasses safe today."

Sin's infinitesimal smirk vanished, and his eyebrows merged in his usual savage frown.

I elbowed Burn in the gut. "I'm going to try some schoolwork with Cassie. Want to help me with that?"

"Can't read." Burn shrugged. "No good asking me."

Scar exited the house, now fully dressed. Thea appeared behind him and handed her keys over to Sin.

I scrutinised the youngest brother. "Then maybe sit in on the lessons and learn instead?"

Burn's eyebrows rose into his dishevelled dark hair. "You'd teach me? Seriously, Lottie. Marry me."

With a sound of irritation, Sin flung open the porch door and stomped outside. He and Scar headed over to the cars while the rest of us watched.

The intensity of his presence eased as the borrowed car climbed the cliff road and vanished. Without him around, I could talk to Thea, breathe more easily. Still, I missed him instantly. He was heading into danger, and there wasn't a single thing I could do about the fact.

An hour on, both Cassie and Burn had reached their limit. We'd chosen a book from the holiday home's stocked bookshelf, and both had taken turns in reading. Cassie had managed well nailing all the simpler words, and even the occasional complete sentence unaided. But the adventure story we'd picked was too complex. We needed a children's book designed for young readers. Burn was a different story. He knew the words when I sounded them out but couldn't easily recognise them on the page. As he struggled, his thumb flicked at his lighter wheel, the sparks dangerously close to the paper.

"Why don't we stop for the day?" I suggested.

Burn sighed then pitched the book across the bright porch, scowling as it landed with a thump. "Sorry. I'm not good at this."

"Ye can be. We just need to work out how ye learn. Not everyone is the same."

He struggled to his feet, his gaze switching to the water in the waves. "Sin tried to teach me back in the hostel, but I haven't improved any. Lost cause."

"Not true. We'll try something different next time."

He dropped a kiss to the top of my head. "It's a waste of time, but you're sweet for trying."

They headed out to the beach to kick around the surf,

and I spotted Thea and Struan returning. While we'd been reading, they'd gone for a walk, and now, joined me in the porch.

Struan sprawled on the wicker sofa, waiting until Thea sat before laying his head in her lap and closing his eyes. His recovery was still exhausting him, which was hardly surprising in the short time he'd had since surgery.

My friend drifted her fingers over his hair but spoke to me. "How do you feel about your dad chasing us?"

"Guilty. Worried. A thousand other things."

Struan wrinkled his nose, his eyes firmly closed. "Theadora told me everything about his threat to ye. Speak freely. I'm not judging ye. I might fall asleep, though."

I glanced from him back to Thea. "Okay, then I'm a tiny bit relieved, too. If he's here, he can't hurt my mother, so I can stop stressing about her for a day or two. I also know that he's determined."

She nodded. "All of them are, my dad included. One sniff of money, and they're bloodhounds."

Struan grumbled. "It's the root of all evil. Then again, if we had money, we could pay off the islanders and it would be one fewer group of people hunting us."

We all went quiet for a moment.

Thea started again. "I had an email from my university this morning. I need to pay to keep my accommodation over the summer. They also sent me the bill for the year to come including my course fees. I'm not going back, at least not now, and never again to finish the course my father picked. But that means I've got to drive to Edinburgh to empty my things from my room."

"I could go with ye," I offered.

"Thank you, but Struan wants to, if he's well enough. It's far enough away from Inverness that no one should recognise him."

I glanced at her boyfriend. With his mouth slightly

open and his breathing steady, he slept.

"It's everything I own, pretty much," she continued. "Clothes, bedding, books, and papers, probably a carload of my life's possessions. It will all get binned if I don't go. They won't put it in storage, even if I pay." She dropped her voice, presumably for the benefit of sleeping Struan. "I own a house, so could take it all there, but it's on the damn island. Struan will never want to go back there. I don't either."

"Just like my mother never wants to leave," I observed.

"To be honest, the house is a burden. I don't want to sell it. It would mean emptying out all my grandmother's possessions, and aside from setting foot in the place again, it's all too much." Amusement lit her eyes. "There's something funny the lawyers told me. Soon, I'll start to receive an income from the rent of everyone who lives on the island."

A laugh slipped from my lips. "Including my da? That's amazing. He'll hate that."

"It will give us something to live on for a while. So long as Struan accepts it, the others will."

A small stab of jealousy pierced me. Thea and Struan were one. Committed. She was a member of the family and pulling in the same direction as them. I was anything but.

I lapsed into silence again, wishing I could be more useful. Do more than bring trouble and cook a nice meal.

As I brooded, a nagging thought occurred. I set my gaze on Thea. "I was just thinking, I get why my da and others on the island fell in with Charterman's plan. He offered them money, which they're still chasing now. But why did your father agree? He owned the island, until he signed it over to ye, so there was a much greater risk."

Thea smiled, continuing her gentle stroking of Struan's hair. "Debt collectors were after him. That's why he gave me the island. So they couldn't have it. Eventually, I think he assumed he'd make me give it back, but fuck him."

I squinted, things not quite adding up. "But he hated the place. Why not just cash in? He knew his mother was dying, so he didn't have to tell her. If he'd just done that, he would've had the money to pay off his debts and probably lived very comfortably. Instead, he enabled kidnap, false imprisonment, and abuse."

Thea opened her mouth then closed it. "That's a very good point. I didn't think of it before. Could it be that he owed something to Charterman so had to go along with his scheme?"

"Maybe. He went to extremes for it." The man had disappeared, leading Thea to report him as missing, presumed dead. But we knew he wasn't. Charterman had told her that on the night he died. Her da had hidden from his debt collectors yet made no attempt to fix his problems. Instead, he'd signed the island over to his daughter, enabling Charterman to continue his scheme.

My friend went quiet for a long moment. "You're right. It doesn't make sense. Perhaps Charterman was somehow blackmailing him."

"Or he was the one who instigated the scheme to claim McInver's money."

Thea shook her head gently. "No, that can't be it. Charterman's son was set up to be the beneficiary."

"Is there anyone ye can ask?"

She pulled a face. "I could call my mother, but she hates me asking her anything about Dad. When I told her he was missing, she moaned about how he still makes things difficult for her even after their divorce."

"Make the call," Struan muttered, apparently not asleep after all. "I'm with Lottie. The more I think about it, the less his role adds up."

Thea found her phone and dialled a number, putting on loudspeaker.

After several rings, her mother answered. “What is it?”

Thea gritted her jaw. “Hello to you, too, Mum. I’ve been chatting with Lottie about Dad, and I had some questions I wanted to ask.”

Her mother sighed. “No, he hasn’t called me. No, I have no idea where he is, and no, I haven’t any interest either. Will that do?”

“Did he ever mention a man called McInver to you?” Thea ignored her complaints.

A pause came. “Where did you hear that name?”

“I’ve been doing a little digging into his past.”

Another half. “Then I suppose you know about Edie?”

Edie... Sin’s mother’s name. Thea and I swapped a wide-eyed glance.

“Yes, but not everything,” Thea said carefully.

“You won’t like it,” her mother warned.

“Tell me anyway.”

“Edie was your father’s one true love. The woman he never got over and the reason I fell pregnant while Augustus was on the rebound.”

I slid my fingers into Thea’s, and she gripped my hand. It was no secret that her parents weren’t a love match, but for her mother to casually throw out there that Thea was the product of a rebound affair was just cruel.

Her mother continued. “I never met McInver, but when drunk, your father would curse him because he stole Edie from him. It’s all very tawdry. If that’s all, I’ve got to go.”

“Wait,” I bit out. “It’s Lottie here. So Augustus dated Edie?”

“Theadora, you never told me people were listening in,” her mother hissed. “But yes, Edie and Augustus were once an item. He pursued her even after she’d threw him over for this other man and had his baby. Edie rejected him, he met me. Theadora was the result."

I widened my eyes more. When Edie fell pregnant, that had to be with Sin.

We already knew that McInver went on a binge of sleeping with women twenty years ago, as that's when Sin and his brothers were all conceived. But now, a new connection was made.

"So your ex-husband hated McInver for it?" I confirmed, a deep sense of unease swirling in my gut.

"What do you think?" she snapped. "And don't think your family is so squeaky clean, Lottie. Augustus had a minor obsession with your desperate bitch of a mother at one point, too. She never stopped chasing him. Got to go."

She hung up, and I let out a puff a breath.

"My mother?" I sputtered. "I mean, of course they knew each other, because they both grew up on the same island, but she never mentioned him."

"Don't listen to Mum. Perhaps they were just sweet on each other as kids? Dad left for college and never looked back."

Struan struggled up and took his phone from his pocket. "This is fucking with my head. Augustus has more skin in the game than just money."

I ticked back through my points to the original purpose of our call. "Ye mean revenge against McInver."

He typed fast. "And two of my brothers are walking straight into that hot mess now."

21

Scar

An aspect I hadn't expected from finding my freedom, even if shaky, was the sense of being utterly fucking lost. We had purpose today, cruising down the road, minutes away from McInver's place, eyes open for any passing islander. But in a week, or a month, what then? I'd need to find work and pay my own way.

Settle down, somehow.

I was a million miles away from that.

I lurched between ideas, my thoughts wild. I hid it well enough, but without some kind of purpose in my life, some structure or control, I was spiralling.

I'd killed someone.

Deservedly, but I hadn't processed it at all. Even when exhausted, I was dogged by the sense of urgency that never left me.

Perhaps if I had an outlet in sex like my older brothers did, and my younger brother talked too much about, but even that was way out there for me.

I'd never been hot for anyone.

It felt as dark a secret as my murderous act.

"We'll leave the car in the same place as before," Sin muttered. "Do what ye need to do then come back. Don't try to find me. We'll tackle this separately and meet when we're done."

I nodded agreement, gazing at the woods as Sin cruised the car to a stop, hidden in the lane.

The plan of attack was that he would approach from the front, knock on the door, and demand entry. Try to get answers. I'd sneak in the back and explore the house.

The *fuck around and find out* approach.

We didn't know what we were looking for, but we didn't know shite about this guy either. Every new piece of intelligence would help.

My phone buzzed in my pocket at the same moment Sin's lit up on the dash. We both read our screens.

Ruin: McInver stole a woman called Edie from Augustus Stewart – Thea's da. Revenge motivation?

I switched my gaze to Sin, ready with a joke about the spurned old bastard, but my words died. Shock tightened my brother's features.

I pieced through the meaning. "After the prison visit, Thea said your ma was called Edie."

He snapped out of his fog and climbed from the car. I followed, watching him with caution. He strode into the woods, and I jogged to keep up.

"Sin."

Shite. This felt bad. And he wasn't slowing.

"Hold up," I tried again. "Your mother dated Thea's father? As well as ... uh, hanging out with McInver?"

"Sounds that way."

I knew Sin's mother was dead, same as mine and Burn's. He never talked about her life, his time with her, or how she died. Then again, none of us went near that dark place if we could avoid it.

I steamed past and stopped him with a hand extended

before we emerged into the parkland on the other side of the woods.

I wasn't small, topping out at six-two, but Sin towered over me. If he wanted, he could knock me aside easily, but instead, my big brother waited.

"I'm worried that you're going in there without a clear mind," I said.

Sin glared at me, then planted his hands on his hips, gazed up, and exhaled. "Right now, I want to rip his head off. Either of them."

"Which is a bad idea because..." I prompted.

"Because I'm going to fuck this up."

"Aye. Our whole objective is to find a way we can live free of all the people who screwed up our past. McInver is key to that. This conversation is important."

If I'd blinked, I could've missed the tiny twitch of Sin's lips. Something I'd said wasn't true for him. The whole objective? Did he have another?

"Take a breath," I ordered.

He rolled his head to the side, regarding me. "What is this, fucking yoga?"

I punched him in the biceps. "No. I just don't want ye to die because ye lost your temper."

He stared at me for a moment longer then swore and looked away. "Okay. Point taken. I'm good."

"Are ye sure?"

He swiped at me with a huge meaty hand. Not a punch like I'd laid on him but enough to send me stumbling. "Give me a five-minute head start then follow."

He took off into the park, and I hung back, listening to the sounds of nature around me.

It was tranquil as fuck here. Shame the place belonged to a perverted old arsehole.

After my five minutes were up, I silenced my phone and got moving, skirting the woods to go around the back of the stately home. I had no choice but to cross open parkland to reach the gardens, but there were plenty of places to hide.

I stole closer until I spotted a side door that would be my target. Not the main rear entrance, where heavy double doors led to a patio, but what appeared to be a kitchen or utility room exit. Breaking cover, I jogged across the gravel and into the alcove. My breathing came harder, and my pulse raced.

If I was caught, McInver would call the cops. I'd be charged with trespass or breaking and entering, but with no priors or criminal record, probably released. That was a risk I was willing to take.

With care, I twisted the door handle, ready to jiggle it and test how many locks were in place. I was no burglar, though. Brute force normally did the trick.

The door opened under my hand.

My mouth gaped in amusement, and I didn't hesitate, slipping inside to the cool hall. As expected, this was a staff area, no elaborate decoration here but functional hard-wearing tiles and plain walls with the faint smell of bleach in the air. I crept along, peering in the first doorway, which was a mudroom, by the looks of things, then to the end where it opened out to a wider corridor. Going left would take me to the front of the house, so I went right instead.

A large kitchen took up a whole corner of the house, with no occupant that I could see, but then I found what I'd been searching for.

A staircase, leading up.

McInver had to have help running the place. We'd already decided that. But surely those people would be managing the main living space only. Which meant upstairs would be safer for wandering.

I ascended fast, keeping my footfalls light. At the top,

a corridor spread out in three directions. I took the central route, going deep into the house. At the end, an ajar door led into a palatial hallway. This was the part designed to impress. Polished flooring, fancy carved wood doorways, that fussy curly plasterwork shite on the ceiling. Here and there, oil paintings broke up the wall space. Important but long-dead people in fancy outfits stared back at me.

I had the sudden, dizzying sense that I was in front of pictures of my ancestors. It didn't feel real, though. I hadn't been born into this life. Maybe I carried McInver's DNA, but his world wasn't mine.

I opened the first door, an empty bedroom inside with the blinds half drawn. It looked like a guest room, though, so I carried on down the hall. The next room was the same, and the third a big bathroom.

A sound reached me.

I froze and concentrated. So far, I hadn't seen a soul around. There were signs of habitation, like a dustpan and brush left by a doorway, but no chatter, no phone conversations. If Sin had been let in downstairs, I could hear none of that.

Probably a good thing, as it indicated he wasn't in an argument or fight.

The sound came again, and I homed in on the room across from me. A sneeze. Light and small.

My uneasiness returned. I'd been half joking when I'd told the rest of my family I thought I'd seen a body carried in. Sin hadn't agreed, which made me doubt myself, but a strong man carrying a slight person wouldn't show much strain.

What if I was right?

I crossed the hall silently and listened at the door.

No further sound came, so I carefully twisted the handle and pushed. Locked.

A grunt or mumble returned.

Young, and female. Not high like a child, though.

In a flash, a picture built in my mind. We'd been kidnapped and locked away. This person maybe had, too. Adrenaline spiked in my blood, and I set a shoulder to the door, twisted the handle again, and shoved.

It gave, and I stumbled into the room.

And stopped dead, staring at the shocking sight.

Heavy curtains blocked the windows, but it didn't conceal the fair-haired woman, about my age, lying flat on her back on a four-poster bed. A cuff on each ankle and wrist connected to chains which spreadeagled her out, securing her to the bedposts.

She was naked.

And from her expression, furious.

Blonde, shoulder-length curls. Pink nipples on full tits. A completely bare pussy, her legs wide and nothing hidden.

Then something nightmarish happened. At the sight of her nude body, a stab of instant, hot lust pierced me. I slammed my eyes closed, horrified at myself.

Never once in my life had I experienced this. Not when Burn found porn for us to watch, or even in real life when a girl had wanted to kiss me at school. Nothing touched me.

Not until this second.

Which meant there was something badly wrong with me.

Not just a murderer but a pervert, too.

More like our revolting father than I could live with.

The woman mumbled something, and I glowered at her once more, spotting tape over her lips. I stomped to the bed and yanked a bedsheet over her nude form. Then I reached for the tape, tearing it free.

"What the fuck do you think you're doing?" she snapped, her accent English. "Put the tape back and leave."

I hauled on one of her chains, following it back to the bedpost. There was no clip but a solid link, so I picked up her arm to examine the cuff.

"Don't worry. I'll get ye out of here," I promised.

"What? No. Stop."

The poor lass was confused. Two days, she must have been like this. I didn't doubt it was her I'd seen carried in.

I focused on the cuff, urgency building, but she snatched her arm away.

"You're not listening. Don't untie me. I don't want to be rescued."

I hesitated, even though my heart pounded. "Who are ye?"

"Breeze. Who are you?"

For the first time in forever, I used my real name. "Camden. I'm not going to hurt ye, I swear. I'll get ye loose then take ye to safety."

Breeze shook her head, her curls fanned out on the pillow. "Seriously, Camden, don't. If you mess up my plans to help my sister, I'll—"

She cut off her sentence with a squeal.

I picked up the footstep behind me too slowly to do anything about it. A hard object smashed into my head, and unconsciousness claimed me before I hit the floor.

22

Sin

Anger brewed inside me, tightening my muscles and increasing the rate of my breathing. My body readying to fight.

From the pose of the guy standing behind me, one of the men we'd seen on our recce and a beefy motherfucker with a dirty scowl on his ugly face, I wasn't the only one.

He'd opened the door to my knock, and when I'd made my demand to see McInver, had marched me to this room then told me to wait. He'd sent a message then stood on guard with me. No conversation, no questions.

Fine. I didn't have any for him anyway.

It was his owner I was here to see. And the old bastard was keeping me waiting.

It was only making my anger worse. Struan's message earlier had done two things. Given me more intel on my mother but also reminded me of the date. We were coming up on the anniversary of her death. I'd had no reason to check the day of the week or even what month we were in, not until I saw that text.

Years had passed, but nothing had changed. Except

for the fact that now, I might get answers.

I cast a look around the space—a wide hall at the centre of the building. Heavy furniture and expensive, old decorations, fucking chandeliers hanging from the ceiling, the smell of dust thick in the air. When we'd been imprisoned in the hostel, I'd tried to teach Burn how to read with one of the few books we had there. *Little Women.* In the story, one of the sisters had gone to a dance, all dressed up. I imagined it was a place like this. Impressive and showy. A world away from our decaying home.

But things had gone wrong for her there. They probably would for me, too.

A door opened at the end of the hall. I snapped my attention to it. A person emerged, hunched over, small, but undoubtedly him.

For the first time ever, I was face to face with my father.

Using a cane, McInver stalked towards me. I held my ground, forcing my breathing to stay regular. When he was close enough, the old man peered up at me. My guard hustled to grab him a chair, placing it behind so he could sit in the centre of the hall.

Like a king before his court, McInver regarded me. "What is your game? Salesman? Thief? Casing the joint for a burglary?" He jabbed his stick to the beefy guy, his gaze still on me. "You're wasting your time. I have cast-iron protection night and day."

I held my ground, curling my lip. "Don't ye know who I am?"

McInver's eyes narrowed. "Child of some maid I've wronged? A long-lost relative? Put away your begging bowl. I'm not interested."

"I'm not begging for anything. I came here for answers." I took a step closer, ignoring the guard as he jerked forward. "Take another look at my face. Tell me what ye see."

"You're going to have to tell me, boy. I don't play games."

"My mother was Edie Stone."

Silence fell in the room. McInver's self-satisfied smirk dropped. "Edie?"

I hated her name on his lips. But this needed to happen. I needed to know.

"Edie Stone. Ye paid for her time. Remember her?"

McInver's gaze dropped to my boots then rose over my long body and lingered on my face. I couldn't read his expression, though I sensed his surprise.

"I recall the woman," he said last. "Big girl. Liked her drink." He squawked out an unpleasant laugh. "Liked other things more. The colour of my money. So what does that make ye? Her bastard? Do ye think you're one of mine over hundreds of other street crawlers?"

My anger burned hot, but I forced control. There were other things I needed to learn aside from what happened to Ma. Whether he knew about us and our imprisonment. I wasn't about to give up the existence of my brothers and sister, but McInver's 'one of mine' statement was telling.

"How many have ye got?" I challenged.

McInver stood, wobbly on his cane. He stabbed it into the floor and paced towards me. A few feet away, he peered up, grunted, then circled me like a decrepit shark.

"Yes," he muttered to himself. "Not bad."

After he'd done a whole circuit, he prodded me in the chest with his stick. "Edie sent ye then, did she? Whether you're mine or not, I admit I'm curious. Where is she now?"

My heart thudded. "Edie died years ago. You're to blame."

I didn't know how much I believed that to be true. McInver had rejected my mother in favour of Burn's. She died long after her entanglement with this man, except this had been my only lead, aside from the possible clue in Struan's text.

McInver made an off sound and returned to his seat. "You're implying I hurt her? Cheeky welp."

"Am I supposed to believe ye didn't?"

"Believe what ye want. I don't owe ye any of my truths."

"Then who might have? Who else knew her? Anyone else here?"

He beckoned over the guard, who stooped and listened as McInver whispered in his ear. The second man returned to his post, still glaring daggers at me, but tapped out something on his phone.

My emotions rioted. I had other questions, more to discover, but if McInver really had nothing to do with Ma's death, it'd been another year with no answers. I was failing her memory.

"I understand now why you're here," McInver said. "Ye came to challenge me like one of my stags out on the hill. A buck charging at the dominant male. Is that it?"

"No."

"Aye, lad. Ye did. Now you'll answer some of my questions. How old are ye?"

I curled my lip, but if I gave him information, maybe he'd do the same. "Twenty. I was born in December."

"Where?"

"Aberdeen. When was the last time ye saw Edie?"

He tutted. "Impatient. What did she name ye?"

"Sinclair."

He jerked his head back, then his gaze distanced as if he was remembering twenty-one years ago when my mother was here. She wasn't the only one. Struan was born two weeks before me, so his mother would have been around the same time. I shuddered, pushing those thoughts away.

"How tall are ye?"

"Six-seven. Do I have brothers or sisters?"

"Brothers, sister, who cares. So big!" He cackled. "A much better proposition. This will set the cat amongst the pigeons. Disrupt all their plans."

"Whose plans?"

He smiled, revealing missing and browned teeth. "You're not the only one sniffing around me, boy. I know what ye all see. My fine home. All my piles of cash. They're lining up with their wheelbarrows. Coming here and pleading their case. Promising me the world. Flattering me with pretty words and slutty girls."

The only people I knew interested in McInver were the ones who'd imprisoned us. Charterman, who was dead, and Augustus Stewart, his friend who owned the island we'd been taken to.

"Who else is sniffing around ye?" I challenged.

"Silence. Let me make my plans. If ye want to be in the running, you'll quickly get used to my ways. I make the rules here. You'll speak when you're spoken to."

"Who said I'm interested in your money?"

McInver laughed his high cackle again, the sound disturbing. "Ye must think I was born yesterday."

"All I want to know is what happened to Edie," I demanded.

McInver's guard jumped to stand directly beside me, and the old man's expression shifted to a savage sneer.

"Talk to me like that again and you'll have the measure of me. Bring him in."

Someone stumbled into the rear of the hall, and I twisted around. My anger rushed, and panic rippled under it.

Scar was on the floor, a dark-red mark at his temple. A second guard stood over him.

With a double-barrelled shotgun pointed at his back.

"Found him in the locked room," the new guard

reported. He held up Scar's hunter's knife then slid it into a pocket on his belt.

My brother raised his furious gaze to me then snarled at McInver. "You're a fucking monster."

"Silence."

"No. You're a dirty old bastard. Who the hell have ye—" He moaned and clutched his head, the guard behind him lowering the butt of his gun from another hit.

I took a step his way. The guard pressed the gun's barrels to the back of Scar's head, a warning in how he stared at me.

I swung back to McInver. "Let him go."

"Why should I? He's been snooping."

"He's here as my backup. Tell your dog to get off him."

The old man uttered another high laugh. "Backup? Against ye, he's a scrawny wee shite. Bring him closer," he snapped.

The guard yanked Scar to his feet, and my brother shook him off then strode to my side, weaving slightly. I stared down at him, sharing his palpable rage at both of us being caught like this. The guard kept his gun trained on my brother, staring down the barrels now, finger on the trigger.

Before, I hadn't felt any real concern, aside from the risk of losing my temper. McInver was no threat, and I could easily have overpowered the man watching me. One swift hit and he'd be down.

But a shotgun blast at close range would kill Scar.

Things had turned deadly in a heartbeat.

McInver examined him. "He's all scarred. Not mine, this reject. If ye were hoping to pass him off as another of mine, guess again. I'm not so easily fooled."

"Let him go," I gritted out.

"He's an intruder. I'm within my rights to deal with him as I see fit."

"And how will that be?"

McInver's beady eyes twinkled. "Dependant on your behaviour." He gestured from me to the first guard. "Give him your phone."

I opened my mouth to refuse, but the second guy nudged his gun into Scar's skull.

I had no fucking choice but to hand it over.

The guard took it to McInver who curled his lip.

"Don't give it to me, fool. Take his number then give it back."

The guard held the screen up to me. "Unlock it."

Fury rose. "There's no lock on it."

I'd instructed all my family to keep their phones locked down, but I'd left mine open.

"Amateur." The man dialled a number, waited, presumably for it to connect with his phone, then handed it back.

McInver stood again and strolled closer, suddenly less reliant on his stick. "Your mother came here in much the same way ye have. With expectation. With big eyes over my treasures and a want for my wealth. I paid her well for her time, and it seems she gave me a bonus. Tell me now that ye think you're my blood."

"I wish I wasn't."

McInver's face crinkled in the semblance of a smile. "At last, a son I might be proud of. Just like me in my youth. Braw and strong. Determined. If ye want answers, Sinclair, if ye want to hear all I know about Edie and her activities, then next time ye come you'll do it with your cap in your fucking hand and no surprises. I want that fire tamed and on my side. And by the way, that name of yours? It's mine. Sinclair Irvin McInver. If ye had any doubts, your mother has given ye a message from her grave. Take your friend and come back when I call, alone this time. Now get out of my sight."

23

Lottie

Lunchtime came and went. None of us ate, everyone distracted and listless, waiting for news. I'd had Thea map the route to McInver's house on her phone so we had a realistic timeframe of the earliest they could return. Even spending a couple of hours there, they should've been back by now.

Against the breeze, I paced the sea wall, watching the access road and trying not to panic.

My mind conjured images of the islanders finding them. A car chase. A wreck.

Struan called Gordain to find out if he'd seen any more of my father and his cronies. He had. They were still hanging around the cabin, presumably waiting for us to show, so at least that worry reduced.

Other dangers remained. Of McInver setting guard dogs on them or calling the police. It had all been a horrible idea, too high-risk. I knew they needed answers, but there were different ways of getting them. I could have gone in and talked to the old man. Then again, Thea had met him once, and he'd been vile to her.

I choked on my own too-fast breath, trying to imagine if Sin would go all out to protect me or just leave me alone. I couldn't be sure. Even after last night...

An engine roared, and I spun around. Thea's borrowed car hurtled down the road, two men visible in the front. I clapped my hands to my mouth. They'd returned. They were okay.

"They're back!" I called into the porch.

But as I hustled to where Sin pulled up, I revised my opinion on how okay they were.

They climbed out, both glowering at the other.

Scar clutched his head, his features contorted in pain. "This is fucked up. We shouldn't be here."

I reached them, the others right behind me. "What happened?"

Scar swung around to me. "We need to go back. There was a woman. We had to leave her."

I took his free hand. "Slow down. What woman?"

"In a bed, chained up." His gaze slid to Cassie, and he pressed his lips together.

The little girl ran to Sin and hugged him. He set a hand on the back of her head, allowing it, his features flat, and steely determination in his eyes.

I wanted to hug him myself. So much. But I wasn't allowed. He'd reject me faster than I could blink.

Scar sucked in a shaky breath, still clinging to his open car door like he couldn't bring himself to close it. "She was a prisoner like us, but worse. She was N-A-K-E-D," he spelled out. "Obviously only there for one thing."

"She was what?" Burn muttered over my shoulder.

Struan gave a low reply, filling him in on the word he hadn't been able to spell quickly.

"Holy shite," Burn replied. "That's messed up."

I squeezed Scar's fingers. "Did ye talk to her?"

"Aye. Her name's Breeze."

"And she didnae want your help," Sin added.

Scar shot him a look then returned to us, his confusion clear. "Yes. No. She couldn't have been thinking straight. We can't leave her to him."

"Ye saw McInver then?" Struan asked.

"Aye. He loved his tall, scary son here." Scar smacked the roof of the car. "If ye won't drive back, I will."

Sin shook off Cassie and rounded on his brother, fury breaking through his control, his movements fast and precise. "And what? Get shot this time? You're lucky to have got away with a couple of hits to the head. I agree we need to help that lass, but we can't just drive back to the place. They'll be better prepared this time. I'm not risking your neck for a stranger's who told ye she didn't need it." He snapped his attention to me. "Scar's hurt. He was knocked unconscious then took a second hit from the butt of a gun."

Wide-eyed, I drew Scar's hand down from his temple, revealing a dark bruise spreading into his hair. It was far worse than the one receding on my brow. "God. They knocked ye out? Ye could have a concussion."

"Ex-fucking-actly." Sin pushed away from the car and stormed to the outbuilding next to the house. "Don't talk about going back there now. It isn't happening," he snarled over his shoulder.

Scar glared after him then closed his eyes as if the light hurt.

I wrapped an arm around his waist, guiding him with me. "Come into the house. Give us the full story. We'll work something out."

He let me lead him, and I sent him inside with the others. To my left, the door to the outhouse which contained all the sports kit swung in the light wind. I stepped over and took a peek inside.

Sin had stripped and was pulling on a wetsuit. He

zipped it up then snatched a surfboard. Without raising his gaze, he spoke. "If I don't head out into the water, I'm going to lose my fucking head."

"Are ye hurt?" I asked.

"No. Go tend to my brother. He needs ye."

"And ye don't?" The words were out of my mouth before I could stop them.

Sin propped his board against the shelving unit then backed me against the door. "Don't offer, or I'll take every bit of my anger out on your soft body. Believe me, Violet, ye don't want that."

Except I did. I'd absorb every blow and gladly. The fact he wasn't asking said more about him than me. I folded my arms and hid my shaking. "Use up the worst then find me later."

He gave an outraged laugh then left me for the beach, entering the water with a smooth glide on his board.

I watched him for a moment then went into the house.

On the sofa, Scar accepted a mug from Burn, concluding a sentence. "...one massive fuck-up."

I perched next to him. "I need to check ye over. Are ye dizzy? Do ye have a headache or double vision?"

"Aye, my head is pounding. It doesn't matter, though. We were wrong about McInver. He isn't harmless. His guards were ready and waiting for us. Fucking armed, too. But that wasn't the worst part. At least we were able to walk away."

While I took a look at his injury, Scar recounted the full story of finding the young woman locked in a bedroom. Naked. Chained up.

The picture he painted was horrifying. Clearly the old man wasn't done with abusing women.

"I don't understand why she didn't want you to free her," Thea said.

"Something to do with finding her sister. Maybe McInver took her, too. I've no idea, but I can't leave her there. We couldn't help her. McInver's guards saw us off his land." He swung a look between us all, beseeching us. "Sin's right that if we go back, it's high-risk. But I can't ignore what I saw. What can I do?"

I swallowed, hating the thought of another victim just left there. "A tip-off to the police could see her rescued."

We'd spent so long avoiding the authorities, this felt wrong, but it was the only solution I had.

Struan regarded him. "I fucking hate the cops, but Lottie's right. They'd go there and search for her."

Scar slowly nodded. "I could tell them exactly what room. They'd find her and maybe arrest him."

"It would need to be anonymous," I said, working through the idea. "But then how will we know if it's successful?"

"We could stake it out and watch the police come and go," Thea considered.

Struan snorted. "No fucking chance you're going anywhere near that place, sweetheart."

Scar shook his head, closing his eyes as if the act hurt. "Sin won't let any of us go back. Apart from him. McInver demanded that. He liked Sin and took his phone number so he can call him in. He talked about other people wanting to claim his money, but it was like now he had this impressive son, he somehow had the upper hand."

We all went quiet.

"McInver claimed Sin?" Struan grated out.

But it was Thea I'd locked on to. She'd paled.

"What is it?" I asked her.

"When I went there before, it was with Charterman and his son, Henry. My dad was missing, but only because by that point he'd been scared off by the debt collectors. So if Charterman isn't the one pushing a relative onto McInver now, it has to be my dad."

We swapped a glance. Earlier, her mother had implied our parents had a fling. It'd set my mind racing, though I'd buried it behind worry for Sin and Scar.

For a day of trying to uncover mysteries, we seemed to only have accumulated more.

Thea tried calling Henry but got no answer. Scar concocted a message for the police, deciding it couldn't be sent from our location in case they tracked us.

I busied around making an early dinner, needing to use my hands and dispel some of the tension in the house. It only rose when Sin came in from carving up the waves.

After storming upstairs for a shower, he stomped into the kitchen. "Thought I told ye not to wait on us all."

I cocked an eyebrow. "And I said I like cooking. Unless ye plan to use the energy fuelling that temper in a better way, don't come at me."

He held my gaze in one heck of a stare off, broken only when Scar entered the room. Sin's focus snapped to the dark bruise on Scar's head, then he abruptly turned and crossed the kitchen to take a glass from the cupboard, pouring himself a drink.

I watched him, realising something about his shitty mood. It was fear affecting him. He'd witnessed someone injure his brother with the hit from a gun, and he hadn't been able to stop it.

It must've driven him insane.

"Lottie," Scar said. "After we've eaten, I'm going to drive up the coast to find a village with a payphone, then I'll make my call to the police from there."

He was telling me for a reason. “Want me to come with ye?”

“Would ye?”

I reached up and brushed back the dark hair falling over his bruise, checking to make sure it hadn’t grown any. Scar let me fuss over him, far more compliant than his big brother.

“Always. How’s your vision?” I asked.

“Twenty-twenty. Worried about me fainting on the road?”

I gave up a small laugh. “Maybe we should rethink. If for whatever reason ye can’t drive us back, I’ll be no good. I don’t mind speaking to the police on your behalf, though. It might be easier.”

“Actually, that would help. I’ll write out exactly what I saw and what the lass said.”

A dark shadow fell over us. *Sin.* “You’re going to call the cops?”

I folded my arms. “Got a better idea?”

He chewed on that. “No. I’ll drive. Or maybe it’s your turn behind the wheel, Violet. About time ye learned.”

Somehow both threat and promise were loaded into his words. If he was taking me for a ride, I was beyond ready to challenge him in return.

24

Lottie

I ate quickly then readied to leave. After a day of being stuck in, no matter how lovely the spot, I was burning up to get out of the house this evening.

Sin strode to the car, but Scar paused me.

He handed over a folded piece of paper. "Your script."

I scanned it then pocketed the sheet. "You're not coming?"

"Mind if I don't? Sin's mood is doing my head in." He jerked his chin at the sea. "Burn and I are heading out for a surf. All I need to know is that the police take the report seriously. That they'll go for her."

I gave him a soft smile. "I'll make sure they do."

He let me go, and I hid my boosted emotions. I didn't want to admit it, but being alone with Sin worked for me.

We drove out of the bay and up the coast road. Sin put his foot down, and we sped along, passing signs for Dunnottar Castle, and then for Stonehaven, the nearest big town.

But we didn't stop.

There had to be a public phone box here, but Sin kept

on driving. The farther we got from our temporary home, the more my worry built.

Scar had cried off. Had he been asked to? Maybe Sin had made a decision about me. He was taking me to my father. Or he was going to leave me somewhere, away from the family. I hadn't hugged Cassie goodbye. I didn't have my things. Unless he'd packed them for me when he'd been upstairs, and my bag was in the boot. I curled in on myself, wishing I was wrong, but holding in my words.

If he was rejecting me, nothing I could do would change it.

Half a miserable hour later, signs told me we were approaching the city of Aberdeen.

A long time ago, I'd asked him where he came from. It was here, I remembered him saying.

Fresh questions rose by the dozen, but I only allowed one. "Your hometown."

A short grunt of agreement was my answer.

Sin cruised through suburbs of dark stone buildings, his focus forward and his pissed-off expression not changing. In fact, his mood only seemed to darken the more we explored the city.

The route felt undirected, as if he needed to be here, but didn't want to commit to an actual location. We cruised around quiet streets, then the busier town centre. Past a working harbour.

At a busy junction, we crossed a cobbled bridge. Under us, a wide river flowed from an industrial area with huge ocean-going boats moored at dockyards along the banks.

Victoria Bridge, the sign read.

Over the water, we took a left into a road lined with workshops and warehouses, closed now it was after working hours. Sin abruptly halted. I peered up at the building next to us. It looked like accommodation of some sort, though neglected.

"What is this?" I asked.

I hadn't entirely given up the feeling he was going to kick me out, but his energy wasn't directed at me. It swirled around him like a storm cloud.

"Did ye hang out here as a boy?" I tried again, picturing a stern little dark-haired lad, taller than his friends, the same frown stamped on his forehead.

"Go use the phone." Sin pointed across the road to a lone phone box, graffiti decorating the wall behind it.

I watched him for a moment then climbed out, Scar's urgency over the woman he'd seen directing me. Sin's car door opened behind me, but I ignored him, sucked in a breath, and entered the box.

I dialled nine-nine-nine, unfolded my page of notes, then requested the police from the operator.

The call handler greeted me and asked for my emergency. As succinctly as possible, I explained that earlier today, my friend had visited a relative but had deep concerns over something found in the house.

I described what Scar had seen, repeating myself when the surprised woman on the other end of the line asked for clarification.

I left out the part of the woman, *Breeze,* refusing help.

"Will ye send someone out to find her?" I asked.

"I've taken the details down and passed it to our dispatch. They'll send a patrol car out to the address."

I breathed a sigh of relief. "Is it okay if I call back tomorrow and ask if she's been found?"

"I'll provide a reference number for the report. Quote that and we'll see what we can do. It would be better if ye told me your details as the witness to any potential crime."

I shook my head, not that she could see. "Sorry. I can't do that, but I'll take the number."

I'd propped the door of the phone box open with

my foot, the odour inside not all that pleasant, and now, gestured through the gap to Sin, wiggling my hand to show I need a pen.

He reached inside the car then brought me a pencil. I scrawled down the number on the back of Scar's notes then hung up the call.

"Done. They're going to pay him a visit."

Sin just stared, somehow both imposing and uncomfortable-looking at the same time.

"Want to explain to me why we're here?" I asked.

"No."

I chewed my lip. "We could've made this call closer to home. Coming here was important to ye, aye? Talk to me."

"I said no, Violet."

With a hand curled around my upper arm, he marched me back to the car, then he sped us away from the city. This time, he didn't linger over any of the sights.

Ten minutes beyond the outskirts, he pulled over in a vacant car park and killed the engine, climbing out. Then he yanked open my door.

"Get in the driver's seat."

I blinked at him. "Were ye being serious about the driving lesson?"

He waited, not dignifying me with an answer.

My stomach tightened. "I don't have a provisional licence."

"So what? If we get stopped that's the least of our concerns. Get in the damn seat."

Something was affecting him, probably what caused him to want to return to where he'd grown up. Maybe that combined with seeing his father for the first time was messing with his head. Still, it didn't give him an excuse to be mean to me.

I held my gaze on him in a challenge. "Is this lesson to help me or to humiliate me when I can't do it?"

"Want to learn, don't ye?"

I did, but I had a bad feeling about this. Even so, I trotted around the car and climbed into the driver's seat. I was way back from the steering wheel, though. My short body needing nothing like the space of Sin's massive one.

He reached under me and yanked on something that slid my seat forward. Then he adjusted the headrest, scanned me, and slammed my door closed. In the passenger's side, he extended his seat as far back as it could go then snapped on his seat belt.

"Twist the key to turn the engine on."

I obeyed, and the motor thrummed under me.

He set a hot hand on my knee, and I jerked, heat flooding me. Sin pointed at the pedals by my feet.

"Clutch, brake, accelerator. Left foot only for the clutch. Right foot alternates between the other two."

In short commands, he instructed me on how to get the car moving—depress the clutch, engage the gear, and raise the clutch while simultaneously pressing down on the accelerator.

Flustered, I messed it up repeatedly, the car stalling each time.

I wanted kind words from him on how this was just muscle memory, and I'd get it eventually, but he didn't say anything.

Pressure built.

Another stranger reaction happened, too.

The hardness of his treatment was *working* for me. Getting me hot alongside my nerves. His low, snapped orders hitched my breath. His firm, careless touches scalded.

It was utterly unreasonable for my body to respond like this, but I wanted him.

I also badly wanted him to say *well done* when I finally worked out the balance and got the car to move across the car park successfully. Instead, he made me do it again until

I was circling the space in second gear.

On another pass, he gestured to the exit to the road.

"Out there? I don't think—" I started.

But Sin took hold of the wheel and steered straight out of the exit.

I squeaked, throwing glances around me to the dual-lane road. A car came the other way, passing us fast.

"Holy shite," I bit out. "I'm stopping."

"No you're not. You're going to speed up."

I glared at him, but for some reason, accelerated rather than braked. With my gaze now firmly on the road ahead, I sensed rather than saw Sin's approval.

"Clutch down."

"Why?"

"To change gear."

"No! I can't look down at the stick."

"Hit the clutch, Violet. I'll move it into third."

I shifted my pressure from the accelerator to the clutch, unable to stop from glancing down to make sure I had the right pedal then snapping my gaze back so we didn't crash. Sin adjusted the gear lever, and I slowly brought the clutch up while adding pressure onto the accelerator.

It didn't stall.

I gave a small yip of pleasure. "I did it."

"Now go faster."

My breath sped along with the car, but I followed orders, a tiny bit addicted to the buzz of being behind the wheel. Around us, hedges led to open fields, and there were few other cars around, a whole other lane available if they wanted to overtake me.

I edged the needle higher.

Sin made a sound almost of amusement. "Clutch down again, Speedster."

I moved my feet, and he changed the gear again for

me. We were flying along now.

On the journey up, I hadn't really paid attention to our route, but I got a heady rush of being the one in control of where we were going and what we were doing. Temporarily, my frustration lifted. Driving was fun.

The road zigzagged ahead, so I found the brake and slowed, ready to take in the curves. Then I made the mistake of glancing left.

The sea glittered under the evening sun.

It was a distance away, but then I remembered how close we'd driven to it coming out. Farther on, we'd be right on the cliff.

Forcing my attention forward, I concentrated on staying in my lane. The road climbed a hill, passing a large sign for Stonehaven and its harbour.

"In a minute, I'll pull over."

"No."

"I'm not driving on a cliff."

The farther we travelled, the closer the sea drew.

"I'll talk ye through it."

"Really? When you've barely said a handful of words to me all evening?"

An engine roared, and a car flew past, so fast it shook us. I squeaked in fear and gaped at it as it sped off in the distance.

"I don't like this now." My voice came out small, the adrenaline wearing off. "I don't know what to do other than drive in a straight line, you're not telling me anything, and I'm scared."

He sighed. "Chase down that car. I'll break the fucker's face for ye. Will that do?"

"You're an idiot. This is dangerous. I'll kill us."

"You'd be doing me a favour."

For God's sake. "I'm stopping."

We hadn't passed a lay-by in a while, but I was done.

A tiny farmer's track appeared on the left, so I braked and swung off the road, bumping over the uneven ground. I kept going, too fast, crossing a tiny bridge until we reached a narrow field full of crops.

Right at the top of a cliff with a sharp drop to the sea.

With no idea how to safely stop, I jammed on the brake. The car jerked and made a horrible noise.

"Take it out of gear," Sin snapped.

"What does that mean?"

"Hit the clutch."

I stamped on the pedal, and Sin joggled the gear stick then yanked on the handbrake. The car settled, and Sin leaned across me to turn off the engine.

My heart sped, and my panic peaked.

Yanking open my door, I flew from my seat, turning to snarl at Sin. "I am so done with ye."

He climbed out after me and rounded the car, resting a hip on the bonnet in such a casual way it made me want to grind my teeth.

"You're done with me?"

"Yes! With ye and your attitude. That was mean. I was scared, and ye did nothing to help me. Look at where we are! I could've driven straight over that edge." All the things I'd repressed rose to the surface in a hot wave of hurt. I prowled a step closer. "You're angry all the time. Ye have nothing nice to say unless it's to do with sex. Ye hate me but want me. I'm not allowed to touch ye yet every night I wake up with your arms wrapped around me. It's messing with my head. So yes, I'm done."

My hands shook, and I hid them behind my back.

Sin's gaze snapped to my chest. His mouth fell open in a cruel smirk that was nothing like the smile I was so desperate to see. "Strip naked and I'll let ye blow me while I drive us home."

"Fuck off. Ye won't let me touch ye? You're never seeing my body."

The smirk dropped. "Don't issue ultimatums. Run your mouth again, and I'll take ye over the bonnet of this car where anyone passing will see ye screaming as ye come around my dick."

I was such an idiot. That was the only explanation for the burst of sheer want that spread through me.

"So ye do actually want to fuck me then?"

He gave up a crazed laugh. "Yes, I do. Your body is my obsession. I think about ye constantly."

"About having sex with me," I confirmed.

Sin strode the short distance until he was right in front of me, blocking out the sun with his huge form. "Imagining it makes me weak. Having ye naked and me filling ye up. It's the only thing I want. The one good thing that's getting me through this shittiest of anniversaries."

My anger receded another degree. "Anniversary of what?"

"It doesn't matter."

It did, though. This was something big and unrelated to all the other pressures and problems we faced.

Slowly, I raised my hand and set my fingertips to his chest. My heart hammered. Under his black t-shirt, his did, too.

I pushed lightly, propelling him backwards until we were next to the car, and I switched our positions so I could stand on the doorframe, bringing me nicely to his height.

"Your mother's birthday?"

"Death. Tomorrow."

"And the places we drove around?"

"Were all the ones I remembered her best."

We watched one another, just breathing the same air while the weight of what he'd told me settled. I could tell the bereaved boy I was sorry he lost her, but that changed nothing.

"Ye scared me," I finally said, repeating the worst of my hurts. "Make it better."

Sin's dark eyes took me in, then he curled a possessive hand around my waist. I hitched a breath, letting him come to me. With a rough tug so I half fell on him, Sin took my mouth in a bruising kiss. I found my balance and kissed him back, careful not to grab at him, though I badly wanted to.

Instead, I rested my forearms on his chest with my fingers curled into fists.

His mouth moved on mine with aggressive, needy strokes. I matched his moves, fever for him building with each sweep. He cupped my cheek, then his fingertips slid around the back of my head, holding me still.

I opened for him, remembering how much I liked his tongue. Immediately, he plundered my mouth, giving up a groan of lust that sent my mind into freefall. He slid his hand under my shirt to take a handful of my breasts.

His fast, steady heartbeat thumped under my clenched fists, picking up when he pinched my nipple and moulded me in his palm.

He slicked his tongue onto mine, and I moaned with utter need.

Sin broke our kiss. "Turn around, bend over, legs apart."

Urgency decorated his words.

God, I needed this. Except... He was out of control. He'd lost everything from his manners to his sense of safety. I knew him. He was a protector through and through.

I needed to take the reins. "Not here."

Sin swore and backed up a step, releasing me. "Violet."

"Sinclair. I'm not losing my virginity in a field."

"Who says—"

I held up a hand. "From now on, I don't want anything less than your best."

I was done with the anger, but not with him. Him, I wanted endlessly. Had from the minute I first saw him.

A muscle in his jaw ticked, and unknown thoughts played out behind those dark eyes. With a curl of his lip, he put voice to them. "I'll take one from ye now. The rest can wait until we're home."

"One?" My words cut off as his lips landed on mine again.

Sin grabbed my thigh, drawing it around his hip. Then his hand slipped behind my waistband and straight into my underwear.

Giving me no pause, he sank two fingers into my heat then withdrew to toy with my clit. I gasped at the spike of pleasure and dropped my head to his shoulder. Sin rumbled an urgent sound and upped the pace, focusing on me with exacting pressure, hitting the centre of me with repeated demands. His huge body hid what he was doing to me from the road, not that I cared.

It was too good. Almost too much.

He kissed my face, nudging me to give him my mouth once more, all the while driving me wild with his fingers.

I was in such trouble with this man. We'd gone from upset and clashing to passion in a heartbeat.

All he had to do was touch me, and I splintered. I craved him, needed him, ached for him.

I moaned as the tremors of my climax spread, dazzling me with a fast, hard orgasm. Sin clamped me to him, easing the pressure but keeping his fingers moving until my spasms ceased.

He withdrew his hand, took his fingers to his mouth then, nudging me to look at him, licked each one clean.

Dizzy, I took a full breath, too stunned to speak.

Then he jumped into action, yanking me around the

car to set me, a little more gently, in the passenger seat. He leaned over to clip in my seat belt, kissed my chest, neck, then my mouth, then jogged to climb in his side. We were back on the main road before I could blink.

I didn't kid myself that I had him tamed. He wasn't an animal. But I was starting to understand myself better, and what I really, badly wanted now was to lose myself in the storm of his making.

25

Lottie

I barely noticed the journey home. All I knew was the burning need rising in me. The promise behind our clinch. On our much quieter stretch of coast, we trundled down the hill to the surf house.

Inside, Scar appeared in the hallway. "What happened?"

Halfway up the stairs, Sin leading me, I called back to him, "Report made. They'll go get her. We'll call them tomorrow to find out what happened."

He hollered out his thanks, but my attention was firmly on the man thundering up the final steps with me in tow.

In our room, he locked the door, then backed me to the bed, his lips taking mine in a now-familiar claiming. When we'd been in this room and situation last, I'd been afraid. Needy but cautious. That wasn't the case now. I was compelled. Driven. This had to happen.

I sat on the mattress and reached to pop the button of Sin's jeans. This time, he let me, though I stopped after

"Take me out," he muttered against my lips.

I reached for his dick, gasping at how hard he was. I stroked him, and he made a sound of need and let me pump my fist up his length before he withdrew.

"See what ye do to me? Only ye."

In the half light of the room, Sin stripped his shirt, followed by the rest of his clothes in quick succession until he stood in front of me fully naked.

I tugged down my leggings and knickers. Then I reached back and unclipped my bra, sliding the straps off my arms and casting it aside. I was left in just my long top, and...that was enough. For now.

Sin moved between my legs and brought his mouth to mine for another kiss. He took hungry pulls then moved to my cheek. My throat.

I arched my neck to give him access, loving this.

Badly, I wanted to caress his dark hair. Feel how silky it was now it was growing out from his buzz cut, then move on to his muscles. His strong arms made me weak. Touching them would be a whole new sensory experience, except...he wouldn't like it.

I kept my hands to myself.

At my chest, he reached the line of my shirt then kept going, finding my nipple through the material and grazing it with his teeth.

His fingers drifted up my thighs and gathered the hem of my top. I bit back my immediate reaction to tell him to stop and closed my eyes instead. Sin drew my shirt up my naked body, revealing me completely. He made a hungry sound and took two handfuls of my breasts, thumbing my nipples at the same time. Then he ducked his head and sucked first one, then the other.

He stroked my belly, laying his lips on the soft skin. Then he tongued my belly button.

I wanted to love it, but I stiffened.

"Open your eyes," he asked, gruff.

I gazed at his expression, at the rapture in his focus on me.

"What's wrong?" he asked.

"I have stretch marks."

He returned his gaze to my belly, then brushed his thumb over the tiny silver lines. I had them there, on my breasts and thighs, and even on my calves. They'd alarmed me when I first found them at maybe twelve or thirteen years old, and my parents had openly discussed them, stating I was putting on weight too fast for my body to cope.

"Your body is incredible," he said. "Every inch perfect. It's like ye were designed to drive me insane. All these wee marks do is show me how the curves I'm so fucking crazy about filled out to perfection."

I allowed a small, slightly astonished laugh which turned into another moan as he kissed each area of stretch marks. Heat streaked through me, and pleasure bloomed every place he touched me.

Then he returned to my face, laid his lips on mine in a sweet caress, and eased the shirt over my head.

It was the moment I should be freaking out, and mild nervousness gathered. But then he did something which short-circuited my reaction.

Sin took my hand and placed it around his biceps.

I widened my eyes and felt up his hard muscles, the power in them doing something silly to my brain.

"Touch me. Distract yourself. Keep going," he said, low and gruff.

Slowly, I grazed up and over his shoulder, utterly enraptured with the ability to lay a hand on him. Gone was the attitude from earlier. The man with me now was working through as many barriers as I owned.

I traced my other hand up his neck, brushing over the side of his face then down to his scruff-shadowed jaw.

"Tell me what to avoid," I asked softly.

For a beat, he just watched me. "Just don't grab me too tight."

I had any number of ideas on why he feared touch, but his answer didn't fit any of them. I lightened my touch.

"What do I need to know about ye?" he asked in exchange.

It surprised me into silence.

My problem wasn't the same. Except... "Don't shame me," I said.

He tilted his head. "Your body? How could I? You're a fucking goddess."

With that, he gripped me under the arms and boosted me up the bed. Then he ducked to press a kiss to my thigh, another landing higher, at my hip.

"So listen up," he said with a possessive, hot glance at the apex of my thighs. "I'm not going to mess around. Going to touch every part of ye. Fuck ye with my fingers, my tongue, then finally my dick. If ye want to keep your virginity, tell me now before I lose my mind over ye."

"Lose it. Don't hold back. Do I have to keep my hands to myself?"

He pressed his lips together, breathing hard through his nose. Some extremes of need and emotion playing out that I couldn't miss.

He might have let me touch him, but he wasn't sure about more.

Purposefully, I interlaced my fingers and stretched my hands above my head to grab the headboard. It was so alien to put myself on display like this, and yet at the same time easy, because it made him comfortable.

Sin's focus fell to my exposed breasts, and he grinned devilishly. He sank down to suck both of my nipples into peaks in turn, moulding my plump flesh in a way that had him even harder against my leg.

I writhed under him. Heat bloomed until I was panting and a mess of need.

"Where's your toy?" he asked.

"Bedside table."

He crawled over and found it, turning it on with an instant buzz. "Keep playing with your tits for me."

He picked up my knee and pushed it out, then dropped his head to kiss and bite at my belly before moving on south.

I was too far gone on the path of need to feel self-conscious now. I pressed the vibrator to one nipple, squeezing the other while he trailed a fingertip over my clit. Electricity zapped me from his touch. I was so ready to come. A few touches and I'd be gone.

He bit my thigh at the same second he pushed a finger inside me.

"So fucking wet. So ready for me."

"You're so much bigger than me. Six-seven to my five-two. We'll never fit."

He laughed against the juncture of my legs. "Your greedy cunt will take my dick."

He added another finger, his tongue sweeping a hard circle over my clit, spiralling pleasure through me. Mindlessly, I spread my legs, needing everything he could give. Arching against him as he upped the pace, finger-fucking me faster and faster.

He ducked to kiss me right on my lower lips, sliding his tongue inside me alongside his fingers.

"Tell me you're not done with me. Tell me ye want this."

"Sin," I warned.

Inside me, heat spiralled in tight coils.

Sin kissed my clit then licked me. "I hated ye saying that. Tell me."

I cried out. "I want ye. Everything with ye."

He sucked my clit into his mouth, plunging his fingers in and out of me.

My orgasm struck, and I moaned. Sin kept moving, working me through it. I gasped, revelling in everything he made me feel, then I cried out again as he pulled back, knelt between my thighs, and guided the blunt end of his dick to my aching, wet centre.

At some point, I'd closed my eyes.

I sprang them open now.

It was the only cue he needed. Sin jacked his hips and sank inside me.

For a moment, all I could do was stare at him, open-mouthed. He did the same, gripping my hips.

The uncontrolled lust in his expression stole my shock. I rotated my hips, impaling myself farther though not all the way.

I hadn't known what to expect. Maybe for pain, definitely for it to be strange.

But the weight of him, the solid length of his dick inside me, only felt right. He gave me a second to adjust then drew out before surging back in.

I moaned with unexpected pleasure.

All of this was alien. All of it vital.

He thrust in and out a few times, features contorted. "You're so tight. Use the vibrator on your clit."

"But ye already made me come."

"You're going to again, this time with me deep in ye. I want to feel it. But we need to get there first."

A thrill of fresh need burned through my veins. I moaned and directed the vibrator straight to my clit, gasping again at the blaze of feeling.

Sin kept up a steady motion, his arms rigid either side of me. Each thrust buried him a little deeper. Each inch drove me wild.

The problem of his last couple of inches were in how

thick he was at the base. My body had never done this before. We had to learn how to fit together.

He dropped forward and kissed me, giving me time to adjust while he loved on my mouth.

Finally, he was fully seated, his groin flush against mine.

I was dizzy with it all, wholly obsessed with the sensation.

"Holy fuck." He stared down our bodies. "You're taking me."

"That feels incredible. You're pressing against all these points, God," I babbled. Then I drifted the toy lower so it touched him, too.

He growled then snatched it, bringing it away from his dick. "Do that and I willnae be able to pull out. Ye already feel too good. I'm fucking desperate to fill ye up."

A darker undertone played out in his words.

We'd messed around with his cum. I'd taunted him with it.

He'd liked that, too.

The lack of protection. The risks it brought.

I hadn't needed an aphrodisiac with him, he turned me on with just a look, but this was something else. A deep need we were toying with the edges of.

It connected us on a level I barely understood.

"I want that," I confessed, easing the vibrator down a little. "I want everything you've got. No holding back."

Sin swore then ducked to kiss me. Then he bit my jaw. "If I do this, you're mine. No going back. No running from me. No betrayal. I won't give ye up. You're mine to do with as I please."

I nudged his face so I could see his eyes. "You're mine, too."

Sin jerked his hips, sliding almost completely out before slamming back in. I moaned loud, shocked at the intrusion, loving every touch.

He upped the pace even more. His gaze darted between my chest, which jiggled with every hit, and my face. He took a grasp of my breast, so I plumped both together with my arms, propping them up for him while I kept up the action with the vibrator. Sliding over my clit and touching him, too.

Sin fucked me harder, the muscles of his neck taut. His expression rapt.

With my knees wide, all I could do was take it. Every blow. He hit the same places inside over and over, and it was unbearably good. Building towards a crash. I was barrelling in the direction of another release, maybe too fast. The intensity startled me.

I shifted the vibrator to my thigh, but Sin snatched it and pressed it back straight on my clit and to the base of his dick.

I yelped, but it was too late. My second orgasm hit in spasms.

At the same moment, Sin groaned and stilled, dropping his head, his arms shaking. Inside me, his hefty dick pulsed.

He came? Oh fuck.

He withdrew and jerked his last over me, painting my pussy with ribbons of his cum. Then, with rapt fascination, he rubbed his fingers into the mess, pushing it inside me, his focus fixed on what he was doing.

After everything we'd done, this final part of the act gave the most intense burst of pleasure. I couldn't have imagined it or dreamt it up. It was everything.

Explosive. Somehow, life altering.

He gave up a deep sound of pleasure, then collapsed down onto me. Still conscious of his touch issues, I kept one hand by my side but shifted the other to brush gently over his hair. He hugged me, burying his face against mine.

I didn't want to move, and apparently, neither did he. We'd changed everything between us, and I never wanted to go back.

26

Sin

Downstairs, I found my brothers in the living room. Violet slept, but I'd forced myself out of bed. Scar had known everything I'd seen at McInver's, but I needed to give my brothers the chance to ask questions of me.

At the table in the window, Scar drew an outline on Burn's arm, our youngest brother laughing at some video on his new phone. Scar's tattoo kit was spread out around him.

I took the armchair and regarded Struan. "Where are the lasses?"

"Cassie went to sleep ages ago, and I left Thea in our bed. Tired her out."

He didn't need to say more. The arsehole wore a smug grin.

I was having a hard job controlling my own.

"Check this out. He nailed it." Struan extended his arm and displayed new ink work. The surfer against a rocky island in a circle. It was neatly done, the lines tight.

I raised my eyebrows at Scar. "That's fucking amaz-

Our tattoo artist shrugged, keeping his focus on Burn's forearm. "It's okay. I'll get better with each I do."

"Seriously, I want mine next. You're a natural."

He didn't smile back. Something was wrong.

I squinted at him. "Got a problem with me? It was the right call not going back into the house. I know ye don't agree, but I couldn't choose a stranger over ye. We were outnumbered. Outgunned. Violet's idea to let the police handle it will work."

He set down the pen and swore. "It's not that. I wanted to break your fucking face when we drove home, but I know you're right."

"Then what?"

He dropped my gaze.

"It doesn't matter." He picked up the tattoo gun, tilting his head at Burn. "Ready?"

Burn's grin was instant. "Lay it on me. Take my tattoo virginity."

He beamed out excitement, but Scar's frown only deepened. The buzz of the gun took over the room, interspersed with the flick of Burn's Zippo.

"Tell me what ye saw of McInver's place," Burn asked Scar halfway through. "Start with the kitchens. Was there a laundry room? What kind of cooker did he have, gas or electric?"

While they talked, Struan gestured to me, and I switched my gaze to him.

"I spoke to Gordain McRae again. The islanders left this afternoon for a few hours but returned to hang out at the house. He asked if we wanted them moved. They're on his land so he can kick them off."

I still didn't trust the castle-owning mountain rescue man, but he was doing us a solid all the same. "Better we know where they are."

Struan pursed his lips and nodded agreement. "He

spoke to them. They aren't talking to him about us now. Nothing more about Lottie."

"They don't want the cops involved. The minute that happens, they lose their leverage over us. They need to catch us to have any chance of cashing out on us."

He watched me. "I'm not so sure. They aren't giving up."

My thoughts turned inwards. The problem of Violet's father needed solving. For all of our sakes, but most of all, hers.

It felt like there were several different threads that needed pulling together. I wasn't the cunning or devious type. I could wait and plan, but I was better in a confrontation where I could see my opponent's strength.

"Going toe to toe with Forbes Hunter will be a fucking trip," I admitted.

Struan paused again, and I glanced over at him.

"My strength is coming back," he said. "My head's clear."

A soldier, presenting for battle.

"How's the pain?" I asked.

"Bearable."

Something passed between us of solidarity and respect. We didn't use his nickname as much as the rest of ours, but Ruin was a dangerous man. Powerful and fearless. Loyal, too. He'd let me take command without argument, believing in me to protect him while he needed to recover.

"Good to know," I told him.

"Include me in your decisions."

"Always have."

"No, I mean as a body on the ground. I want to end this war against us as much as ye do. I need for my lass to be safe. I want to do that with me at her side and not dead. So count me in." He angled his head at me. "Like ye want to keep Lottie."

"What makes ye think that?"

"Tell me ye aren't dreaming up ways to save her from her da."

From across the room, Burn laughed. "If the noises floating down the stairs earlier were anything to go by, he's all in. Which is fucking annoying because I have to stop staring at her now."

I rolled an unimpressed look his way. "Mention her tits again, and I'll brain ye."

He ignored me, and his expression transformed to one of bliss. "I always wanted a mother and father. Ye two are the parents of the group. Cassie already thinks that."

Struan shook his head. "Back to our immediate plans, that text I sent earlier—Thea spoke to her ma. She's who told us about Augustus Stewart having a connection to your mother."

I sneered, hating the thought. "Good to know."

Burn grimaced. "It's fucked up how intertwined our parents all were. We were scattered to the wind, but every time one of the living ones speaks, they reveal yet another pair that was fucking."

"Shut it," I snarled, really not wanting to think about it.

Struan sighed. "Next thing, Theadora needs to clear her shite from her university room. I'll go with her. It's fucking miles away in Edinburgh, so we'll be gone a full day."

"Sure you're up to it?"

"The alternative is she goes with Lottie."

He pulled an expression of no *fucking way*, and I had the idea I was making the same face.

"When are ye going?" I asked.

"Within the next few days."

I nodded, but I didn't like it. The idea of our group

breaking apart, even for a day, felt wrong.

"Done," Scar announced.

At the table, Burn examined his new tattoo. "Fucking A. You're up next." He pointed at me.

I quizzed Struan instead. "Will Thea get one?"

"Like a brand? Fuck, yeah. I already told her she has to."

Burn choked out a laugh. "Told her? Like she doesnae own your balls."

Struan lowered his gaze at the challenge. I ignored them both.

"Do mine," I said to Scar, "then be ready for another."

I was teetering on the edge of upturning everything I believed about Violet. She was mine, there was no going back with that, but I needed to see she felt the same.

A little loyalty test wouldn't hurt.

I took my place at Scar's station, watching as he shaved a patch of skin on my arm, freehand drew our brand on my biceps, then set his needle to my skin.

"When you're done," Burn told us, emerging back from the kitchen with a bottle of whisky, "we're going to hit the waves for a midnight surf. Lottie's branding can wait until we're back. Bonding time, aye?"

Scar lifted his head. "Pretty sure it's bad to get new ink wet, but I've got some plastic shite to cover them with."

"All of us?" I lifted an eyebrow at Struan.

He stared me down. "I'm sick of doing nothing, so aye, I'm coming. Scar can cover my wound with the same plastic shite."

Burn whooped. "I'll start a fire on the beach. Plenty of dry wood ready for incineration."

"No," the rest of us chorused.

More than once, Burn had slyly commented on starting fires, usually with some kind of distant gaze and a disturbing smirk. Scared the shite out of me.

"Not now," I added. "It'd be too visible, and we don't want anyone coming down to investigate."

Less happy, he passed the bottle around. I took my share and wallowed in some fucked-up emotion, trying to block out the fact that tomorrow was Ma's anniversary, while needing this moment with my brothers so badly.

I carried the weight of their emotions. Wanted to make things better for them. For the lasses, too. Struan needed to have his wish of keeping Theadora and the two of them staying safe. Burn needed freedom, though I had no clue how we'd clear him of the police charges against his name. Scar was a mystery. He claimed Keep's death didn't bother him, but something was affecting him.

I let him scratch his scar into my skin and waited my moment to ask.

An hour later, the bottle of whisky was long gone and the rest of our beer supply drained.

We were inked up, in wetsuits, and entering the dark sea. It was a calm evening, so low risk of being smashed into the rocks either side of the bay. Each of us had our surfing beacon to see where the others were. Struan in blue, mine green, Scar's purple, and Burn's a fiery red.

Just like old times on the island where surfing, and seeing Violet, had been the only joy in my days.

I caught waves, watched Struan to make sure he wasn't going to drown, Burn to be sure he wasn't about to head in to set fire to shite, and waited for my chance with Scar.

He wiped out, his light disappearing beneath the surface, then rushed up with a splash of seawater to straddle his board.

I paddled over, but Scar surprised me, speaking ahead of me asking.

"I think I'm like him."

"Who?"

Moonlight cast him in black and white. The surfing beacon at his wrist flashed purple.

"McInver."

"You're going to have to walk me through this one."

He peered over at our brothers, then dropped his voice. "I'm different to the rest of ye. I never stared at Lottie. Never lusted over any lass. Until I walked into that room at McInver's house."

I opened then closed my mouth.

"It's so fucked up," he continued, his shoulders hunched. "She was lying there on the bed, her arms and legs spread out and held open by chains to the four corners. I could see everything. Her tits." He darted his gaze to me and then down. "Her cunt. Things no one should see without permission. She could do nothing to hide herself. It was like he'd arranged her like that so he could climb on, fuck her with minimum effort, then go."

He curled his hands into fists, pressing them into his board. "It was fucking horrifying, and that was the moment my body decided to wake up and be interested. I wanted her. Got hard over a lass for the first time ever. Do ye see what I mean? I'm a monster."

No fucking way.

I grabbed his board to steady it, holding him where I could see him. "Don't ye dare compare yourself with him."

He pushed me away with a snap of aggression. "Don't diminish it."

"Camden. What did ye do when ye saw her? Help yourself? Rape her like he would? Did ye want to?"

He snapped a wide-eyed look my way, his mouth open. "No! I covered her up and tried to unchain her."

"Would ye ever hurt a woman like that?"

"Ye know I wouldn't."

"Then it sounds to me that ye had a normal animal response which ye overrode with the fact you're a decent fucking human being. When I was twelve, everything made me think about sex. A woman walking along the street, minding her own business. A teacher old enough to be my grandmother, but with cleavage that stretched her blouse. Shite, any display of fruit that resembled the shape of tits. It's a normal part of sexual awakening."

He lifted his gaze to me again, uncertainty in how he held himself. "Really?"

"The difference with McInver is that he doesn't see women as humans. He abuses them because he thinks they're not worth respect. You're nothing like him in any way. None of us are."

He sagged. "Holy fuck."

"Does that make sense?" I checked.

"I think so. I mean, I'm not getting turned on by fruit bowls. It was just that one image."

"Maybe you'll be into tying your girlfriend up one day. So long as it's consensual, it's no one else's business. There's nothing wrong with ye."

He went quiet, and I stayed by his side. Our brotherhood had been forged in the worst of circumstances, through kidnapping, false imprisonment, and acts of violence against us. I'd do whatever it took to make sure it went on stronger.

Finally, he took a deep breath and sat taller. "I need to tell the others about Keep. It's another risk factor, so we should all be aware."

Without pause, he whistled with his forefinger and thumb. The surf lights curved our way, our brothers paddling in.

"Problem?" Struan asked.

Scar took a breath. "I killed Keep."

For a beat, silence, then Burn choked out a laugh. "It was ye? I couldn't picture how she'd done it. Fallen on her damn Taser."

"It was me. And it wasn't an accident. She was screaming how she was going to end us. Let them at us. She was going to fucking sell Cassie. Or ye, Burn. If we'd been locked up again, we would have lost the chance." Scar's eyes went wider still. "I'd never let her or anyone else hurt ye. I ran at the bitch, grabbed the hand holding the Taser, and stabbed her in the leg. She must have pressed the button herself. The second I let go, bang."

All of us laughed, crazy, outlandish sounds.

Struan moved his board closer and gripped the edge of Scar's. "Did it actually pop like that? I wish I'd been there the minute her heart gave out. I've never wished violence on any woman, but she was the exception. Fucking evil rapist-enabling, profit-hungry bitch. Ye did the world a favour."

Scar stared at him. "I'm a murderer."

Struan and Burn shrugged, and somehow, this, the explanation about the death of our prison keeper, made the evening complete.

"Join the club," our oldest brother said with a savage grin.

We surfed for a while longer, taking advantage of the waves and the mild night. Relaxing together like we'd once done in stolen moments on the island.

Whatever our differences as brothers, however fucked up our experiences had made us, we'd always have this. The shared love of the water, and the freedom it gave us when that was our only grounding.

Peace stole over me.

For a long while, I let my brain empty of all but this. I had my family. Violet. It felt...good. Almost complete. If only I could make them safe permanently.

Struan's blue surf light curved towards me, Scar's purple one out a little deeper.

"Where's Burn?" Struan's voice broke the calm.

I sat up on my board and scanned the dark. Waves lapped my board.

No red-orange light flickered.

No slightly insane younger brother carving the surf.

"Did he go inside?" I replied.

"Don't think so."

I cupped my mouth. "Scar," I yelled. "Can ye see Burn?"

The purple light stalled, then a voice returned. "No. Fuck, where is he?"

A tendril of panic wormed through me. "Burn," I bellowed.

My brothers took up the call, echoing his name into the night.

No reply came.

Nothing but rushing water. Even the sea birds had gone quiet.

The silence felt ominous.

In no scenario had I ever worried about him in the sea. Or any of us. We were all strong swimmers. Able to handle the currents around the island, let alone this calm bay.

"He wouldn't have gone in." Scar paddled closer. "He'd want to stay out as long as he could. What if he hit a rock and slipped under the surface?"

"We'll be able to see his board," Struan said, his words tense.

"Split up. We have to find him." I pushed away, picking a direction. "Scar, check around the pier. Struan, take the shallows. I'll go—"

My words cut off as, on the beach, a bright flare burst upwards from the sands.

We all snapped our gazes to it.

Fire crept over something, orange flames crackling, the base of them a blue-green.

Beyond it, our youngest brother danced back, cackling out a laugh. He whooped and swung his leg through his blaze, squirting something into the base that made the flames rush.

"What the fuck," I bit out.

Then I was moving, this time towards the beach. Whatever fear I'd felt evaporated and was replaced with other strong emotions.

I powered through the water, Struan and Scar at my back.

As soon as I hit the pebbles, I dragged my board free, tugged off the ankle leash, then stormed over to Burn. "What the fuck are ye doing?"

His gaze found mine, and his delighted grin spread. "The night called for a fire."

"Are ye insane?" I snapped.

An easy shrug was my answer. "Little bit."

Burn directed a stream of lighter fluid from a yellow can at the burning timber. The flames rushed over the fuel, getting stronger.

I squinted, recognising the bones of an old rowing boat I'd seen next to the house. "Seriously. Put it out now. Before someone sees."

"Who? It's the middle of the night, and we're miles from anywhere. One small fire isn't going to hurt."

"Burn!" I snapped. "Kill it. Now."

His grin dropped. Firelight flickered over his features. "I don't want to."

"Listen," I tried again. "If someone sees and comes

to investigate, we're in trouble. We need to extinguish it. Sorry, but it's a risk."

Struan made a noise of irritation then advanced on the fire. Barefoot, he drove his heel into the centre of it. The broken hull of the boat splintered, singed pieces falling away.

Charred pieces flared. Some extinguished where they fell with wisps of grey smoke.

Burn stared wide-eyed then growled. He planted his bare foot into the remaining section of the boat. Over and again, he stamped into it, the fire still burning.

Sparks scattered, flying upwards, little fireflies against the now-dark beach.

One landed on Burn's head.

"Your hair!" Scar yelped.

Our pyromaniac didn't move, his chest rising and falling.

Scar snatched Burn's arm and dragged him to the water, the smell of burning hair acrid in the air. Scar shoved him down and scooped seawater over his head.

"Are ye fucking mad?" he snarled. "That could've scarred ye for life. You're lucky it's only taken a chunk from your scruffy, damp mop."

Struan grabbed a smouldering plank and hurled it into the sea. I followed suit, clearing the evidence from the beach. One by one, the remnants disappeared into the surf. Then the blaze was finally out, darkness returning.

Scar released Burn who stormed back to the house, pissed off but apparently uninjured from his ordeal.

As we'd worked, I'd kept an eye on the coast road high above the house, but no headlights appeared. It seemed we'd gotten away with it. Not that the fact helped my pulse rate any.

My peace had been broken, and I had only one way to use up the fresh energy in me. And a warm lass to help me over the fuss.

27

Lottie

The bedroom door snicked open, and I shifted under the bedsheet, lying on my side. I'd woken alone and hadn't gotten back to sleep. From the window, I'd spotted the men out on the water, the sight of their surf beacons a blast from the not-too-distant past.

Sin was easy to pick out. A flash of bright neon green.

It was easier to know it was him who'd entered the room now.

He rounded the bed then pulled back the sheet, revealing my naked body.

After what we'd done earlier, and from every night we'd been in the same bed, I was an addict. Of him touching me. Of how he made me feel.

Of his cum, for certain.

Sin gave up a groan and knelt on the mattress behind me. He held back from laying his hands on my body, but I felt his gaze all over me. He smelled of the seawater he'd played in.

I slid my knee higher, knowing how it put everything

He murmured something too quiet for me to hear, but the tension in his voice told me everything.

"I'm not asleep," I said.

"Thank fuck. Ye have no idea how edible ye look. Your arse is a peach."

My voice came out in a shudder. "If ye want to fuck me, ye don't have to wake me. Just do it. I want that, too."

Any opportunity. Every chance. I wanted him inside me.

A rustle came like he was stripping, but I didn't move to look. Then Sin's body curled around me, his knee landing between my legs, and his ultra-hard dick pressing against my backside.

"Seriously?" He landed a kiss on my bare shoulder, sending shivers down my spine. "If I come to bed and you're naked, that's a sign?"

I arched my neck to give him access to kiss me there. "It is now."

He made a low sound of pleasure and travelled his open-mouthed kisses down my back until he laid his lips on my arse. He stroked his hand over my cheeks, dipping his fingers between to find me wet and ready for him.

God, just the lightest touch alone, and I was on edge. Needing everything.

"Ye smell of smoke," I mumbled in an attempt to stop from begging him to make me feel good.

"Burn lost his mind and set a wee fire. It's out now. I took a shower downstairs but I can take another."

"Don't go anywhere."

"Christ, woman. I just want to slide right in."

"Then do it."

He paused, and I wiggled in anticipation.

"You're not too sore?"

"A little, but I don't care."

He gathered my wetness on his fingers, then drew

them back to my tight rear hole. "If ye were, I could take my pleasure another way."

His fingertip penetrated me, and I tensed up, my eyes flying open.

Sin rumbled a laugh then moved so his thick cock was between my legs from behind. He held my hip and slowly thrust against me, sliding through my lower lips but not pushing inside. "I intend to claim every part of ye, Violet Hunter. Another time and you'll have me every way there is."

Then as if he couldn't wait a second longer, he snaked a hand around me to grasp my breast and simultaneously fucked into my pussy.

I gasped, the size of him still so shocking. My body gave way, opening for him much easier now, as if knowing the pleasure was only going to get better. He stretched me, and every nerve ending lit up.

"Couldn't even imagine this," he gritted out and withdrew his hips to thrust again. "Ye were made for me. Made to take my dick."

I moaned in agreement, stifling it in the mattress.

Sin pumped in and out of me, each hit generating sparks. He pulled lightly on my nipple in the way he'd done previously that drove me wild, keeping up the action in time with his thrusts.

I imagined waking like this, to find him inside me, giving me an orgasm. He read my body so easily, knowing exactly how to tease me.

In this position, he was out of my reach, which could be his preference. I just had to take it.

In minutes, he had me gasping, and he ran his hands over my soft belly rolls then down to my thigh. Grasping my knee, he drew my leg back over his. Leaving my pussy open to his attention.

"If ye touch my clit, I'll come," I warned.

"Is that a threat?"

He pressed firmly, laughing low at my instant spasm, but then he moved on, feeling over my lips where he was taking me.

"Put your hand between your legs," he ordered.

I moved mine alongside his, and he interlaced our fingers, showing me what he was feeling while he fucked me.

For some unknown reason, that simple act hit my heart. He was holding my hand. It added to the overflow of emotions, and I needed to channel it. I dragged his hand to my clit and, together, we rubbed hard circles.

I was already close just from having him inside me, and I gasped out, my movements stuttering as my orgasm danced closer. Sin took up the slack, his rhythm never faltering.

Delicious waves flooded me. I contracted around his dick, the pleasure that much more intense with him inside me.

Sin kept up the pressure until I went limp. Then he grabbed both my hips and reared over me, pushing me down into the mattress with his weight. He fucked me like a piston, relentless and hard. Our skin slapped together, and my breathing came out fast and sharp, his in desperate pants.

He dipped to lay his teeth on the back of my neck—a bite that turned into a kiss. His hips working double-time. Every slide hitting me deep.

The kiss was abandoned when he braced himself on me and thickened so much I cried out. At the same second, he came with a shout and stopped moving, enabling me to feel every pulse of his dick. The sensation of his cum coating me inside.

This time, he'd finished right where I wanted him to, and I moaned again, loving every bit of what we'd done.

Sin dropped onto me, breathing hard for a long minute. Then he gave a huff of a laugh, kissed my shoulder, and withdrew.

I twisted to look at him, and he grinned at me, rolling me onto my back.

With purpose, he put my legs together, lifted my feet, and set them on his shoulder, one arm banded around my knees to hold me like that.

Not letting the essence of him slip away.

"What are ye doing?" I demanded on a breath.

Still holding my legs up, Sin curled his lips in a smirk. "Play with your nipples. Pull on them like I do."

I'd already come, but I glided my hands to my breasts, taking hold of my nipples.

Sin watched for a moment then ran his fingers between my legs. He dipped one into my slippery wet core, a grin forming on his lips.

"Like feeling yourself inside me?" I asked.

Slowly, he nodded, moving to work my clit again with our combined wetness. I parted my thighs to give him space.

Sin played with me, taking his time over stirring me up again.

Pretty quickly, I was panting, then arching up as another climax hit. It was gentler than the last, but the rush just as addictive and sweet.

Sin growled and pushed my legs wide, his dick hard again. He slid inside me and fucked me without pause. Blown away by too much pleasure, I barely had a mind to think with, but even so, I kept one hand back in the pillows and placed the other gently on his back.

Sin jacked himself then orgasmed once more, his lips hot on mine. Doubling down on what he'd already done.

"I want my cum so deep inside ye it doesnae escape," he confessed. "I want to keep doing it. Fucking constantly."

Breathless, I carefully turned his head so I could see

his eyes. Then I held his gaze.

"You'll get me pregnant."

"I know."

"Intentionally?"

For several loaded seconds, he just stared. "Ye want me to as well."

I did. So badly. Which made no sense. We weren't dating. We had no future. But I wanted his baby growing inside me. To raise a little boy or girl that looked like him. I'd do it well. Love them and keep them safe. Right all the wrongs of our childhoods.

Seemed to me he had the exact same drive.

Sin kissed me, blowing my mind yet again.

Then he stood and hunted for his clothes. "Up."

"Where are we going?"

"Downstairs. Scar's waiting. There's something I'm going to do with ye. Don't clean up. I want my cum inside ye while we do this."

I sat up and reached for a long shirt and knickers, hopelessly gone for how damp I was. At the door, Sin stopped and pressed me into the wood. Standing up, he had so much farther to duck so he could kiss me, so I stood on a chair, bringing myself closer to his height. He kissed me and cupped me between my legs, groaning into my mouth at the wetness that was driving me wild.

"Ye make me insane," I said against his lips.

"The feeling's mutual."

"What are ye going to do to me?"

Sin pulled back then drew my gaze to his arm. Plastic wrapped a new tattoo. I'd noticed it in bed but hadn't examined it closely until now.

"I need to know you're mine."

"And you'll do that how?"

"By branding ye, Violet. Marking your pretty, soft skin so the whole world can see, and so neither of us will ever forget."

In the window, under the light of a lamp, Scar waited, his expression knowing but patient. "Took your time," he grouched, then patted the seat. "Sure you're up for this, Lottie?"

I wasn't a fan of pain, but this test compelled me. I wanted to belong. I'd seen Scar's work. Sin's version. Knew Thea would get one to tie herself to Struan.

So I curled a leg under me and sat.

Sin moved in behind me.

Scar showed me his stencil. "Where? I'm getting better, but it's different putting this on ye than it is one of my hairy arsehole brothers."

Choices. I could hide it under my clothes or be bold and wear it proud.

I stared down at the surfer against a dark island—Sin, where I first fell for him.

"Forehead," Sin grumbled.

I spluttered a laugh and pointed to my upper arm. "Same place as his."

Scar shrugged and prepped my biceps, taking his time over getting the stencil in place. Then he offered Sin the tattoo gun.

Oh hell. What had I let myself in for?

28

Breeze

Thuds from outside my hiding place echoed through the halls. Car doors, followed by an engine. They were leaving?

Behind my gag, I breathed too fast. I hated the cops, they'd let me down too many times, but I'd been almost ready to scream for them.

I was in over my head and I didn't know how to get out.

But they were gone. I'd missed my chance.

The lid to the wooden box I'd been stuffed in opened above me, and I peered up at the sour-faced guard. One meaty hand snatched me under my armpit and hauled me to my feet, my skin twisting in his grip. Vicious bastard.

An hour ago, I'd been chained to the bed and dozing when he'd marched in. Without pause or explanation, he'd untied my restraints, thrown a dressing gown over me, winding the cord around my head and between my teeth, then dragged me down the corridor to a different room.

I'd been stuffed into the blanket box, threatened with a knife to my thigh, and closed in.

In the dark, I'd waited. Then came the static report of a police radio and footsteps.

I'd kept silent.

All of this would be wasted if I didn't find my sister. I'd suffer anything, worse than they'd dealt out so far, if only I got news. A clue or a trail I could follow.

Back in my bedroom, the guard unwound the cord and freed my mouth. He yanked the gown off me, leaving me naked again.

"Back on the bed. Legs open. Let the dog see the... cunt."

I scowled but obeyed, no point in arguing this now.

For days, since I'd been picked up for this job, I'd been here, only allowed off the bed for short breaks. Restrained. Flat out. *Ready.*

But no one had come. Not since the dark-haired boy with a handsome, scarred face had tried to free me. I'd wondered endlessly about him since. Dead or alive? Knocked out then killed and buried in the gardens? I hoped not. He seemed kind. The world needed more people like him, even if his interference hadn't been useful for me.

Perhaps he'd been the one to call the police.

I only realised the guard had said something else to me when he yanked me to look at him.

"What?"

"He's coming now. Remember what he likes and you'll still be able to walk afterwards."

My mouth dried, and I could only stare as the guard fastened my restraints again. I'd been prepared for any outcome. I knew what coming here meant, and it was worth the cost. Virginity was a man-made concept. It had no value to me. Still, the thought of getting fucked for the first time by some old creep who bought women like they were something to be used and thrown away terrified me.

I'd never admit that to another living soul. No one needed to know the real me.

The guard stood back and swung his gaze over my ankles and wrists, grunting approval to himself at the work done.

The door opened, and cool air swirled up my legs and to the juncture of my bare thighs. Instantly, the guard snapped straight and backed off to stand by the wall, his body language respectful and subservient.

In the time I'd been here, he hadn't taken a grab at me or tried to rape me, so I could only assume McInver had him on a short leash.

Or maybe the elderly man was more evil than I'd imagined.

My skin crawled, but I remembered the instruction and kept my gaze upwards. Vacant.

"A pretty one," a voice came.

That wasn't McInver.

I clenched my jaw to stop myself from staring at the newcomer.

"Young, nice tits, ripe. I asked for a virgin, but I never trust what they send me."

The second voice was definitely McInver. I'd only seen him once, but I'd never forget how he sounded.

I felt his gaze on my body, and I couldn't stop my muscles tightening. My nipples hardened of their own accord, and I wished they hadn't. I didn't want the men talking over my naked form to think it was anything else.

They kept on coming until they were right next to the bed. I made out the shape of them at the edge of my vision. Small, crooked McInver, and a taller, dark-haired man. Not young, but not elderly either.

I was meat on the slab, laid out for them to pick over.

"I wanted a brunette, too. Not like this one, nor the girl ye brought me, Stewart."

The second man chuckled. "Augustus, please. I'll have Esme dye her hair for you. It's not a problem."

The old man snorted. "Such desperation to get my money. I notice ye didn't have the boy with ye, the one your business partner offered up."

"I'll bring him next time. Henry is your great-nephew. He's entitled to know you," the other man commented, Augustus Stewart, I gathered.

McInver's gnarled hand landed on my knee. I cringed, trying to keep still and soft. His rough, bony fingers slithered up my thigh, pushing my legs open wider.

His avid gaze slunk to the centre of me.

Panic sent treacherous shocks up and down my nervous system. Fight or flight impulses. But chained up, I had no chance but to freeze.

The mattress depressed at my side, and McInver leaned over me, inspecting the goods. His gaze centred on my face.

My fingers trembled. I couldn't stop them.

"If ye want anything from me, then I have conditions you'll meet to the letter," he ordered Augustus Stewart. "Now go wait outside until I'm done."

Footsteps led away, and the door closed.

McInver tilted my chin, and I couldn't help focusing on his ugly, devilish eyes before I slackened my vision once more.

He groped my pussy and thrust a fingertip inside me.

Revulsion and shock iced me over.

"Well, well. A dry little virgin after all. What a surprise, slut. I know what to do with ye," he said, deadly calm. "I know exactly what you'll be good for, and it isn't me."

He was rejecting me? All this, and I was going to get sent away without the chance to investigate and start my hunt.

Inwardly, I screamed in outrage and unwanted fear.

He popped his finger into his mouth to suck away my taste, and smiled.

"Yes, girl. I'm saving ye. Not for me. Not for the heir Stewart is here fronting in the hope of getting my money. No, someone he doesn't know exists."

An awful, evil smile crinkled his lips. "I'll save ye for my son."

29

Lottie

A low rumble of thunder resounded across the bay, a heavy, dark sky hanging over our stolen holiday home. Despite it being early afternoon, it felt like evening. The storm had been rolling in for hours, building up electricity in the air.

In the porch, I curled up in my seat, unnerved but not willing to move. Sin and Scar had gone out for a run to the shops and to try for an update from the police. I didn't like them being away.

I'd chickened out of going along, providing a list instead. I hated storms. I'd even stopped Burn going out on the water in case he got struck by lightning. He already had a chunk of hair missing from his head that he declined to explain. Sin had murmured that it was his own fault before he'd reluctantly left us.

The patter of footsteps came from behind me, then Cassie burst into the porch, her soft toy dog clamped under her arm, and dove onto the cushion next me. I extended an arm so she could cuddle into me, and the little girl

"More thunder," she whispered.

I kissed her black curls. "We're safe here. Stay with me, and we'll watch the storm until it goes away."

Lightning flashed across the sky, bright and deadly against the dark-grey clouds. A crash followed. Cassie yipped in fear, and I jumped, too, my heart pounding. We hugged each other.

"Storms are good," I repeated the mantra I rehearsed whenever I got scared. "They clear the air, so it's nice and calm after. Look at how pretty the sea is here."

Cassie gazed down the beach, where foamy waves dragged over the pebbles, tossing seaweed. The storm aside, I loved it here. The beauty and isolation of it all, and how far I felt from danger. More thunder rumbled, and Cassie ducked back down.

"Why don't we play a game to take our minds off it?" I suggested.

She gave a fast nod, wedged against my boob. "What kind of game?"

"I-spy?"

"How do ye play that?"

I peeked down at her. "You've never played?"

Cassie's background was an enigma to me. I'd tried gently asking her about herself, but the six-year-old either couldn't or wouldn't answer. Burn had said the same. The most we knew was that she'd been in foster care and she didn't think she had parents at all.

It broke my heart to imagine her with no information on her early life. No one holding the stories of her first word or when she took her first step.

It also worried me that someone might eventually come looking for her, but I didn't have the faintest clue how we'd protect her against that.

I taught her the rules of I-spy and started her off. Then it was her turn.

"I spy with both my little eyes, something beginning with C."

"Cassie?" I booped her button nose.

"Nope."

"Clouds?"

"Still nope."

"Um, churn? Like the sea is doing?"

"Noooo. Do ye give up?"

I nodded and marked a point in the air on our imaginary scoreboard.

Cassie clapped and rose up on her knees. "It's a car."

My heart leapt, and I twisted in my seat to look at the access road. A swift chill followed. Sin had driven Thea's borrowed Kia, leaving the temperamental Ford in a space the other side of the house. The vehicle approaching was neither of them.

A stranger was here.

I stood and guided Cassie to the front door. "Car approaching. Everyone stay out of sight," I hollered into the depths of the house.

Burn stuck his head out of the kitchen. In his hand, he held a razor, and the sides of his hair had been shaved, leaving just the top long. I sent Cassie skittering to him. Struan sloped downstairs and sat near the bottom, menace in his pose, his dark gaze full wolf.

I stepped back into the porch and closed the door behind me, fluttering my hands over my belly as two people approached the house. They were older, maybe in their fifties, and wearing the loose, comfortable clothes of holidaymakers.

Still, they could be anyone.

Forcing back nerves, I exited the porch and smiled.

The woman stopped dead on the path. "Oh! Are you the cleaner? I know we're early, but I wasn't expecting anyone to be here."

I cocked my head to one side. “No, I’m here on holiday with my family. Can I help ye?”

Thunder rolled again, and I hid my flinch.

The man planted his hands on his hips. “What do ye mean you’re on holiday? We’ve got this place booked for the next week.”

Shite.

We’d always known this might happen. Someone could show up to kick us out. But unless they were the property owner, I had a chance of getting rid of them.

I widened my eyes. “That’s terrible. They didn’t tell ye?”

“Didn’t tell us what?” he snapped.

“When we booked this place, the rep explained they had only just taken over management of it. The previous company went bust, and all other bookings were cancelled. The rep assured us it was available.”

Both husband and wife’s jaws dropped in identical gapes.

The wife recovered first. “You’ve got it wrong. We’ve had this booked for months. We’re staying here now, so you’ll have to leave.”

I frowned and shook my head. “No. Why should we leave? We were here first, and our booking is valid. I’m sorry you’ve had a wasted journey, but that’s not our fault. The company who took your money should have contacted ye.”

Part of this was true. It was how Sin found the place.

They swapped outraged looks. Rain started in a steady patter.

The husband leaned forward, his face purple. “Now listen here, I’ve not just driven three and a half hours for some chit of a girl to send me away. For all I know, you could be squatters.”

I took a shocked breath. “You’re so rude. I’m sorry for the mix-up, but we’re not leaving. I’m going inside now. I suggest ye contact your holiday company."

I turned. A hand grabbed my arm.

Oh God. If Struan could see, or Burn, they were about to burst from the door and issue threats rather than acting this out. The conversation had to end.

I tore my arm from the man's grip and backed up a couple of steps.

"At least let us inside to work this out," his wife pleaded.

The rain came down harder, trickling down my neck.

"There's children in the house. I can't allow that. Really sorry. Hope ye find somewhere else to stay." I reached the door of the porch and darted inside, locking it behind me.

The man grasped the handle, twisting it but with no effect. He slapped the glass with the flat of his hand. "This is outrageous."

I threw myself in the front door and slammed that closed, too.

Four people stared back at me.

"What did they say?" Thea asked.

"They have this place booked. I told them it'd been cancelled and to take it up with their agent. Hopefully they'll just leave." I rubbed my arm where the man's fingers had dug in.

Struan's gaze locked on to the move. "Did that arsehole touch ye?"

"He tried to stop me coming in, but I got away."

He clenched his jaw and marched to the door, peering through the glass inserts. "I should've gone out."

Thea hummed disagreement. "The last thing we need is aggravation and a police report. Well done, Lottie. You did good."

The others echoed her sentiment.

Cassie curled her fingers into mine. "Will we have to

leave again?"

"Maybe." I hugged her to my side. "Don't worry. We'll stay together either way."

At least I hoped so. But I couldn't say anything different to a girl who'd lost everything and only just found people who could really love her.

Struan took out his phone and sent a quick text. "I've told Sin and Scar to hold back until our visitors have gone. Sin's going to go spare at ye being hurt."

"I'm not hurt," I said, but he moved into the living room, watching out the window. Burn went with him.

Thea put her arm over my shoulder and guided me to the kitchen, Cassie alongside.

My friend pulled out a stool for me at the kitchen counter. "Proud of you. You stood up for all of us."

"My heart was pounding the whole time."

"I probably would've crumpled and told them we'd leave within the hour." She gave a soft laugh. "You stood up for your family. You're the best."

My family...

For days, I'd done nothing about my parents. It had been enough to know that my father was nowhere near my mother, which made his two-day countdown meaningless. We'd had more than enough of our own problems to handle here.

Cassie helped herself to a drink, and Thea offered her a snack.

I stared into space and brooded. Thinking about home gave me an uncomfortable sensation. I hadn't come to terms with the fact my mother had an affair, or considered whether it really mattered to me. It made sense my da hated me. It also gave me the small inkling that he might not be my biological father, but thinking along those lines felt nebulous and dangerous. Would I be relieved? Or angry at suffering under his hand all those years when I hadn't had to?

On the day Sin made me throw my phone down the cliff, he'd said that my mother wasn't worth my care. She'd enabled the abuse by the simple act of not walking away.

I switched my gaze to Cassie, the fragile, fine-boned little girl, and tried to imagine a world where I'd let anyone hurt her. She wasn't even my blood, and I knew instinctively that I would protect her until the last. Even against Sin, not that I thought he'd ever be like my da, but the comparison was where I stumbled.

My mother hadn't picked me.

Faced with seeing her child hurt, she had chosen to remain with our abuser.

My upper arm tingled under the loyalty tattoo I'd had done last night, concealed under my long-sleeved top. Sin had scratched the first of the ink into my skin, but Scar had taken over and drawn a perfect design on me.

It had me rethinking everything about my wants and needs and where I owed allegiance. My mother was a grown woman, able to make her own choices. I hadn't been. Her new baby wasn't.

Realisation settled. First, I wanted to protect her baby, and second, I needed the chance to have a family done right.

A family like this one. Sin and his brothers and sister. Thea, my best friend. I couldn't betray them for the sake of my mother.

The whole time I'd been here, I'd wanted Sin to ask me about my motivation. In a heartbeat, that changed.

I couldn't tell him.

I didn't want him to care about my problems because they wholly conflicted with his.

If I told him I needed to protect my unborn baby sibling, he'd want to help me with that.

Everything had shifted again, and still, I had no clear

way through my problems. Only that handling it left me perfectly conflicted.

"Thea," I said.

My friend twisted around from where she was making a sandwich.

"My mother had an affair but didn't leave her marriage," I said without preamble. "Why bother? Guilt? A roof above her head? Why put up with how awful my da is?"

Thea pursed her lips. "My parents stayed in a crappy relationship for longer than necessary. I think people get stuck in their situations and can't get out."

"But they did eventually call it a day. My mother refuses to even talk about leaving Da. Yet he's vile to her. And to me."

Thea handed the sandwich over to Cassie and directed her to take it to the living room but to stay out of sight.

"He beat you," she said softly once the little girl was clear.

"Both of us. Not all the time, but often enough."

"I hate him for it."

"I do, too."

"Tell me about it."

I blew out a breath. For years, I'd wanted to share this with someone, and Thea had earned my trust over and over. "He doled out his anger through his fists. He was always worse in the summer holidays and at Christmas. That was when the real damage would be done. Other than that, drinking didn't help."

Thea tilted her head. "I don't remember seeing you with bruises. He made you hide them, then."

I furrowed my brow, something clicking together in my mind. "Not really. It was more to do with the timing that ye never saw. Now I think about it, it always coincided with ye and your da leaving. When we heard you'd arrived,

Ma would encourage me to spend time with ye, though I was never allowed to invite ye to the house. Da would get progressively angrier over the duration of your stay. I'd try to be out of the house as much as possible, but on the day ye left, I'd naturally be back indoors. That's when he'd flip."

A moment passed between us, and my childhood memories turned to something only an adult could see. My whole perspective had changed.

"My father was triggered by yours," I said slowly. "The man he knew had slept with his wife."

Thea made an unhappy sound. "Or was still sleeping with her. Why are we assuming the affair was a one-time deal? Dad hated Torlum, so even though he'd moved far away, he never took my mother on his visits back. Only me. I thought it was to visit my granny, but what if there was more to it? What if he used the time to see your mum and their affair kept going?"

We stared at one another, so different in several ways, but maybe not as much as I'd thought.

"What if he's your dad, too?" Thea uttered. "It would explain why your father is so angry at you."

I opened and closed my mouth, the conclusion there in my mind, too.

"Weird how much I'd love that to be true. It would make sense, but there's no real evidence," I admitted. "I know people say we look alike, but we only suspected the affair because your mother said so. She could have been wrong. Augustus was meant to be obsessed with Sin's mother. How likely is it that there's yet another connection between the generation that came before us? How badly can they have screwed up their lives and ours before we could even walk?"

Thea clasped my hands in hers, calming my rambling. "I don't know. I can try to find out?"

I gave a single, sad shake of my head. "No. I'll ring Ma and get it from her. I'm done trying to protect her. She did nothing of that for me."

She took her phone from her pocket and handed it over. "Without jumping to conclusions, I have an offer. If we share a father, we share a grandmother, too. Have Granny's house. Move your mother in there. She'd be independent, and it's furnished. Offer her it, please."

A thump came at the back door. Both Thea and I jumped and turned around. The kitchen opened onto a small courtyard with the cliff right behind it. In that exit way, Sin stared right in at us.

Still holding Thea's phone, I rushed to let him inside.

He crowded me, rain-damp and furious. He took my face in his big hands. "Are ye okay?"

"I'm fine. Where did ye come from?"

"Down the cliff. We hid the car at the top. Scar's waiting with it. Struan said in his text the man grabbed ye."

"That couple have gone," Burn called from the depths of the house. "They made angry phone calls, then the rain forced them back into their car. They've given up."

I took a breath to tell the story, but then the phone in my hand rang. I stared at it then turned to Thea.

"Who is it?" she asked.

I held up the screen, displaying the name *Henry.* Charterman's son, and the rival for McInver's inheritance. Another person who could add a piece of the puzzle.

Except I barely had time to hand over the device, because Sin was towing me through the house and upstairs.

Looked like there was a conversation we needed to have alone.

30

Lottie

Sin closed our bedroom door, engaged the lock, then spun me around to pin me to the wood. Without pause, he stooped and fitted his mouth to mine, his hands sliding over my body with fevered urgency.

"Where did the man touch ye?"

"He only grabbed my arm. I'm fine."

He pulled back, examining the wrist I'd raised for him, checking under my sleeve for any marks. Then he laid his lips on my skin, erasing the memory of the man's grasp. There was no easiness about him now. Only harsh need.

Sin had been worried for me, this time. Whatever Struan had said in his message, it had panicked him. He'd descended the damn cliff to get to us.

Sin's lips took mine once again. Emboldened, I looped my arms around his neck. He broke the kiss, breathing hard.

"I want ye. Right now."

"Then have me."

He took the waistband of my leggings and underwear and stripped them off me. I stepped out of them and shed my top, my heart rate speeding now for entirely different reasons than the storm or the intruders. He sank his fingers over my damp core, and a dirty smile took his lips.

"Always ready for me."

"Always want ye."

He gave a pained groan. "Undo my jeans."

I obeyed, yanking them down, his huge dick springing free. But before I could touch him, he hoisted me into his arms. Automatically, I wound my legs around his waist. But I clamped down on the urge to tell him no, I was too heavy. It would only make him glower at me.

Besides, I needed this.

He pushed me against the door once more, then brought his blunt end to my entrance.

"Kiss me," I demanded.

Sin's mouth landed on mine at the same second he thrust inside me. I gasped, and he swallowed the sound. All morning, I'd carried the ache from where we'd had sex multiple times. It felt like a delicious secret. Now, the feel of him inside me obliterated any pain.

Sin jacked his hips until he was fully seated, then issued a warning. "I just need to take."

I nodded, breathless with need.

All the signal he required. My words unleashed his control, and he pinned me to the door then fucked me hard and fast. It was all I could do to cling on, absorb the relentless drive. Loving his desperate sounds.

He pistoned in and out of me like this was the last time we'd get to do it.

His actions charged me up. Again and again, he slammed into me with raw power.

Thunder rolled again, but I was too far gone to feel fear.

Just when the tight coil of my orgasm built, Sin gave up a sound of desperate, masculine pleasure and stilled.

He breathed hard, his chest rising and falling.

"Put your legs over my shoulders," he muttered, low.

I gawked at him. "What?"

Without pausing, he moved away from the door and lifted me under the arms so I could swing my legs up. I rested my ankles on his broad shoulders, my thighs flat to his chest. He was still inside me, but the angle totally different, my knees up and all my weight on his arms.

I gripped his biceps, alarmed but desperately turned on by his show of strength.

Sin's lips curved in a wicked smile, and he jerked his hips up into me.

I swore, the drag of his penetration slower and different for me having no purchase to control it. He repeated the action, dropping me slightly so he could push fully inside.

Bright pleasure flared.

"Yes. There," I breathed.

He drove harder, hitting the same high-up spot over and over. "Like this?"

I had no words. They'd been stolen by desire.

Taking care to keep his moves constant, Sin fucked me until I had to close my eyes against the onslaught. I loved being at his mercy. His to own. Electricity zapped me, and I stifled a whimper.

Then my climax struck, stealing every sound.

Keeping us up, Sin surged and pounded into me a few more times before following me over the edge. Jerking inside me and spilling his cum.

Breathing hard, he carried me to the bed, laying me flat on my back. Still lodged inside me, he wrenched aside my bra and stooped to suck my nipples.

His hand snaked between us and strummed my clit.

We'd both already come, but urgency still directed his moves.

The angle made this tricky, the difference in our heights giving him less space to work, so I drove my fingers into his short hair and yanked his head up. Slowly, I took hold of my nipples, gesturing for him to concentrate lower.

He straightened, one hand gripping my hip so he stayed embedded within me, the other working my clit.

I pinched and tugged myself, and he picked up speed, driving me insane. Nothing beat this. The devotion of him to my pleasure. How his thickness stretched me, how right it all felt.

He stroked me until I was crying out once again. I dropped back, reeling. Blissed out. *Happy.*

Half hard, Sin lazily pumped into me a few more times, staring down my body. When my spasms ceased, he collected me in his arms, moved us up the bed, then spooned me, his arms clamped around me and his cheek pressed to my hair.

I fixed my bra and tucked my legs up over his, keeping his cum inside me where we both liked it to be.

For a long while, we just stayed like that until our breathing regulated.

He slid his hand between my legs, trailing a long finger down to my centre. "I have this idea that if I make ye orgasm after I have, your body will take my cum even deeper into ye."

I smiled, loving his caress. "Maybe it does."

"I used to think about this on the island. Every time I jerked off, it felt wasted. I wanted to be inside ye."

"Seriously?"

"I'm going to make ye come again."

He dipped his finger inside, gathering wetness, then used it to toy with me, playing with my clit and seeking out my G-spot. I let him do what he wanted, more than happy to just exist like this. Living for the memory he'd given over. The two of us in that bleak place, linked by need we'd dreamed about and now shared.

Soon, he'd made me climax for a third time, my whole body relaxing down after, spent, but perfectly at ease.

I could've dozed, but I wasn't ready to give up the moment. Once it ended, who knew if we'd ever have another like it.

With light pressure, I stroked his arm. Sin put his hand on mine and pressed it more firmly.

"I like your touch. Think I need it."

My heart thrilled. "Why was it a problem for ye before?"

"My mother took drugs and used to crush me to her. She didn't realise she hurt me."

"God."

He took my hand and grazed it over his hair then down his face, carrying out his own touch therapy. My skin on his. He trusted me, maybe.

Captivated, I lived in the moment, giving myself entirely to him.

"Put your arms around me?" he asked.

I slid one under his neck and the other around his shoulders, holding him loosely. He shifted so he was over me, hugging me back.

"Tighter," Sin demanded.

This embrace had been my dream. A loving, close hold. I buried my face in his neck and clung on.

"Harder. More." His voice came out strained. His grip on me stiffened.

"This is enough," I said softly.

"Hurt me."

"I'll never do that. I care about ye."

"Crush me, Violet. Dig your nails in until I bleed. Try to break me."

Something had changed. He'd gone too far in tackling his problem with touch. Our sweet, joyful cuddle turned dark. "No."

Sin pushed up from the bed, bracing himself over me with his forehead touching mine. "I'm asking for it. I want it. It's..."

"It's what?"

"The only way I feel loved."

My breathing stuttered.

I kissed him, aching for his admission and for everything forming between us. "That isn't true. You feel it in how I hold ye gently. In the things I do for ye."

I'd loved him for over a year. It had started as a crush but only got stronger once I knew him. Now, living together, sleeping together... I let it all rush in. The power of it could break me, but I didn't try to control it.

So many things could destroy our future, but our present burned bright.

Sin made a sound of pain and fitted his mouth to mine, kissing me like he needed me to breathe.

We kissed away his demons, replacing them with love.

He parted my legs, knelt in the gap, and slid inside me, filling my channel, slick with his cum and my arousal.

He groaned into my mouth, caressing me. "Love feeling this."

"More," I commanded.

Sitting up, he lifted my legs to his shoulders so my feet were around his ears and drove his huge dick into me once again. I was soaking wet from him already, and we were only going to make it worse.

This time, Sin worked me slower, his thrusts paced for maximum impact. He'd taken me in all kinds of ways. Hard and fast, making me come first, delivering that after. But this slow, steady assault was something entirely different.

We never stopped kissing. Moving. Mouths fused. Bodies melded.

We were making love.

The realisation spiked my heart rate, and yet another orgasm snuck up on me, generated by Sin's constant pace. I gasped against his lips and let it take me under, drowning me in pleasure.

He groaned and stilled, his dick thickening even more before pulsing inside me. My climax had ignited his. We were so perfect.

And so perfectly fractured. The world made us so.

He hugged onto me again for a long, silent while.

No more thunder came. The storm had abated while we'd got lost in each other. But the danger hadn't gone. Too much still lurked, threatening us from all sides.

"I was going to call my mother," I said, needing to explain the phone he'd seen me with.

Sin was silent for a moment then slipped out of me and reached for his jeans, drawing the quilt over me first.

Then he took his phone from his pocket. He dialled a number and held it to his ear. "Gordain, aye, we're good. What's the latest?"

The older man's voice rang out clearly on the line, and I tucked the blanket closer over my nakedness.

"They havenae returned. My nephew tracked them out of the Cairngorms. Looks to me like they've gone home."

God, he meant Da. Inwardly, I crumbled, knowing that soon, my mother would be in danger again.

My time to wait it out had ended.

Sin thanked the man and hung up. "While we were out, Gordain sent me a message saying your father left. He's been monitoring them. Every day, they've been driving out looking for us, one always remaining at the base. But at lunchtime today, all of them left." His careful gaze scrutinised mine. “They’re going back to Torlum.”

I shivered, unable to stop it. From the moment I’d intercepted Sin and his family, me calling home had been my biggest potential betrayal. Yet now, I had to do it. Not only for the information I needed, but to warn Ma, whether she did anything with the information or not.

A new and desperate thought screamed. Of going there and taking her away by force. If only it would do any good. I couldn’t kidnap her to keep her and the baby safe. She had to want to do it, or Da had to send her away. There was no other choice.

With no let-up in his stare, slowly, Sin held out his phone to me. “Make your call.”

I swallowed. I had to ruin everything between us, because I couldn’t let him hear. Couldn’t let him take on my mess. He’d come back to the island with me, and I wouldn’t let that happen.

“I need to do this in private. I promise I won’t put your family at risk.”

He pressed his lips together, some torment playing out behind his dark eyes, then he stood in one fluid motion, released me, and reinstated his clothes. Without a backward glance, he left the room, shutting me in alone.

I moved quickly so nerves couldn’t stop me, and dialled home. Ma answered.

“It’s me,” I spluttered. “Listen, your husband is on his way home. He won’t be happy. Ye need to leave.”

She clucked her tongue. “Don’t call your father that.”

“Is he? My father, I mean.”

“Violet!”

My words kept tumbling. “I know about your affair. It makes sense now why he hated me. Did ye stay with him because of guilt?”

No answer came, only the sound of my mother’s rapid breathing.

"I'm not his, am I?" Fat tears sprang to my eyes, everything I'd ever known twisted on its head. "He's not my father, and he hates us both because of that."

"How did ye find out?" Her voice came out tiny.

My heart tore.

Fuck.

"Does it matter? Who did the deed, then? Tell me."

"Ye don't need to know."

"How can ye say that? Was it Augustus Stewart?"

She went completely silent. It gave me all the answer I needed.

I pushed on, hurting from the inside out. "I'll take that as a yes. If ye care about me at all, you'll leave Da."

"I can't leave my home," she whispered. "It's all I have. Everyone I know is here. Ye want me to go to the mainland, but I could never do that."

For the first time, she'd given me an inkling of understanding. She put up with it all for fear of starting over.

I clutched the phone tighter. "Is that all? What if we lived in another house on the island? Thea will lend me her grandmother's place."

Ma went quiet once more.

At her hesitation, I continued. "He's on his way now. He'll be there in the matter of hours, and he hasn't found my friends, so ye know what he'll be like. It's not just your life, but the baby's that's at risk. Don't let him harm them like he did me."

"You're blaming me? You're responsible for his anger. Just tell him what he wants to know. Every day, he rings me, demanding to know if you've made contact. Needing to know where ye are, and shouting at me because I'm holding back. Ye can stop this, Violet. Just give them up! They are not your family. Think of your baby sister."

My cry came out as a croak. "It's a girl?"

"She is, and lucky, too, he would've killed a boy."

I took in a rush of breath. "Because this baby isn't his either."

Her silence confirmed it. Thea had been right. The affair was ongoing.

Ugly tears poured down my face, my head hurting with the pressure. I hated the situation my mother was putting me in. Both of them were putting me in. It was utterly hopeless.

Heart-shattering.

If I gave up the location of Sin and his family, the real one, and not a house we'd left, my father would be ecstatic. He'd try to imprison them again to get the money he felt he was owed. Maybe Ma was right—he'd be in such a good mood, he'd spare her any pain.

Until the next time.

Abandoning a part of my heart, I closed my eyes and let my words flow. "Here's your choice. Either come away with me or stay with him. Whatever the consequences of your decision, those are on ye. Da is a violent, sick bastard. Ye can never make him happy enough that he'll change. Not for good."

To the tune of her pleading, I hung up the call. Then I burst into fresh tears I thought would never end.

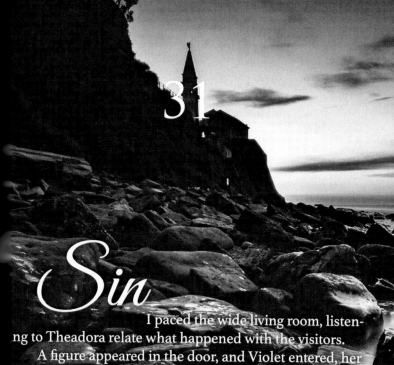

31

Sin

I paced the wide living room, listening to Theadora relate what happened with the visitors.

A figure appeared in the door, and Violet entered, her eyes red and her gaze downward. She handed my phone over, then took a seat by herself.

Thea faced her. "I was just explaining what those people said. You thought they'd go home, right?"

Violet grimaced. "I hope so. But we can't know for sure."

"Do we need to leave?" Burn asked.

I was so distracted by Violet, it took effort to force my mind back on the matter in hand. "From my experience, they'll make a complaint to their holiday company but won't get a reply because it's stopped operating. Our worst problem will be if they've gone to a pub to bitch to locals about it."

"Will they call the police?" Thea asked with a glance at her boyfriend.

"I don't think so, not if they believe the double-booking story. The cops won't do anything for them. Only if the homeowner realises we're here illegally will the police intervene." I turned my attention on Violet. "Unless there's a reason for us to leave sooner, I suggest we pack up enough so we're ready to go, but not panic."

Her gaze touched mine as the others talked. I'd given her my phone and walked away. She could've made any call.

Violet gave a tiny shake of her head.

A week ago, I wouldn't have believed her, but I did now.

Thea brought our attention back to her. "We have another problem. Henry's phone call was a warning. He implied that he knows one of us drowned his dad. It didn't matter to him that Charterman was evil. Henry now wants to claim McInver's estate, just like his dad did. In other words, someone is pulling his strings and has persuaded him to go up against us. It has to be my father. Henry likes money, but he's lazy. There's nothing vicious in him. The language he was using on the call didn't sound like him at all. He said that McInver was dying, and he'd be gone in a matter of months. Then he ranted about how none of you deserved a penny of the old man's cash. Even though he knows his dad imprisoned you for it. He's been poisoned. He said his sister was helping him, but I know it's my dad, too."

I felt Struan's gaze on me and turned to see his expression darken. "Another set of enemies," I said. "The cops are the most dangerous."

"Then maybe my dad, with Esme and Henry," Thea said.

"And the islanders last, headed up by my father," Violet concluded.

Burn scrubbed his face over his hands. "How does this end? If you allow Augustus to claim the money via Henry, the islanders still want their share. The cops will never go away. As long as my name is in their system, and Struan's face on their watchlist, we're screwed. Permanently."

People swapped glum expressions. I couldn't allow this to continue. In Violet's words, I was done. I couldn't allow my family to be threatened, which meant only one thing.

Today was the anniversary of Ma's death. It felt only fitting I end this now.

A screech resounded in the room. Cassie jumped up from the sofa, her eyes wide and little fists clenched.

"This isn't fair," she squeaked. "Why won't they leave us alone? Why won't they all go away?"

Violet reached out, instant emotion crinkling her lips in the face of my sister's outburst.

But Cassie backed away. "You're going to disappear, aren't ye, Lottie? Just like always. Like Ma, like the lady at foster care. All of ye will be taken by those people, and I'll have no one. You'll be dead!"

She burst into tears, her chest heaving with sobs.

"None of us are going to die," Burn told her. "I told ye, we're a family. No one's going to change that."

He sent a warning glance my way.

We'd spoken too openly. In other conversations, we'd made sure our sister was out of earshot. Protecting her from the worst of the unpredictable life we were living.

But his words fell on deaf ears. Her hysteria mounted, and she repeated her fears over and over.

"I didn't think she remembered her mother," Violet uttered.

"Cassiopeia," I said, loud enough to break through her cries. "What do ye see when ye look at me?"

Her crying reduced, but she didn't speak. Couldn't.

"A protector," Burn said firmly.

"Strong and thick-skulled," Struan added.

"Devoted to those he loves." Violet's turn now.

Scar sat cross-legged in front of Cassie. He pointed at

me with his thumb. "Someone who gets what he wants. Do ye see what we're saying?"

I joined him on the floor, sitting beside him and taking up too much space. "We've been talking about some scary things, and I'm sorry you've got upset. You're six, so I'm not going to lie to ye. You're not a baby. Things could get messy, but the fight is worth it, because it gets us to a future where we're safe. Tell me what that looks like."

She scrubbed her fists under her eyes, her breathing shuddering. "We have a house by the sea. You're my da, and Lottie's my mother. My brothers and sister are with us, and we go surfing and eat nice meals together and watch TV."

My big heart cracked open.

She hadn't asked for toys, or money, or days out. All she wanted was what we had now, but with the security to know it wouldn't end.

I placed my hands on her upper arms and fixed her in front of me. "I'll make it happen. I promise ye. Just be patient and remember that end goal. We're a family, and no one can take that away from us."

"Say ye promise."

"I swear it."

Cassie threw her arms around my neck and squeezed. I stiffened, waiting for the wave of panic to hit me at her touch. Except it didn't come. The little lass moved on to hug Scar, then went to Violet who was waiting with a cuddle and tissues to blow her nose.

"Hey, after we've packed up, how about we take a walk on the beach?" Violet offered her.

"We can play Frisbee?" Burn offered.

The three of them got up.

"Just keep an eye on the road. Any sign of another person, run back inside," I ordered.

They headed upstairs, clattering around until the

fast-packing had been done. Then they headed out. I took to the porch to watch them, my mind churning over what to do next.

Scar appeared in the doorway, his gaze dark. "We're going back, aye? To McInver's?"

I sat heavily on the wicker sofa. "We don't have a choice."

Struan passed him and eased himself down on the sofa next to me, his mouth open as if he was hurting. Surfing had probably injured him.

"We have every choice," he argued. "We could get in the cars, drive south to England, and start over somewhere far away."

"Run away? Like we're scared? This would always be hanging over our heads."

He glowered at me. "I'm not a coward. I'm with ye either way. I'm just saying fuck McInver and his riches. Let them squabble over it. We don't need to be part of that. We'll find our security another way."

Scar stood in front of us, gripping the windowsill at his back. "Breeze is still there."

At Struan's questioning glance, he continued.

"We called the police, and they said they'd been to the house and made enquiries but found no evidence of concern. Nor did they have a missing person by that name to back up the report. In other words, they were easily persuaded to go away." He fixed his gaze on me. "We can't wait long. I can't stop thinking about her."

"We won't," I promised.

Scar's shoulders sagged, and he gave me a nod, then stepped from the porch to join the others outside.

For a minute, Struan and I sat in silence. I watched Violet play with my family. Burn threw his arm around her shoulders, and she ruffled his hair, grinning at him before shoving him away to catch the Frisbee Cassie threw. Burn didn't take a sly glance back at me. It was genuine affection now.

Struan jerked his chin at the scene. "Good to see you've settled things with Lottie."

"Why do ye think that?"

"You're looking at her the way I look at Theadora. You've flipped the switch. She's yours."

"How does that work, I order her to stay and lock her up?"

He barked a laugh. "Ye Neanderthal. That's one way, or ye could just ask her."

I didn't answer, and he sobered.

"I'm pissed off with ye," he said.

"What for?"

"I asked that ye let me in on your plans, and you're keeping shite to yourself."

I knew he didn't mean Violet, but the wider unfuck-our-lives plan.

I worked my jaw, balanced on a line of handling this myself and...not.

He watched me for a moment. "Today is the last chance for Theadora to empty her room in Edinburgh."

The woman in question exited the house, casting her gaze over us. She squeezed Struan's hand, then stepped outside to join the others.

"I thought ye had longer."

"So did I."

"What happens if she doesn't go?" I asked.

"University policy is to chuck it all and charge for the privilege. She's tried calling the caretaker service and the accommodation team, but they just said the same thing. Get it by the cut-off date or lose it. The flat gets emptied by contractors, cleaned or redecorated, then let to someone new. They deal with skip loads of junk left every year so won't do shite to help."

Down the beach, Thea jogged in to take part in the game.

"You're not going, are ye?" I said.

"No. We're needed here."

My heart fucking ached again. Thea was giving up a roomful of her possessions—everything she owned that she hadn't taken with her when she came back to the island for Struan. I knew that, like the rest of us, she didn't have a childhood bedroom filled with memories.

It was a brave decision, and it cemented even further the sense of family we'd created.

"So I ask again," Struan intoned. "Include me in your plans."

I hadn't told anyone else this, but he was right. Sacrifice didn't only go one way.

"McInver could have information on what happened to my mother."

He watched me, lips apart, and recognition in his eyes. "How she died?"

I inclined my head.

"What do ye know already?"

"I was told she OD'd. Which I believed as she was high half the time and desperate the rest. But the cops laughed about prostitutes getting murdered by their customers. Makes me think there was more at play."

My brother pursed his lips, considering this. He shifted in his seat, his hand at his side, over his operation wound. "McInver was a customer, what about Theadora's da?"

I curled my lip. "Tell me exactly what Thea's mother said."

"That Augustus's one true love was a woman called Edie who McInver stole."

I stared at him, then swore. "What kind of bullshit is that? One true love?"

"Apparently so."

I stood and paced the porch. Ma had boyfriends but never for long. She always wanted the rich guy who got away. If Augustus had been sniffing around her, I'd have known. I never forgot a face and I'd seen his picture in Thea's grandmother's place.

"She's full of it," I decided. "More likely he was a paying customer."

He shrugged. "Probably. There's something else she said that's upset the lasses. She said Lottie's ma slept with Augustus, too. It's what Burn meant about the generation before us all being mixed up together. Thea's wondering if he's actually Violet's father."

This was breaking my brain. "Does she know that as fact?"

"No. But Thea wants it to be so."

I stared into space for a moment, thoughts colliding. Over Violet's life turning upside down. Over how I'd never had information on any of Ma's clients, but now I had another name to add to my very short list.

"It's just bollocks that, growing up, none of us knew each other. Yet all of our parents had been this fucking enmeshed. My mother hated Burn's ma because McInver chose her as a favourite. Your ma knew mine, too. Now Thea's da?" I put my face in my hands, rubbing my eyes and my thoughts leaping from one fact to the next. "And ye know what this means? Augustus has a motive. He could have hurt Ma for rejecting him."

Slowly, my brother nodded, getting up to speed with my spiralling. "Finally, I know where your mind is at. I get why you're so set on meeting with the dirty bastard who fathered us. You're trying to solve the mystery of who killed Edie, and ye think by interrogating him, you'll find out. I get that."

"Don't tell me to stop."

His eyes gleamed with dark intensity. “Wasn’t going to.”

“Good. Then we understand each other.”

My phone buzzed in my pocket, and I pulled it out to see a name onscreen. One I hadn’t put into the address book. *McInver.*

I showed Struan then answered the call on loudspeaker, teeth clenched. “What?”

“Sinclair,” he greeted me. “My namesake. Come here tonight, nine PM. Don’t be late, and don’t bring any of your so-called backup. I’ll have them shot on sight. Just yourself, my lad.”

“Why should I?” I didn’t know why I was arguing, I’d go either way.

“Because I told ye to. But don’t worry, there’s something in it for ye. An offer I’m going to make, if ye behave yourself. But also, information. Augustus Stewart will be here, too, and I think ye know his name. If ye want to know who murdered your mother, you’ll come.”

He hung up, and my heart thumped too hard.

Murdered. She had been killed. This wasn’t just a paranoid fantasy of mine.

I went to put the phone away when a message came in.

Unknown: Lottie? I’ll do it. I’ll leave him and live with you in the new house. I’m sorry for everything and I’m ready to make a new start. Just you, me, and the baby. Please tell me when you see this.

Her ma. My heart pounded.

Surely Violet wasn’t pregnant already. Why did I want that to so badly be true?

Then a second message appeared.

Unknown: I had my scan, by the way. Your sister is growing perfectly. She can’t wait to meet you.

My hope guttered out. But when I turned to Struan to

fill him in on McInver's call, my brother lurched forward, clutched his chest, then collapsed to the tiled floor.

32

Lottie

With a giggle, Cassie gripped my fingers, pulling me with her to retrieve the Frisbee from the pebbles. I loved her laugh. Loved how she'd bounced back to happiness so easily. All I wanted was to keep it like that for her.

A bellow came from the house. "It's Struan."

Instantly, all of us stood tall, and my heart thundered. Then I was running.

In the porch, Sin knelt over his brother, lying flat out on the tiles. I pushed my way through and dropped to the floor beside him, next to a panicked Thea.

"What happened?"

"We were talking, and he just collapsed." Sin pulled back to give me space.

"Wake up, baby," Thea pleaded, taking his hand.

A quick check of his chest movement showed me he was breathing, so I put my fingers to his throat to check his pulse. He was hot, far too warm.

"He has a fever," I glanced at Thea. "Did ye notice this

"No. He's often hot. I didn't know. Should I go get the thermometer?"

"No need." Struan's too-fast pulse, coupled with his fever, and the fact he'd passed out, wasn't painting a good picture. Plus I knew from touch alone that he was dangerously overheating. "Struan?" I said. "Can ye hear me? I'm going to look at your stomach."

I peeled back his shirt. His stab wound had been healing, but he'd covered it with a film of plastic, and underneath, red marks streaked out from the injury site.

To my touch, it was hard.

"What's wrong with him?" Burn asked from the doorway.

I sat back on my haunches, wishing I knew more than my scant information. "I'm pretty sure he has an infection."

Thea's expression crumpled. "But he was taking antibiotics."

"They've stopped working. He probably needs a different kind."

Everyone exchanged glances.

I continued on, swallowing back the worry over what I had to say. "He needs a doctor. We have to take him to A&E."

The consequences of this weren't small. The police would undoubtedly come back for him at the hospital. Thea would get another interrogation. Perhaps this time they wouldn't let him leave.

But the alternative was risking his life, and that wasn't happening on my watch.

I fixed Thea in my sights. "Go get your phone and his, your bag, and your car keys." Then I turned to Sin. "Help me get him into the car. Which is the nearest hospital?"

Sin ran his arms under his brother and lifted him. "Aberdeen," he gritted out.

Next, I addressed Scar. "Get the postcode for it so

Thea knows where to go."

"I'll go with them," Scar offered.

Thea jogged back into the porch, her face pale. She took Struan's hand, moving with him as we travelled to the car. Sin put him in the front seat, reclined the chair, and belted him in.

Tyres crunched over gravel, the sound coming from the top of the slope.

Three cars descended the single-lane access road.

The first two were police cars.

"Get in the car," Sin snapped to Thea, then he sliced a hand at Burn, a deadly calm over his expression. "Hide."

Burn vanished, but the rest of us were in plain sight. We had no chance of getting away. Cassie hugged my waist, peering out from behind me. My pulse skittered, and fear clamped my belly.

The cars came to a halt and boxed us in.

This was bad. We had to get Struan away. Fevers could be deadly if left too long.

"Sin," I warned.

His gaze locked on mine, a warning in his eyes.

He ducked to whisper something in Thea's ear, and she climbed in the car as the newcomers exited theirs. Two cops from each police car, and a lone man from the third.

"I'm Officer Kate Thomas from North East police," the first cop hailed us. She centred on Sin. "I have a couple of questions. Can I take your name?"

Sin nodded to Thea, and she started the engine.

"Engine off, please, miss," another cop, a beefy motherfucker, snapped.

But my friend didn't hesitate. She floored it instead, reversing in the narrow gap between the cars, the civilian jumping out of the way. On the narrow stretch of concrete, she turned and sped up the hill, gone before anyone could try to stop her.

The police exchanged a glance, but the head honcho shook her head subtly. One stepped aside and spoke into his radio.

If they were calling it in, there was nothing we could do. All we needed was for Struan to get to the hospital. If that was with a police escort, then it only brought him to the door faster.

But still, everything was going wrong. The five who'd just showed up were closing in on us like we were very much of interest to them. They peered at me, Sin, and Scar.

Then they zeroed in on Cassie.

Sin stepped forward, drawing the attention onto him. "I'm Sinclair. Our friends had to leave. How can I help?"

Officer Thomas stepped up. "Sinclair…?" She left a space for him to give his surname and pursed her lips at the lack of response. "We've been called in today by Mr Harrison, the owner of this property. He reported squatters. Can I ask for what purpose you're residing here?"

Sin's gaze touched on the civilian man, then came back to the officer. "We needed a place to stay for a few days. We've done no damage and we're prepared to leave. No need for ye guys."

He'd done this in the past, I knew, and had obviously decided the holidaymaker argument wasn't going to fly, but it didn't stop the fear that froze my heart.

Officer Thomas ran her cool gaze over him then came to me. "May I take your name?"

"Violet Hunter," I whispered. There was no reason for me to hide. Even if Da had made claims about me, I wasn't a child. They had no reason to be interested in me.

Officer Thomas made a note in the pad, then repeated the question to Scar.

"Camden McInver," he replied, though I couldn't smile at the fake surname.

Then she gestured to the tiny girl hiding behind me. "And this is?"

Sin sidestepped to me, completely concealing Cassie. "None of your business. Give us a few minutes and we'll be gone."

Officer Thomas scanned me again, presumably deciding that I couldn't be Cassie's mother. "I'm afraid I'll need a name for the little girl. For safeguarding purposes."

Sin gave a single shake of his head. "Not happening."

He turned and marched us back to the house, closing the door behind us. But the homeowner, Mr Harrison, planted his boot in the doorway to stop us shutting them out.

"Don't think you're staying, lad."

"Grab the bags," Sin said to me and Scar. He folded his arms and stood sentinel, staring down Harrison. "I said we'd leave and I'm a man of my word."

The crackle of police radio made it to me upstairs, and I hustled to collect our things, Cassie a terrified shadow at my side. There was no sign of Burn, and we jogged back downstairs, most of our possessions thankfully ready to go. We'd have to leave all the food and any other items left strewn around, but it was a small price to pay, so long as we got away together.

Scar took the bags from me and moved out with a muttered comment about loading the car.

I opened my mouth to speak to Sin, but Officer Thomas stuck her head in the porch, the homeowner moving aside.

"Everyone outside, please," she asked.

I followed Sin, hating that I didn't know his mind.

In the bright afternoon sunshine, the police officer crouched and peered behind me.

"Cassiopeia Archer?" she said.

Cassie took a rush of breath. "How do ye know my name?"

Dread curled down my spine.

Footsteps sounded behind me, and the second cop closed the front door with a clank, shutting us out of the house. We must've left the back open and he'd come through to block us. Oh God.

The woman continued talking to Cassie who remained half hidden behind me. "We've been looking for ye, sweetheart. Your social worker reported ye missing from your foster care placement. She'd rang and rang but got no reply. We visited but found the place empty."

"I don't like my social worker," Cassie squeaked.

The cop ignored that. "So many people have been worried about your whereabouts. Don't worry, we'll take ye somewhere safe."

Cassie squealed and backed away, pulling me with her. From behind, a cop scooped her up at the same second two moved in on Sin and the lead cop fronted up to Scar.

"Stop!" I yelped, struggling to take her back.

The officer holding Cassie spun away from me and jogged to the police car. I chased after him, but I couldn't free her. He was too big, blocking me with his body.

"She's our sister," Scar snarled. "We're the only family she's got."

Sin gave a deadly roar and charged, dislodging the hold of the police. They tackled him, taking him to the ground with a crash.

Right in front of my eyes, Cassie was fastened into a child's seat in the back of the cruiser, next to a woman I hadn't noticed. The cop slammed the door and circled the car, getting out of my way. I dove forward and jiggled the handle, desperately trying to reach her.

It wouldn't open.

"Lottie!" Cassie cried. "Help me. Please."

"Get the fuck off me," Sin yelled. "Let her go!"

I smacked the glass, hearing the sounds of struggle happening behind me, but I couldn't look around. Worse was happening here. They were taking her.

The woman next to Cassie spoke to her in calming tones. A social worker, if I had to guess. This was no accidental discovery. The police had come prepared. But how?

With a roar of the engine, the police car moved off, climbing the hill and taking Cassie from us.

Sin gave an awful roar. The police must've let him go as he charged up beside me.

But it was too late. Cassie was already out of sight.

"We've lost her." Tears streamed down my face. She had to be so scared. We'd promised her everything, and it had all been taken away.

"As I said," Officer Thomas argued with Scar. "If what you're saying is true and she's your sister, go to the Inverness child protection service and talk to them."

"How is that going to make this better? How do those kind of people ever fucking help? All they do is destroy families," Scar shot back.

"All we're doing, and all they will do, is to act in the interests of the child," she replied, louder and firm. "I have the right to charge ye with child endangerment, possibly even kidnapping. Tell me how Cassiopeia came to be living with ye."

The three of us stilled, and memories crowded my mind on how Cassie had been brought to us. The prison island the family had been held on. Their keeper and jailor both dying. We couldn't explain any of this without implicating Sin and his brothers.

All my anger left me.

It was hopeless.

We'd lost her and we couldn't get her back.

Likewise, the two men had gone utterly silent.

I swiped away my tears. "We love her. We'd never hurt her."

Officer Thomas glanced between us, her frown deepening. "Be that as it may, without a court order and proof of kinship, she cannot live with ye. There's also the matter of your breaking and entering this property, too. Mr Harrison?"

The homeowner shifted closer, his expression pained. "I didn't know they were going to take your lass," he said to us.

The policewoman grimaced. "Is there damage to the property you wish to report?"

"None. Looks cleaner than usual."

"We didn't break in," Scar offered, his tone sullen. "The code was easy to guess on the key safe."

The homeowner lifted his chin in acknowledgement, his discomfort plain. "If they're going to leave, that's good enough for me."

The officer widened her stance, her hands on her hips. She gestured to me, Sin, and Scar. "There's an alternative open to me. I can record the child's absence as a delay in returning her from a family visit. Tell me what happened to her foster carer."

None of us answered.

"The accommodation had been ransacked," she continued. "Know anything about that?"

It suddenly hit me that they'd been to the island. Visited the hostel.

The prison keeper was buried there.

They could arrest all of us here and now.

The officer looked from each of us to the next, then worked her jaw. "I don't like any of this. Not from the first phone call reporting the girl missing, not that dive she was supposed to be living in, and not the lack of answers from ye all now."

"She deserves better than that dive. Don't do this to her," Scar bit out, falling silent again as Sin sliced a look his way.

A moment played out, then Officer Thomas nodded to her colleagues who backed off. "If you're truly related to her, go to the child protection service and talk to them. If ye can prove you're family, you'll get visitation." She glanced between me and Sin. "If you're able to provide a stable home, ye might even be able to take her on officially. But ye can't just take her and run. Whatever the circumstances, these services are in place to protect her."

"Protect her?" Scar spat. "They did a shite job up until us."

"If ye have concerns, there are processes to follow."

Sin's brother shook his head. "Fuck your processes. They failed her. You're failing her now."

"This is the law, Mr McInver. I promise ye she'll be safe." She eyed our car, bags piled in the back and the doors open. "I need to ask ye to leave now. Don't return here. If you're homeless, I can provide a contact—"

I didn't hear the rest. Blood rushed in my ears, and I trudged to the car, climbing into the back and shoving bags out of the way.

Cassie's rucksack was half open, her soft toy puppy peeking out.

An idea hit me fast. "Scar, give me your phone."

From the front, he handed it over, low and out of sight between the seats. I grabbed the dog and worked quickly.

When I was finished, I stepped out and jogged to the policewoman. "Wait. This is Cassie's. All her clothes. Her hair gets matted easily, and I have shampoo and conditioner in there that helps. And her plushie puppy's in there, too. She won't sleep without it. Can ye take it to her? Tell her I knew she'd need it."

The woman offered a small smile, some spark of humanity under her lawful exterior. "I'll see what I can do."

There was every chance they'd find the phone concealed in the Velcro pouch in the toy's belly before Cassie did, but it was my only hope. In the car, Scar raised a single eyebrow, and I nodded.

Sin didn't even look up. Instead, he gunned the engine and drove us away from the happiest home I'd ever known.

Everything had fallen apart. Thea and Struan were gone. Burn had vanished. Poor, terrified Cassie taken.

My brain began its usual path of dissociation to protect me from the tragedy.

Despite that, I had the awful feeling that I'd never see the family together again.

33

Scar

Sin thundered down the cliff road, then abruptly swung into the open gate of the farmer's field, tucking the car behind a hedge. We stopped with the old Ford wheezing in protest.

Sin swung his furious gaze around to me. "Call Burn."

From my pocket, I extracted our brother's phone. "Can't. I found this on the table. Do ye think he's still in the house?"

He swore. "No. We had an agreement that if the police came, he'd scale the cliff and run."

If he'd seen Cassie carried off, Burn would have fought tooth and nail to stop it. It had been all I could do to hold back from fighting the cops.

Lottie unclipped her seat belt, scanning the field. "We need to find him. He must be here somewhere."

But as she spoke, a police car crawled along the road. They passed the entrance to the field, paused, then reversed. Over the loudspeaker, the arseholes hailed us. "Clear the area, please."

Sin growled, snapped at Lottie to clip herself in, and

drove back onto the cliff road.

The police car tracked us away from the coast and into the central Highlands, finally abandoning us far from our hidden bay.

Sin glanced in the rearview, then pulled over.

The sun was lower, evening closing in.

"What can we do?" Lottie asked him, her expression dull.

For a beat, he was silent. Then he twisted to her and held out his phone. "I'm going to McInver's. You're going to call your father and tell him exactly where I am. And why he's chasing me."

She stared, her lips apart. "No."

"Yes."

This had been Lottie's act of betrayal. The threat he claimed she held over us, and he was offering it to her on a plate.

Still, she refused to take the phone.

Sin tossed it to her lap. "For fuck's sake, do as I ask. Tell him we're the heirs to a rich old guy who lives in the Great House." He recited the address.

A tear spilled down her cheek. "I don't want to. I can't."

"Ye can and ye will. Free your mother. Get everything ye want." He jabbed his finger at the phone. "Look at the last message received. It came in from your mother a second before Struan collapsed. She's agreeing to live with ye."

She found the message, her mouth open as she read. "If she'll leave him, I don't need to give Da anything."

"Ye do. He'll come after her. He needs to get his way. Ye know I'm right."

"Sin, don't make me do this."

Then he twisted the knife.

"If ye care about me at all, you'll do this one thing."

They stared at each other, until finally, the lass broke.

Glassy-eyed, Lottie stabbed a number into the phone, lifting it to her ear. "Da? It's me." She repeated the words Sin had given her, listened for a second, then hung up the call, devastation in every move.

With zero emotion, Sin turned to me. "I'll drive to McInver's, then you'll take the car and deliver Violet back to the ferry for Torlum."

I shrugged. "Whatever."

Everything was fucked up. It had all fallen apart, just like always happened. I'd lost my mother, then my grandparents, and now my family.

It's what happened when I cared about people. They left.

Silence held in the car, and Sin drove us deeper into the Cairngorms. We passed the junction to the lane that led to McInver's land, but this time, Sin took us to the main entrance. Tall pillars and gold-tipped railings guarded the open gate.

He pulled over and, with the engine still running, exited the Ford. No backward glance. No words of farewell.

Lottie cried out then dove from the car, running to intercept him. She threw her arms around him, forcing him to stop. For a heartbreaking moment, my brother froze up, but then his ice cracked and he hugged her back.

I dropped my gaze, rounding the car to take the driver's seat while they had their moment. It was too hard to watch. We were all broken. Destroyed.

Some part of me had badly needed Lottie and Sin to work out their differences. For them to be a couple. He adored her. We all did. They'd become the heart of our family, and I couldn't bear for that to shatter.

But the next time I peered up, Sin spun away from Lottie and stormed through McInver's gate without a backward glance.

She returned to the passenger's seat and burst into tears. I wanted to wrap her in a hug. But I'd been given my orders, so instead, I got us the fuck out of there.

The engine's rumble and the tyres on the road were the only sounds.

Lottie curled up in her seat, silent and apparently shellshocked. After a few minutes, she spoke.

"I love him."

I winced and kept my gaze on the road. "We all know that."

Her attention fell heavily on me. "I'm one hundred percent in love with him, and he sent me away."

"He wants to protect ye."

"Do ye know what he said?"

I tilted my head to invite the answer.

"That if I had his baby, I was better off far from him and away from the danger that's always around him. That I should live with my mother and have the life I wanted."

"Lottie, are ye pregnant?"

"No, or I don't think so. That isn't the point." She made a sound of frustration. "Stop the car."

I pulled over, ignoring the horn blast from someone behind. They overtook us and sped on up the road. I turned to Lottie.

She stared in the direction we'd come. "My father was in a pub when I called. He hadn't made it back to Torlum with the other islanders. Which means he'll drive hell for leather to get here. Maybe arrive as soon as in an hour." She focused on me. "What were ye going to do after dropping me off?"

I didn't hesitate. "Return here for Breeze and to help Sin. I'll wait for McInver and his men to be distracted then grab her." Whether she liked it or not.

Lottie took a rush of breath. "I'm staying, too."

"Ye can't go in there. He's fucking evil. If McInver

catches ye, he'll hurt ye."

"Understood. That's my decision to make."

"Sin will kill me if I don't stop ye."

She glowered, her blonde eyebrows diving together. "I survived one abusive bastard for my entire life. I can take being hurt. But I can't stand back while the man I love is voluntarily walking into a trap. He needs someone to have his back, and I have to try."

A phone buzzed. Wide-eyed, Lottie picked it up—Sin's, left with us. She raised it to her ear. "Thea? It's me. How is he?"

I stared at her, needing to hear about Struan.

"Awake. Thank God." Then she listened, and her shock grew. A moment more, and she thanked her friend then hung up.

"Ye didn't tell her about Cassie," I said.

"There's nothing she can do about it. I'll share that with her later. Listen, Struan woke on the journey to the hospital. He was desperate to tell Thea about Sin's last phone call before he passed out. Her father is with McInver, and Struan thinks Sin has a personal vendetta. He wouldn't speak to me. He left his phone. Don't ye see what's happening?"

It all slotted together. "Sin will have McInver, Augustus, and your da in one place at the same time. He's trying to end this."

She smiled, but it wasn't happy. "Turn the car around. He's not doing this alone."

34

Henry

Bloody bored, I hunkered down in the hard seat, glowering at the people across the room. Esme, my sister, perched on the arm of Augustus Stewart's chair, my dead father's business partner. Every time I saw the two of them together, it gave me the icks. I didn't think she was flirting, or maybe I hoped not, but she was definitely gone for him. Devoted.

So gross.

I jumped my gaze around the room—anything instead of staring at their love-in. Besides, this place was giving me big ideas. McInver had collected all kinds of valuables over his ancient lifetime. Earlier, Augustus had given me a tour of the place and pointed out a gallery of oil paintings of long-dead members of the McInver clan. As a great-nephew, or second cousin, or whatever my claim, they were my relatives. One day soon, I'd have my own portrait up on the wall here.

Sweet. My handsome face recorded for history.

Dad had wanted it. Esme had even claimed our father had specifically married my mother so they'd have me. An heir to McInver's line. I'd literally been made for this.

Esme also said Dad had divorced her mother to enable it, so I owed her big time.

Not that I needed much convincing. Dad's death had left us penniless. The fucking idiot had burned through his savings and remortgaged the house because he believed his big payday was coming.

No more money equalled no uni fees, no Porsche, as I couldn't afford the repayments, and the likelihood that I'd need to get a job.

I shuddered dramatically. Screw that. Entry-level jobs at university were for poor people. I'd be laughed at by my friends.

"Is he going to take much longer?" I asked Augustus.

The older man rolled his gaze my way. "He'll take as long as he takes. You'll sit there quietly and be the obedient boy I promised him."

Esme's eyes flashed a warning. "Don't fuck this up for us, Henry. Dad died to make this happen. If McInver asks you to bark like a dog and lick your own balls, you'll do it."

Bitch.

I huffed and stared out the mullioned window. Something felt off. McInver didn't like Augustus, I was pretty sure. When we'd arrived, the old man had cackled something about a fun evening ahead, then ordered us to sit in a side room off his great hall while he made arrangements. I wrinkled my nose, thinking it through. If he'd really been poised to make me his heir, as Augustus believed, why hadn't he looked my way? Today was my second time of meeting him, and in the first, he'd sneered at my blond hair and said I couldn't be related to him.

Unease set in. I wanted that money. We needed to be prepared.

"Hey," I said to Esme and Augustus. "What if he doesn't like me? I'm pretty sure he has other relatives. Men my age." My old friend, Theadora, had clued me in on the fact.

Was it weird that she and her father were on opposite sides?

"Mouth shut. Now," Esme snipped.

Augustus's expression darkened. "Don't mention them."

"I really think we should consider it. Struan, Thea's boyfriend, is a thug." I'd met him in a bar when he'd warned me off Thea, and when I'd left them, I'd heard him mention another name. "He said someone called Sinclair looks like McInver, too. Maybe he—"

Augustus leapt up and marched across the room. He fisted my t-shirt and hauled me to my feet. "What do you know about him?"

I jerked out of his grip, staggering to avoid falling over my chair. "Not much."

"That boy is never to be mentioned in this house, do you understand?" Augustus continued. "His very existence is a blight. He's been ruining lives since before he was born."

"What the hell? How can a baby ruin lives?"

My sister let out an exasperated gasp. "You are so naïve."

I widened my eyes at her. "If you're so smart, clue me in."

"Why bother? As if you're going to suddenly shed your dumb-blond persona. This is exactly why Dad never trusted you with any information."

"Both of you, silence," Augustus shouted then dropped his voice to a creepy growl. "Sinclair Stone is mine to deal with. Do you understand? He will not threaten everything your father spent years building toward. All I intend to deliver in his memory."

I squinted at him. "How? Are you planning to off

these other guys if they turn up?"

I'd made a mistake. I'd known Augustus Stewart for years, but I'd never seen darkness in him. Dad had been a drunk, passing out in his office each night then bitching and moaning until his next binge started. His aggression had been nothing to the flash in his business partner's eyes now. A still and empty pool of hatred. It sent a curl of primordial fear over my nervous system.

I recoiled, but my back was against the wall. My floppy hair in my eyes.

Augustus kept coming until his face was an inch from mine. "I'll do whatever it takes to reach my goal. You'll smile and obey, just like your sister, and McInver will be mine. Anyone who gets in my way will be dealt with. I will succeed."

New feelings flickered in me. The sense that I was in over my head. Augustus had changed from talking about my inheritance to his goals. From our acts to his victory.

I centred on one thing. I was on the side of a monster, not in his path. All I wanted was the money, I just had to hold that in my mind and keep my mouth shut.

Augustus held me in his rabid focus then returned to his seat, hiding away all that venom once again. "Esme," he said with a tone of command.

My sister sank to her knees at his feet.

Augustus placed a hand on her head, like she was a pet. "Well done, child. So obedient," he purred.

"Daddy?" she replied. "May I help with your stress?"

My jaw dropped. What the fuck?

Augustus smiled and stroked down her face, drawing his thumb over her lips. She caught it and sucked. Horror chilled me.

"You may, child," he replied.

She reached for his belt, and their relationship took a whole new and revolting direction in my mind.

Oh fuck, no.

35

Sin

Fist, flex. Fist, flex. I kept up the action with my hands, staring down the guard left to watch me. Unlike last time, today, I'd walked straight up to McInver's front door. My guard had escorted me into the great hall, offered a seat in the centre of the space, and told me to wait. That had been an hour ago.

It was coming up on nine PM, McInver's invite time, and I sensed the weight of someone's gaze on me.

Around me, closed doors hid rooms. Anyone could be in them. Fear didn't touch me, only breathtaking anger at what had happened to my family.

And who I held responsible.

Ahead was what looked like a throne, elaborately decorated with a high, carved back and a purple cushion with gold fringing. At the base of the front feet, metal links glinted. No doubt for McInver to sit in and lord over me.

A plain, single seat waited three metres to my right. Like mine, it faced McInver.

Someone else would be joining me.

Footsteps came from behind, and I peered back. Two

new guards took up positions at the back of the hall, one carrying a shotgun, like my escort was. A fourth marched to a side door and opened it, beckoning to whoever was inside.

A man entered and was led to the vacant seat beside mine.

I stared with unhidden hatred at Augustus Stewart. Thea's da, maybe Violet's, too. Complicit in our imprisonment.

With him, two others emerged, a man and a woman about my age. Blond and with expensive looking clothes. Likely the Charterman kids, as Thea suspected they were working with her father.

Stewart stared straight ahead, not acknowledging me. He would, before the night was out. I'd make sure of it.

Finally, McInver himself hobbled down the hall and took his throne. A cruel smirk appeared, and he cast his gaze over the room, settling on me with a revolting expression of fondness.

Fuck him and the games he was playing. Whatever this setup was leading to, I wasn't interested.

I only wanted answers, and I'd take them in blood.

"Well, well," he started. "Look who we have here. At long last, my meeting can begin." He flicked his fingers at the younger man and woman who hovered at the side of the hall. "Girl, take notes. I want this recorded in the family annals."

She scoffed, but Augustus Stewart tutted at her.

"Obey him, Esme."

Darkness boiled in me, my suspicions confirmed. Esme Charterman had stabbed my brother. I lowered my gaze at her, breathing through my nose. She didn't peek in my direction, clipping away to collect a pad and paper from the room.

McInver folded his fingers on his lap. "For many years,

I imagined this day, bearing the constant weight of ancestral expectation. We survived the English! We kept our lands and flourished. Yet it isn't enough to simply thrive. The ghosts of the past hound me non-stop to pick my heir. The burden was great. They did not know what they asked of me."

Stewart dipped his head. "You have done wonders with the mansion and the estate. Your ancestors will look down on you with pride, and your decision—"

"Enough," McInver snapped. "Your nose is brown enough already. Do not interrupt me again if ye have a hope of being in the running."

I choked out a laugh. "What the fuck is this? The McInver show? Get to the point of why ye demanded I come here. Ye know I'm not interested in your money."

Amusement curled the old man's lips. "That fire. Stand up for me again, boy."

"Fuck off. I'm not your puppet."

He let out a giggle, pointing his cane at Stewart. "What do ye think of that, hey? Surprised?"

Stewart summoned a cool smile, but it was for McInver alone. Still, he wouldn't set his gaze on me. "Very good, sir."

McInver's humour dropped. "This isn't light entertainment. Pay attention to the gravity of the situation. Feel it pulling ye down like I do." He dropped his head and took a couple of shallow breaths, then righted himself. "You're both here today because soon enough, I will shuffle off this mortal coil and everything I own will be bequeathed to one of ye. Either ye Sinclair, my flesh and blood, who has never known a decent home or relaxed in an embarrassment of riches. Or ye, Augustus Stewart, by way of that fair-haired twit over there."

At a minute gesture from McInver, the guards either side of us snapped to attention and marched to take hold of my and Stewart's chairs. They yanked them away, forcing us to stand.

The old man remained seated, a self-satisfied grin spreading. "Learn this: ye will obey me. Which brings me onto my challenge. It is in two parts, the first, your argument, and the second, your obedience."

I sneered at him. "You're not getting it. I won't take part in any challenge. I'll never put any effort into impressing ye."

McInver held his gaze on me. "Not even for the sake of your sister?"

My blood curdled.

Too fast, things started to slot together in my mind. His reference on my last visit to brothers and *sister*. Singular. His knowledge that I'd been raised in poverty.

Cassie's kidnap by the police had been no accident. Never once in my life with my mother had police come along without a court document to evict us as squatters.

He knew exactly what had happened to Cassie because he had been the puppet master.

The guards either side stilled, focusing on me. I'd taken a couple of steps and barely realised it. "It was your doing. Your fault the police took her away."

McInver shrugged. "Ye called the police on me, it was no trouble for me to call them back. Besides, ye looked a little too comfortable in your seaside home. I see my flaw now in leaving ye to be raised away from here. Ye lack an instinct for greed, which I appreciate, but ye also lack cunning. If I'm to model ye into anything more than a scrappy brute, I needed to get your attention."

My breathing came fast, my blood pumped harder. He'd had us followed, and in retaliation for trying to free Breeze, he'd had Cassie taken.

I'd been outplayed when I hadn't even realised it was a game. "My attention? By torturing a wee lass?"

"Would ye rather I picked one of the others? Your pretty blonde sweetheart? Or your scar-faced boy? Just think, with my money, ye could fix the face he's been wearing for years."

For years… "How would ye know that?"

McInver raised his shoulders. "Maybe he wasn't such a surprise when he darkened my door."

"You've seen him before," I bit out.

"How stupid do I look? I remember each bitch mother who came crying to me with fat bellies or squalling bairns. They wailed all the more when I turned them away. Camden's mother tried to leave him here. Lucky for him she returned that night to take him from the doorstep where he'd spent the day in the sun. I knew him then, I also know exactly how he got that deep scar and who carved it into him. The threat he faces that is far worse than me. Yes, my lad. I ignored it all, then ye returned and finally interested me. Ye, I'd lost track of. Your claim of being born in Aberdeen is incorrect, but it seems that's where ye ended up. I originally found your mother in a small village far to the west. I plucked her from obscurity and set her up in a flat. Treated her well until she overstepped her usefulness. Stupid bitch thought she might replace the woman I'd lost in my affections, but after I turned on her, she fled from me."

Hatred rushed through me.

I wanted to kill him. For my mother, who he'd set on a life of homelessness and prostitution. For my brothers and sister he'd watched struggle while he had the means to provide for them all.

But McInver's gaze had skipped from me and onto Stewart.

The second man stood deadly still. If he'd been part of my mother's life, truly loved her, then I hoped he was hurting, too.

"Now starts my challenge," McInver told him. "Tell

me something that will impress me. A dark deed. Some devious doings to get me going. Here, Stewart, ye may have an advantage, so make the most of it. But first, I'm going to give ye an incentive."

From the doorway McInver had used, one of the guards brought in a new person.

A struggling, angry, naked woman.

Gagged, and with her hands tied behind her back, she padded on bare feet then spun around and shoulder barged the guard, her bobbed blonde curls swinging. He grunted at the attack but picked her up with ease and carried her over his shoulder to the centre of the room. McInver stepped from his throne and shuffled to the side, indicating for the guard to continue. The guard manhandled her to the huge, carved seat, extending her hands above her head. A second guard handcuffed her through a gap in the chair's tall back, then both men knelt to secure her feet to the base of the throne's front legs.

This had to be Breeze, the lass my brother found.

Constrained to the seat, she wrenched at her bindings, eyes wild with fury.

McInver watched on in delight, then turned to us. "Symbolic, no? She will be your prize and the second part of my challenge. The proof of your obedience. Not that I imagine it will be difficult to take her, eh?"

Horror and revulsion mixed together with my anger. "Ye want me to rape a woman?"

"Rape? That bitch in heat was sold to me by a brothel. And for a pretty penny, too. Her cunt is virgin territory, which I've confirmed myself, but I'd bet everything I own that her plump little arse and pouty lips are well used to receiving cock."

Stewart moved in on her, pausing for McInver's approval. He tipped her chin up. "I tell you my dark deed, fuck the girl, then you'll give me what I want?"

Breeze glared at him and wrestled away from his touch.

"Your deed, yes, but your boy will be the one to service her, unless he's afraid, like your opponent," McInver said. "After all, when I'm dead and gone, he will need an adviser with a backbone. But I have to be sure he can get it up to keep the family name going."

Stewart glanced around to Henry Charterman. The boy cringed in on himself, obviously uncomfortable at the requirement.

I missed the rest of their exchange. Instead, I scanned the room, looking for opportunities. An exit strategy. Considering my choices.

Scar would return after dropping off Violet—a trip I couldn't think about, my loss so acute it cut me in two. But despite the time I'd been kept waiting, Scar wouldn't be back for at least a couple of hours. I couldn't rely on his help.

I also couldn't leave his woman behind.

"Not a peep from ye," McInver's voice drew my attention back. He stared at me. "You'll get your turn. Augustus, give me your worst. If you can't impress me, if there's nothing in your darkened past that beats the things I've done, I'll have my guards throw ye out."

Thea's father nodded like there was anything normal about this request. "I've stolen."

McInver snorted. "Better than that."

"I've...taken a woman after she refused me."

"Better, but still. More."

Stewart breathed through his nose, his nostrils flaring. "I've killed a man. He was half drowned, and I put an end to his miserable life."

My stomach lurched. He had to mean Charterman. He'd been pulled from the water, and we'd all assumed him dead. Struan hadn't killed him after all.

Across the room, the Charterman kids paled.

"You killed my dad?" Henry asked.

His sister pressed her fingers to her mouth.

"What does it matter? The old drunk couldn't help you," Stewart sneered back.

McInver lowered his gaze, and his guards moved in on Stewart. "Yawn. Final chance for your best."

The man's lip curled. Finally, he looked my way. His gaze was empty of anything but darkness, like staring into a void. "I killed a woman. This one, I think you'll like."

I felt rather than saw McInver's approval of this attempt, but I didn't take my eyes off Stewart.

McInver had pushed him to this, and I needed to know why.

"Weave your tale," McInver crooned.

"Once upon a time," Stewart commenced, "I was in love. I used to leave my island to visit this girl. The most stunning beauty you've ever seen. Long legs, long dark hair. We were so happy together, even remaining a couple after I went away to university. She'd sworn to save her virginity for marriage, and I accepted that. I'd have given her whatever she wanted. Then one day, she vanished with barely a word of goodbye. I hunted for her for years."

On his cane, McInver stepped closer. "Callous whore. Ye wanted answers. Revenge."

A vein in Stewart's neck pulsed. "Yes." He smiled.

The old man smirked back, like they were sharing a moment. "What did ye do to her?"

He was talking about my mother.

McInver was drawing the story from Augustus as part of his twisted game. This was the information he'd promised me.

White-hot rage simmered under my skin, and I couldn't draw a deep breath, every muscle primed to react once I knew the truth.

Stewart continued. "I finally tracked her down by way of an accident. I was in Aberdeen for work and I ordered girls to be sent to my hotel. I used a different name, obviously." He shook his head like he was so clever. "She turned up with two others, then tried to run. I chased her down the corridor. She was a mess. Track lines up her arms. Tits shrunken. One smack to the temple, and my sweet little no-longer-a-virgin was unconscious. I hid her out of sight then returned to the other girls, sending one away on a task for me and paying off the other to go home early."

McInver bobbed his head, both hands clutching the rounded top of his cane. "Ye killed her in your hotel room."

Stewart tutted. "Not right away. I paid for her, after all. I had her a few times, all the ways that she'd never allowed when we were young. She begged me to let her go and said she had a son, and that he was the reason she hadn't contacted me again. She knew I'd never accept him. It was for his sake that she'd thrown me over. I asked about the father, and she said she'd been raped. Such bullshit. Prostitutes can't complain about rape. It's an occupational hazard."

He laughed, and my fury almost broke. I needed him to say the final words. To make his confession. If I died killing him, I didn't care.

A voice in the back of my head reminded me of my family. Of lost Cassie. Of Violet heading home. I couldn't allow those thoughts. I couldn't let in the love.

I'd wanted it all, and I couldn't have it. I'd already lost them. My life meant nothing now.

McInver inched forward again, his attention rapt. "Finish the story."

"Her friend came back with the drugs I'd asked for. Despite everything, I couldn't let Edie go in pain. She cried out for her child, then for her drugs, and she fell silent with an overdose of it flowing in her veins. I dumped her body outside the brothel where she belonged."

That was it. At last, I knew.

I punched forward, only to be crowded on either side by McInver's men. They gripped my arms. Restrained me.

"Let me have him," I demanded.

They battled my struggle, trying to force me to my knees while a third held a shotgun at my head. I didn't give a fuck.

Stewart laughed in my face. "He won't let you hurt me. I'm the only one who can run his empire for him. You're nothing better than your slut mother. But I will see you suffer before the night is out. If it wasn't for you, Edie would've come back to me. You're the reason she stayed away. Her dark little sin."

I struggled against the guards, my muscles primed and blood rushing, only focusing again when McInver peered directly into my eyes.

"Calm, boy. You'll get your moment. Ye forget, I cared about her, too."

Vaguely, I picked up on stress in his voice. Anger, perhaps.

It meant nothing to me.

Nothing did anymore, or could again.

Stewart's expression of mother-killing nostalgia dialled back to a more conscious awareness. He watched the old man, fear springing in his gaze.

McInver's guards suddenly released me, the gunman straightening then holding his shotgun out for me.

I didn't hesitate in taking it. Too far down the path of long-held hurt, I crowded Augustus Stewart, grabbed him by the throat, and pointed the gun at his head.

By my side, McInver held up a stalling hand, his guards surrounding Stewart so he couldn't run.

The old man addressed him. "Thank ye for the tale. It

was all I wanted. Violence, and the base animal nature of man dominating woman. But there was a small oversight. Ye dared touch someone that had once belonged to me."

Stewart's mouth opened and closed, but he couldn't form a word.

McInver slowly turned and placed a gnarled hand on my arm. "Your real first test, my lad. This one, I think you'll ace. Think of what he did to your mother. Think of what I can offer ye, and in exchange what ye can do for your bastard siblings when I'm dead and gone. Kill where I instruct, fuck who I choose, be my heir, Sinclair Stone."

I held my finger on the trigger. The guards backed away. The Charterman kids sprinted down the hall.

But out of the corner of my vision, before they reached the exit, it flung open and someone entirely unexpected burst in.

Everything changed again.

36

Lottie – a few minutes earlier

Cold evening crawled over my skin, but my shiver was all for the scene I glimpsed through a window of the Great House. A naked woman tied to a chair. A man with a gun across the wide room from her. Through the narrow slice, I couldn't see Sin or anyone else, but from the fixed attention of the gunman, something bad was going down.

Scar and I had scoped the place, then he'd broken a window on the other side and entered, heading upstairs to find the woman prisoner. Despite every instinct screaming to stop him, I'd let him go.

Except she was here.

If he saw her, he'd run straight into a killing zone.

I fired off a text from Sin's phone to the one Scar carried. No reply came back.

I had no clue what to do now. If I followed him inside, as I'd promised not to do, I could make things worse. Get captured. Become a pawn. But I was no coward. This was my life, too.

In the hall, another person moved into my view, and

I squinted to identify them, but they ducked back as if dragged.

If that was Sin, if someone was planning to hurt him...

I couldn't stand by and watch.

An engine roared somewhere near the front of the house. I paced to the corner and spotted my father's Skoda—a car I knew well.

Da parked up and exited, gazing up at the mansion with his mouth open.

Ice formed in my veins. The chill of the evening had nothing on me.

"Hey," I whisper-shouted.

His gaze swung instantly to me, and my father sneered. "How the fuck are those convicts related to the man who owns this place?"

I curled my lip in intense hate. "That's for ye to work out, I've done my part. Ye need to let my mother go."

He gave an easy shrug. "Already told her to pack her bags. I'm glad to have shot of the both of ye."

Ma was safe. Her baby would be safe. No matter where she ended up, it couldn't be worse than the regular beatings he'd issued.

"And you'll never contact her again?"

"Whatever. Are they definitely in there?"

I nodded, and he rubbed his hands together.

"Before ye go," I paused him, my fear of the man held back behind my frozen heart. "I know you're not my father. Ye never have been in any way. Not by blood, not by love."

"And?" The bastard smirked at me.

I hid my recoil. "You're so twisted up in hate."

"And you're naïve, just like your stupid bitch mother. She fucked around on me, then had the nerve to cry when I found out and paid her back for it. Ye lived in my house, ate my food, and I had to tolerate that for the sake of avoiding a scandal? You're a fat little waste of space. Giving me this address is the only time you've ever proved yourself useful."

I gave a short, hard laugh, years of pain at his rejection melting away. "With all the chances ye had of being a good person, ye chose to be the lowest kind of scum. If I get my way, you'll never see me or my mother again. I hope ye die alone and lonely."

His nostrils flared, but he sniffed and strode away.

I trailed after him, climbing the shallow steps to the front door he'd left open. Keeping out of sight, I gazed into the wide foyer. A grand staircase led down from the upper floor, and big double doors at the back of the space opened into what looked like a huge hall.

Scar was halfway down the stairs.

As my father entered the hall, two others fled.

Without noticing me, they charged outside and sprinted down the steps into the twilight.

Belatedly, I recognised Henry Charterman.

The woman with him looked so similar, she had to be his sister. *Esme.*

I ran after them.

"Stop!" I demanded.

They slowed.

Scar was about to walk into a fight. I had no time for this. Still, I couldn't let the woman who'd stabbed Struan get away with it.

I pelted at them, pulled back my fist, and slammed it into her face.

She squealed and dropped to the ground, blood oozing from her nose.

I'd never struck another person before in my life, but God, that felt good.

"Stay the hell away from my family," I said through gritted teeth, then again set my sights on the house.

In the foyer, Scar peered in the open doors to the hall.

I joined him, staring inside.

At Breeze, naked and tied to the chair.

At my father, frozen in the middle of the space.

And at Sin, a shotgun in his hand and Augustus Stewart in his grip.

37

Sin

Forbes Hunter halted in the centre of the room, swinging his gaze between me and McInver. The guards advanced on him, but McInver stopped them with a gesture.

Choosing stupidity, Hunter jabbed a finger in my direction, talking to the elderly man. "I'm owed money for him."

McInver cocked his head like a bird. "Is that so? Who are ye?"

"Forbes Hunter."

"And why are ye owed money, Mr Hunter?"

Augustus Stewart made a sound of pain. I pressed the barrel of the gun harder into his temple, and he quietened, his hands up in submission.

"That boy lived on my island, rent-free for over a year. Him and his brothers. Caused all sorts of problems for us."

McInver raised his eyebrows in invitation. "Go on."

Hunter didn't back down. "They stole girls. One of them burned a house to the ground. They killed."

"Whom did they kill?" McInver enquired.

"The man who set up the place where they stayed. Charterman." He stood taller. "If I don't make it home safe, my men will report every single thing they did to the police."

If he thought that an ace card, he was stupider than he looked. I barely knew McInver, but I was rapidly getting used to his style.

"We didn't kill Charterman," I informed him. I shook Augustus. "He confessed to it. Everyone here is a witness."

Hunter spared a glance for me, but McInver cleared his throat and drew his attention back.

"Thank ye for the information. I'd wondered what happened to my son in the time he was missing. Now I understand it all. A prison was set up for them, enabled by ye."

"Wait, I didn't say—" Hunter spluttered.

"Silence." McInver moved to my side. His beady-eyed gaze fell on Stewart. "Ye hid them from me. My children."

The man in my grasp didn't answer.

McInver smiled at me. "Let's return to where we were before the interruption. Proceed with your challenge, Sinclair."

He meant me to kill him.

I'd wanted this for a long time. At first, I'd thought my revenge needed to be taken from Charterman, but Struan did that for me, drowning the man. Now I knew different. The real brains behind the operation was here in my grip.

He was also possibly Violet's father.

She was owed the truth for that.

"How long have ye been fucking this man's wife?" I gestured from Stewart to Hunter.

Hunter's expression soured, his lips pressing together. Beside me, McInver cackled.

Stewart lifted his gaze. "Longer than he has."

"Did ye father her bairns?" I continued.

"What do ye mean bairns? There's another one? The first is mine. She claimed she never wanted to carry on his genes." Stewart gave a cruel smile. "She took great pains to avoid pregnancy with him. Lucky she had another man for the job."

The man who'd raised Violet, and beat her, wheezed in anger. "Shut your mouth."

McInver tutted. "Or you'll what?"

Hunter's breathing came faster. "I'll kill him."

"Wrong answer." McInver moved faster than I thought possible.

He grabbed my arm, pulling down my hand with the gun. With both our fingers on the trigger, he squeezed.

A gunshot echoed around the hall.

The blast tore through Augustus Stewart's head, blood and bone spattering the floor.

McInver released me. I dropped the body, tossed aside the gun with a clatter to the shadowed edge of the hall, and backed away. His guards moved in on Hunter who'd screamed and tried to run.

In the panic, a figure entered fast through the hall doors and passed me. Scar ignored the blood and prowled to Breeze, the lass utterly quiet, still chained to the throne. He dropped to his knees and methodically set about releasing her legs.

McInver sighed and raised a hand to signal his guards.

"No," I snapped.

McInver narrowed his gaze. "I told ye my terms. He shouldn't be here. The girl is for ye."

"He's my brother. Your flesh and blood."

"He's of no interest to me."

I spread my arms out, droplets of blood painting my skin. "If ye think ye have a chance in hell of commanding me, ye won't touch a hair on his head."

Scar worked faster, freeing one of Breeze's ankles.

"If I let him go, you're mine?" McInver asked.

It was an easy decision to make. Violet had gone, Struan was in hospital, Cassie had been taken. If Scar could get away, it was worth my life as forfeit.

"I am."

The old man smiled then turned away, taking his attention back to Hunter.

"Release him," he directed his guards holding the man. "We'll deal with Mr Hunter now."

I caught Scar's eye then dipped my head to the door, signalling that the moment Breeze was free, they run and don't look back. He jerked his head in agreement and continued his task, moving on to the final link at the top of the throne that secured her arms.

"How much are ye owed?" McInver said to Hunter.

"Fifty grand," he stuttered.

McInver beckoned in a guard, who listened to his whisper then took off down the room. To the sound of his footsteps, we stood there in the blood-soaked space, the dead man sprawled on the floor, and Hunter trembling.

"He's a piece of shite," I snapped. "He doesn't deserve a payout."

"Because he enabled your imprisonment? Or is there another reason?" McInver asked.

I only cared about how he'd hurt Violet. Drove her to extremes. Ruined her life.

McInver already knew about her—his spies on our house enabled that—but I wasn't about to give him any details. I kept my mouth shut.

The guard reappeared with a stuffed envelope. McInver checked it then held it out to Hunter.

"It's all there. Take it and go."

With a shaking hand, Hunter reached for the envelope.

McInver held on tight. "If I ever hear of ye coming

near my son again, talking about him, or anything that happened on that island, your life is over. Same goes for any of your men. I know your face, and my reach is far. Go. Tell your friends you've won. Never darken my door again."

He released the envelope, and Hunter scrambled to get away, his shoes slipping in the blood.

He fled the hall, and I stared after him.

"You're letting him go?" I asked.

McInver shrugged and turned to one of his guards. "Go get the dogs."

The man jogged away, pursuing the islander.

"What?" McInver asked. "Too brutal? He crossed ye then threatened me. I do not suffer that kind of fool."

I didn't give a fuck about Hunter's life or death, but I knew what McInver was doing. It was all a display of power. He wanted to impress me. Own me.

At the throne, Scar completed his work. He helped Breeze to stand, stripped his shirt and handed it to her to shrug on, then towed her down the room.

The remaining armed guard cut them off, gun up.

"You'll let them go," I snapped at McInver.

"Don't think I will. I've had second thoughts and may have a use for both of them. Not least in controlling ye."

"I said let them go," I yelled.

"Oh, I will. Once I'm sure you'll toe the line."

From the back of the hall, Violet emerged from the shadows, holding the shotgun I'd thrown.

My muscles went rigid. My breathing stopped.

She was here. Hadn't gone back to her island after all.

She pointed the gun at McInver, her gaze and her aim not wavering. "Ye can't have him, old man. He's mine."

If I'd thought myself in love with the brave woman before, her actions now claimed my heart as permanently hers. Even if it fucking terrified me to see her in this place.

McInver scowled but didn't flinch. His gunman advanced to stand beside him, weapon trained on her.

He'd kill her. He'd have to kill me trying.

McInver cackled and took the gun himself. "Oh my. A new pet," he started.

An explosion rattled through the room. Glass splintered and cracked. Dust fell from the ceiling.

Everyone swung in the direction of the blast.

Through the windows of the great hall, orange fire flared bright, scaling the adjacent wing of the building.

"Fire! My house!" McInver screamed. "The paintings. My collection—"

His shouts to his guards cut off, and the old man's muscles locked, his expression contorting. He dropped to the floor, the gun falling from his grip.

"Sir?" a guard asked.

No reply came. McInver's mouth went slack.

The guard switched his gaze to me. "What should we do?"

I swung around to Scar. "Go!"

He was already moving, Breeze with him. He grabbed Violet's arm as they passed.

I came back to the guard, somehow suddenly in charge. "Get him to a hospital. Is there anyone else in the house?"

"No, sir."

"Then call the fire brigade. Get far away."

My family reached the door, then a body stepped in the frame. Burn, a crazed grin on his face.

"Get the fuck out. The place is about to blow."

38

Lottie

Outside, we spilled into the night, the acrid stench of burning in the air. The power to the house went out, plunging us into darkness as the exterior lights extinguished.

"Sin," I screamed.

He hadn't come out with the rest of us.

He was still inside.

Burn landed his hand on my shoulder. "Keep moving, Lottie."

"Not without him."

I had no idea how the youngest brother had got here, but so long as he was safe, I could only think about Sinclair.

In the distance, sirens wailed.

That was fast. Too fast to be the fire brigade, presumably called by McInver's guards.

Breeze ripped the tape from her mouth and spun back to face the mansion, barefoot and panicked. "We can't let McInver die. You have to get him."

"His guards will take him to safety," Scar dragged her

on.

"I need to talk to him tonight," she pleaded. "If he dies, she dies, too."

"We'll work something out, but right now, we have to get away."

Breeze was my height but skinny as a rake. Her expression of outrage and pain spoke of suffering I couldn't imagine.

Burn stared at the petite woman, recognition in his eyes. "What the hell are ye doing here?"

Breeze frowned at him. "Do I know you?"

"Are ye fucking kidding me?" he replied.

Something cracked, and we all flinched.

Burn's puzzled expression broadened into delight. "Everyone, run, now!"

Breeze cried out, and Scar picked her up.

"So sorry. It isn't safe." He looked at me. "The Ford is parked in a lane at the edge of the estate."

"I'll be right behind ye." I wouldn't leave without Sin.

Scar swore but jogged away into the dark.

Something crashed at the other side of the house. If the hall's ceiling collapsed, if Sin had been hurt by a guard and was lying somewhere...

I had to go back inside.

I climbed the first step, ready to do anything for him.

Sin burst around the side of the building. With a rush of breath, he sprinted to me and grabbed me up. The reek of smoke clung to his clothes.

I thumped his chest, tears leaking out. "Where were ye? What happened?"

"The guard carrying McInver dropped him and fled. I picked up the old man and carried him out of the side exit to the grass. Is everybody out?"

I nodded, wriggling free so we could run. "Scar has taken Breeze to the car. He parked up at the lane. Burn..."

I swung my gaze around. "He was here a moment ago. He must've gone after them."

"Are ye sure? Could he have gone back inside?"

"Definitely not." I'd had the main entrance in my view the whole time.

Sin squeezed my hand, and we moved fast through the shadowed landscape. "I can't believe you're here."

"I couldn't leave. I meant what I said to McInver. You're mine. Ye told me to walk away and take care of my family. Well, you're my family now. I came back because I'm in love with ye."

Blue flashing lights lit the night. We sprinted to a thicket and hid. On the main entrance road, two police cars sped past towards the house, fire now visible scaling the walls of one of the wings.

Sin tracked them. "Either someone called them, or they were brought here by a fire alert system." He took a breath then stooped to kiss me. "For the record, you're mine, too. If you'd left me, I would have come for ye because I'm entirely in love with ye. So take this as a warning—I'll never let ye go again. Now let's get the fuck out of here so we can plan how to piece our family back together."

That was all the promise I needed.

We left McInver's estate to burn, our own lives still to be rebuilt. I had him, and he had me, and from that, we'd make everything right.

Epilogue

Burn

A distance from the house, I crossed the cool grass, my back to the flickering, mesmerising fire that consumed McInver's mansion. The flames crawled from the arched windows, reaching up to the floors above. Spreading. Loving their task.

So pretty.

I'd never taken on a building this size before, but the principles had been the same.

Find a starting point, lay on materials, have a fucking good motivation to toss a match and walk away.

I'd been slower to leave because of needing to see it through.

I owed my family for us losing our home. I'd started the beach fire which brought the cops to our door. It was my doing, and I'd had to run to avoid being caught. Yet all of this came back to the fucker who owned this place. He was the real deal. Taking him down was my payback for all the shite he'd laid on us. Lingering here had meant I could be sure my family had got back to the cars where I guessed Struan, Thea, and Cassie waited.

A roar had me glancing back at the road.

More fire engines arrived, the two already here laying a pipeline to McInver's lake. Their job sucked. If something was burning, it lived, dancing along until it consumed itself. Firefighters killed it, or at least stunted its potential.

This place was a house of horrors. McInver a sick bastard. By rights, my fire should have its way.

Shame the man himself had escaped it. He'd hurt so many, but an ambulance had whisked him away to be fixed. Fuck that guy.

No matter.

Now I just needed to reach the car I'd hotwired then follow my family. I jogged over the park, making it to the edge of the woods.

Just inside the tree line, a hand landed on my shoulder. I swung around.

A uniformed police officer loomed over me. "Hold up there."

Fuck.

My heart beat faster.

"Are ye a resident of this house?" he asked.

"No."

"Ye smell of smoke. Are ye injured?"

At my lack of an answer, the officer gripped my biceps, his gaze sinking over me. "Happen to know anything about this fire?"

"I can't tell ye that."

His radio crackled, and he muttered something into it before coming back to me. "If ye don't explain your presence, I'll have reason to suspect you're involved in the setting of this fire."

Arson was such an interesting crime. Very easy to prove the act. Much harder to point a finger at the individual responsible. Particularly if you knew your shite.

"Prove it," I said with a grin.

Springing back, I found my feet and sprinted back the way I'd come. I'd circle around so I didn't lead this guy straight to my car.

From the open park, two more cops appeared. A shout from behind told me mine was in pursuit.

Outrunning them wasn't going to be a problem, I was fucking fast.

"Burn!" Scar's voice pierced the trees dead ahead.

I staggered, changing direction on the spot. I couldn't lead them to him. He'd found his girl. Got away.

Should've known he'd come back for me.

I had to protect my family.

My hesitation cost me.

Something hit me with a jolt. Then I was falling. Hands grasped my arms and held me down, pinning my face to the forest floor while the cops shouted orders to me and each other.

My last words came out silent. "Run, Scar."

The End.

To find out what happens next, continue the series with Scar (Dark Island Scots, #3).
https://mybook.to/DarkScar

ACKNOWLEDGEMENTS

Dear reader,

How are you feeling? I thought I'd better check in because you've just been on a rollercoaster with the island boys. After *Ruin* left us on a cliffhanger, this next episode upped the drama. We know who imprisoned the siblings and why. We've watched them wrestle with their pasts and try to see how they might have a future, and now, they're going into a new fight.

What a ride.

I am having such fun discovering this story as it unfolds. Each twist and turn is news to me, and whenever I think I know where the plot is going, a fresh surprise comes my way derailing what I thought was coming next. This is the first time I've written a story in this style, with an overarching plot that spans several books, and I'm loving every second of it.

Who knew Sin would have a breeding kink? Or that Lottie would share it.

Who'd guess that Burn would show up at the last minute and...do what he did? (Hiding that in case anyone reads this first.)

I can't wait to find out what happens in the next instalment.

Thank you for reading and for continuing to love my Scots. The island boys have such avid fans it's unreal.

As always, I want to thank Elle Thorpe and Zoe Ashwood, Sara Massery, Shellie M, and Liz Parker for being my core team. You guys rock. Cleo Moran makes amazing graphics, Natasha Snow provides sumptuous covers.

Emmy Ellis edits each manuscript until it's shiny. My Street Team are the best and each of you gets a virtual hug. A shout out also goes to narrators Zara Hampton-Brown and Zachary Webber who breathe life into the audio version of these stories.

I have a fabulous reader group on Facebook, run by Liz, with excellent moderation by the awesome Erika and Amanda. Stop by if you want to join in the fun! Or add yourself to my newsletter to never miss a new release announcement.

Finally to my husband and son, you're my whole world and you make every day wonderful. Funny story - Mr V had Ruin's cover printed up as a huge poster which hangs near my desk. Lovely of him! Except our boy enjoys using Struan's face for nerf gun target practice.

See you in book 3!
Jolie <3

ALSO BY JOLIE VINES

Marry the Scot series

1) Storm the Castle

2) Love Most, Say Least

3) Hero

4) Picture This

5) Oh Baby

Wild Scots series

1) Hard Nox

2) Perfect Storm

3) Lion Heart

4) Fallen Snow

5) Stubborn Spark

Wild Mountain Scots series

1) Obsessed

2) Hunted

3) Stolen

4) Betrayed

5) Tormented

Dark Island Scots series

1) Ruin

2) Sin

3) Scar

4) Burn

Standalones

Cocky Kilt:

a Cocky Hero Club Novel

Race You:

An Office-Based Enemies-to-Lovers Romance

Fight For Us:

a Second-Chance Military Romantic Suspense

Visit and follow my Amazon page for all new releases
https://amazon.com/author/jolievines

Add yourself to my insider list to make sure you don't miss my publishing news

https://www.jolievines.com/newsletter

ABOUT THE AUTHOR

JOLIE VINES is a romance author who lives in the UK with her husband and son.

Jolie loves her heroes to be one-woman guys.

Whether they are a brooding pilot (Gordain in Hero), a wrongfully imprisoned rich boy (Sebastian in Lion Heart), or a tormented twin (Max in Betrayed), they will adore their heroine until the end of time.

Her favourite pastime is wrecking emotions, then making up for it by giving her imaginary friends deep and meaningful happily ever afters.

Have you found all of Jolie's Scots?

Visit her page on Amazon and join her ever active Fall Hard Facebook group.

Made in United States
North Haven, CT
04 August 2022

22296090R00198